STATION BREAKER

Thank you to everyone who provided me with notes, corrections and input on this book.

STATION
BREAKER

[COSMODROME]

DROPS OF BLOOD TRICKLED through Natalie Kharitonova's fingertips and splattered into the puddle below. She caught her distraught reflection in the pool of water and the glow on the horizon as a RD-300 rocket engine fired on its test stand, lighting up the night sky over Baikonur Cosmodrome.

Bracing her body against a silver sedan, smearing blood across the door, the roar was a distant hum under the sound of her own difficult breathing.

"Don't run," said the thick-jawed man from the window of the black Mercedes as he rolled up.

Natalie pushed away from her resting spot and stumbled further into the parking lot, trying to find someone to help her.

A minute ago she was reaching for her keys when the two men came to a stop.

"Natalie," the driver had shouted, feigning familiarity.

When she turned to look at who was calling to her, he fired his pistol.

The noise startled her more than the wound. She thought a rock or something sharp had flicked her. It was the growing numbness and the sight of blood on her palms that told her what just happened.

In an instant she knew this was about what she had seen a few hours ago.

It had been a clerical error. As a payload supervisor, normally it was her job to inspect all cargo before being loaded onto the Baikal rocket – except for military cargo.

But this wasn't a military payload, or at least she hadn't thought so. There was no certificate from the Army, much less a liaison officer from Roscosmos.

Clipboard in hand, Natalie had donned her clean room scrubs and entered the sterile chamber just like she did for every other launch. When she saw the plastic case sitting on the table, there was nothing indicating it was military. But when she cracked the seal and looked inside, she realized immediately there must have been some mistake.

She quickly closed the case, but it was too late. The escort assigned to the cargo had re-entered the room, having momentarily abandoned his post.

There were no words exchanged between them. Natalie made a quick exit, not even bothering to throw her garments into the bin.

She headed straight for Supervisor Volodin's office, Roscosmos Chief Zhirov's right-hand man, and told him what she had seen.

He listened carefully, made a call, then gave her a warm smile and told her it was just a mistake. Everything was fine. There had been a mix-up with some sensing equipment.

Natalie thanked him, laughed it off, pretending the best she could. She knew he was lying. Having an engineering background, there was no mistaking what was in the case.

She wasn't sure what she was going to do about it, if anything. Then the Mercedes pulled up and the man shot her.

Natalie managed to weave through another row of cars, but her legs were betraying her. Darkness began to encroach her peripheral vision as she continued to bleed out.

She made one more stride, then collapsed on the wet pavement. Unable to move, yet still somewhat alert, she heard the footsteps of the approaching men.

"Get her into the bag, then place her into the trunk," one said to the other.

Natalie felt their rough hands as they picked her up and laid her inside a plastic pouch – the kind they keep onboard a spacecraft in case of a fatality.

The scent of the material reminded her of a spacesuit, which set off a mental trigger in her mind. She remembered where she'd seen these men before...

Their names were Yablokov and Domnin. They were cosmonauts. They weren't supposed to be here. They were supposed to be getting ready to launch in just a few hours.

That thought faded as quickly as it came. When they zipped the bag over her head, she worried about her daughter, Elena. If Natalie didn't call and remind her, she would forget to start the oven and dinner would be cold.

[1]
SPACE GUN

T-MINUS 4 HOURS:
I think my Commander is insane.

Not the kind of insanity natural to anybody willing to sit on top of a million gallons of explosive fuel – but the workplace shooting kind of nuts.

I tell myself I'm the crazy one. This is Commander Halston Bennet we're talking about. I've known him for years. Yet, a second ago I saw him in the prep room mirror slipping a gun into the side pocket of his spacesuit when he didn't think anyone was looking.

At first I don't think anything of it. Bennet, after all, is the manliest man you'll ever meet; a former Navy pilot, SEAL instructor, and a NASA astronaut before coming to work for iCosmos. Of course a guy like him would carry a gun into space. Military pilots are taught hand-to-hand combat in case they come down in hostile territory. Russians keep pistols on their Soyuz craft in case they land somewhere with wolves – which is just about everywhere there. Maybe Bennet is just planning for any contingency?

Hell, maybe he wants to shoot Martians.

I try to put it out of my mind, but I can't. I should say something.

Maybe it's just a standard operating procedure I don't know about? In that case, telling Renata, our launch manager, that he has a gun won't be a big deal.

But what if it's Bennet's little secret? Maybe he's not supposed to do this, but the piece is his good luck charm?

If I rat him out, he could be out of the company and I'll probably catch shit for being the one that finked on an American hero.

An American hero.

Halston Bennet is the kind of man that made me want to become an astronaut. He's the man I want to be when I grow up. He's also the one that trained me to go into space.

Space.

Holy shit.

Of course this would happen on my first mission.

Hell, I didn't even know I was going until twelve hours ago. I was an alternate for Robbie Carlyle. I got a phone call at 3 AM telling me I needed to get my ass to Canaveral in the next hour.

The official story is Carlyle suffered a sprain while working out.

The real story is that he slipped in the shower getting busy with some girl other than his regular girlfriend.

I've been listed as an alternate six times. After the fifth time the astronaut I was alternating for defiantly refused to show up with the flu, a broken leg or visible cold sores, I kind of gave up and decided I'd be going into space after about the 10,000th rich jerk-off tourist flew out of Mojave in one of those suborbital tin cans they call a spaceship.

Then I got the call.

I'd been waiting for that call ever since I decided I wanted to be an astronaut.

Not because I wanted to set foot on Mars or perform earth-shattering experiments in micro-gravity. But because I wanted to fly things. The faster the better.

My heroes have always been pilots. From Chuck Yeager to Han Solo, I wanted to be the guy at the controls – a guy like Bennet.

Bennet. Damn it. In some alternate universe I was going to be a military guy turned NASA astronaut like him.

Imagine my disappointment when I was seventeen years old and walked into an Air Force recruitment center wearing my Coke-bottle glasses and was told in no uncertain terms the only way I'd see the inside of a fighter cockpit was if there were paper towels and a bottle of Windex in my hand so I could clean it for the guys with perfect eyesight.

Pissed, I worked two jobs that summer; getting up hours before dawn to fold newspapers and deliver them. I can still smell the wet ink and feel the warm newsprint in my hands as it sucked all the moisture from my fingers. After that, I worked at Burger King during the day, getting laughed at by my friends as they came into the place imagining new and ridiculous ways to "Have it their way." Har har, guys.

I used the money I earned to buy myself laser surgery for my eyes. Which was something my parents couldn't afford – trying to raise three kids on one teacher's salary as my mother finished up her master's degree.

With beyond perfect 20/10 vision, I walked into the Navy recruiter's office and was told, sorry kid, LASIK was an automatic disqualifier.

They changed the rule later, but it was too late for me. Uncle Sam wanted no part in making my dream a reality. I'd never be a guy like Bennet, a Real American Hero™.

Dejected and rejected, I decided I'd find other ways to take to the sky. I studied engineering and aeronautics in college and found that as a student you could get cheap pilot training.

I learned how to fly fixed wing, rotary, single engine, multi-engine and even no-engine in gliders and a hot air balloon. One summer, a couple of my flight school pals and I even took a trip to Russia and got to take control of MiGs. I did a crash course in Russian, afraid I'd try to change the air conditioner and end up ejecting myself over Siberia.

To pay for it all, I spent my spare time volunteering for medical studies where they poked me with different chemicals as I sat around playing flight simulators.

When it came time to graduate, my friends all went into commercial aviation. I didn't. Flying a jumbo jet wasn't the same as going to the stars. So I took a job as a science teacher in my mom's school district.

The same week classes started, iCosmos, the private space company with its own fleet of rockets, announced they were accepting applications for astronauts.

I pissed my mom off when I turned in my school resignation after iCosmos hired me. Although, it wasn't as an astronaut at first. They had plenty of former NASA people, like Bennet, who'd gone through their program to choose from.

When the recruiter read the part on my resume about working for various pharmaceutical companies, you should have seen the fiendish look in her eyes when I explained I'd basically been a medical guinea pig.

"Oh, we need those too," she replied.

"Will it help me be an astronaut?" I asked.

"Sure, why not?" she answered in that Northern Californian, non-response.

It didn't matter. Being a test monkey stuck at the bottom of a swimming pool for ten hours in a leaking spacesuit, or finding out what happens when your cockpit chair snaps loose as the capsule goes rolling sideways down a hill, was a lot closer to being an astronaut than flying complaining tourists and neurotic flight attendants on the same route over and over.

The day they finally accepted me into the iCosmos astronaut program, after nearly killing me on Earth nine ways from Sunday, was the second happiest day of my life.

The happiest was today, when I got the call. That all came to a fiery reentry when I saw Bennet, the man who taught The Most Interesting Man in the World how to be interesting, stick a gun into his pocket.

Man up, David. Go talk to him.

Worst-case scenario and he actually is crazy?

He'll just shoot me here on Earth instead of 200 miles up.

[2]
GLITTER MENACE

ACTING AS CASUALLY AS I CAN, I finish sliding my chest unit into place and make sure all the lights are green. I double-check it, even though half a dozen people will take a look before I get into the capsule. Spaceflight is supposed to be routine now, but not that routine.

"What's up, Dixon?" asks Bennet, looking up at me from his wrist display.

"You know, suicide pills are a lot easier to pack," I say in the weakest possible way as I point to the pouch with the gun.

He glances past me and sees the mirror. "Watching me suit up? I didn't know you were into that."

This kind of locker room trash talk is a bit out of place for Bennet, not to mention the fact his son is openly gay and a Republican US Senator elected in no small part because of his father's support.

He's clearly trying to avoid the topic.

I press on. "Seriously. Is that some new SOP I don't know about?"

Bennet takes his time as he examines his readout then walks up to me, standing toe-to-toe, our chest units almost touching.

"Dixon, there are things you need to know and things you do not need to know. I do not have time to tell you all the things you need to know. What I can tell you is that what you thought you saw doesn't exist in your world. Understand? But I'll humor you and tell you that because of certain security requirements for our payload, I'm required to take certain precautions."

He gives me a friendly clap on the shoulder and smiles. "Don't worry, son."

I've seen the cargo manifest. We're just bringing standard supplies to the US-iCosmos Space Station. There are no military or spy agency payloads I'm aware of.

But would I know? A line item that says 35 x 55 x 20 cm box weighing 2.4 kilograms listed as "Replacement carbon dioxide sensor monitor" could be some NRO long-range LiDAR sensor designed to scan foreign satellites or something or other.

"I'm proud of you, Dixon. This is what it's all about. You're going do to fine."

That's the Halston Bennet I know, the man who trained me and dozens of others in the iCosmos program – the guy we secretly try to emulate.

"Gentlemen, you all set?" says Stephanie Peterson as she enters our locker section. Technically part of the cargo, she's a NASA astronaut we're taking to the Station.

An athletic, imposing former Air Force pilot, she's also the man I want to be when I grow up.

"I was just explaining to Yoga Boy how things are going to be."

"You just do whatever Halsy tells you." She gives me a wink.

I want to ask her if she knows about "Halsy's" gun. But by the informal way those two talk to each other, I get the feeling that if he's up to something she'd either know, or be in on it.

Yoga Boy. Ugh. Bennet once caught me doing some stretches before a pool dive and never let it go.

He's a great instructor but never lets you forget who the real men are – the men and women who served in the military and were part of NASA's astronaut program. They were accepted from the best and the brightest. The twee poseurs like myself are just pretenders.

"Astronauts to the press room," Renata calls to us from the door.

"Let's go, Dixon," says Bennet as he gives me a friendly pat on the back. "Time to tell them what it feels like to be about to have your space cherry popped."

It's disorienting the way he just can switch right into the avuncular instructor whose calm voice walked me through my underwater and zero-g training on our 727 Vomit Comet jet.

It's hard to call it a "press room" when at the moment it's a mostly empty auditorium with just twelve internet bloggers.

On a real mission, something besides a FedEx run, the room would be full. Today we get anyone with more than ten Twitter followers and nothing better to do until their parents come home.

It's kind of embarrassing and nothing like the newsreel footage I grew up watching of astronaut press conferences.

Vin Amin, the CEO of our company, insists that we do this before every launch.

"Watch out for that one," Peterson whispers to me, singling out a girl in crutches wearing a glitter-speckled t-shirt and purple streaks in her hair. She looks to be between nineteen and twenty-five.

I pretend everything is totally cool and my hero didn't just emasculate me moments before the most important day of my life. "I'll be careful."

"No, seriously. She once asked the NASA director a question about a contractor funding overrun that he didn't have the answer for. It nearly cost him his job and killed the program."

"Seriously?"

I give the girl a hesitant glance. Leaning on metal arm crutches, from some kind of condition, she doesn't look threatening...

I keep a wary eye on her anyway as Renata starts our briefing. There's also a mischievous curl to her lips, like she's holding back something clever, that I find alluring.

Bennet explains how excited he is to be part of this program. Peterson talks about how thrilled she is to be going to the Station and what kind of research she's going to do.

I make an inane comment about being eager to ride shotgun – actually saying the word "shotgun," and catching myself too late. Thankfully, the joke passes by and I feel pretty sure Bennet isn't looking at me with daggers.

Renata opens it to questions. The menace in the glitter shirt shoots an arm into the air and almost drops a crutch.

Renata manages to avoid her as long as others have their hands up.

There are the predictable questions about what it's like to be an astronaut from a group of people who look like the most adventurous thing they'll ever do is move out of their parent's basements.

I get a couple technical ones about the new version of our space capsule.

Finally, the only raised hand is glitter girl.

I can see Renata's hesitation. "Okay, Laney Washburn, you're our last question."

"My question is for David Dixon. As one of the first astronauts to not have prior NASA or military training, what's it like to be the odd man out in a capsule full of veterans?"

Did she just call Yoga Boy out for being a poseur?

I probably stutter and take longer than I should. "Well Laney, the mission of iCosmos is to open space up for everyone. That starts when a regular guy like me gets a chance to fly next to a couple of real heroes like Captain Bennet and Dr. Peterson."

She smiles at my answer. I mentally clap myself on the back.

Before Renata can end the briefing Laney blurts out another question. Teetering on her crutches she asks,"When will people like me be able to fly for iCosmos?"

By "me," I think she means handicapped.

Gut punch.

I flinch.

I hope Bennet's gun is loaded and I get the first bullet.

Thankfully, Peterson jumps in and saves the day telling Laney that both NASA and iCosmos have a program for making space accessible to all Americans.

Laney smiles at her answer, but keeps her eyes on me. I get the feeling she asked the question just to make me squirm.

[3]
MOVING TARGET

IT WAS A TEXTBOOK LAUNCH, just like the simulator –
except for the part where I'm worried my commanding
officer is going to whip a gun out at any moment and
shoot my brains out.

The Gs were more than I've experienced for a
sustained period, but I've done enough gut-churning
flight maneuvers to not be bothered. The real stomach
twister happens a few minutes after we reach orbit.

Launching to a space station is like trying to throw a
baseball through a specific window of a bullet train as it
flies past – if the train was going 17,000 miles an hour.

You don't aim for the target. Instead, you calculate
where it will be at a specific time, then try to intercept it.
Launch windows are measured in half seconds for this
kind of thing. You don't use a map, so much as a
spreadsheet.

While we were sitting on the launchpad for three
hours, the US/iCosmos flew overhead twice.

If you've ever been out in the middle of the desert on a
moonless night and seen the tiny speck of a low earth
orbit satellite or space station whiz across the sky, that's
what we're trying to intercept. It's not even over the
horizon when the launch computer fires the rocket.

The launch computer controls everything.

Joining up with a space station involves two other computers besides our own: There's the one at mission control in Nashville, watching everything and making sure tracking and telemetry jibe. Then there's the one controlling our destination, the US/iCosmos station, doing things like adjusting the pitch of the solar panels every few minutes so the station will encounter less drag as it reaches the closest point to the atmosphere in its orbit and controlling the tiny little thrusters that move the station out of the path of space debris.

The station's biggest concern is fast-moving objects hurtling towards it – which is exactly what our space capsule is doing.

At 17,000 miles an hour, a 1% margin of error in velocity means slamming into the station at the same speed as a race car at full throttle – enough force to destroy the structure.

Before we even get close, we have to reach a parallel orbit matching its velocity.

This is made all the more tricky because spacecraft, even the fancy iCosmos Unicorn capsules, don't have a lot of fuel to burn.

It's not like the Millennium Falcon where you can just have Chewbacca take you to orbit on a whim and dodge incoming TIE-Fighters without worrying about fuel consumption.

A little spreadsheet is keeping track of fuel, velocity, distance to target and has lots of little triggers to tell us when we need to take a different course of action.

All of this is automatic for the most part. Commander Bennet's job and mine is to watch our big flatscreen displays and keep an eye out for any flashing warnings.

At some point in a normal launch ground control will let him use the joystick to bring us closer to the station before the automatic docking computer takes over. This is really just giving a monkey something to press so he feels he achieved something.

The iCosmos ships have done this kind of thing hundreds of times without anyone at the controls. But when there's human cargo, in this case Dr. Peterson, you want pilots onboard for when all the computers don't agree and letting the ship burn up over the Pacific Ocean isn't an option.

Fifteen minutes after launch I get a flashing box on my console saying there's a problem with our trajectory.

"Commander, I'm getting a warning about our projected path."

"I'm on it. Nashville, this is Unicorn 22, I'm getting a warning that our intended destination is unavailable. Over."

"Unicorn 22, hold steady while we check on this. Over."

I flip through a few screens and realize the US/iC station is sending us a "do not proceed any closer" signal. This would be from the computer system that watches out for any fast moving threats.

"Unicorn 22, we just heard from the US/iC that they experienced a solar flare that knocked out their inbound telemetry sensor. They're going to try a reboot. Continue your orbit until otherwise noted. Over."

"A solar flare?" I check through all my readouts and can't find anything from the Helios satellite. "There's nothing about it."

"Dixon, are you planning on arguing with their computer?" says Bennet. "Which is preferable? They're right or that their computer made a mistake?"

"Good point." I shut up.

I pull up the reentry profiles. If we can't dock with the US/iC then we'll have to return to Earth. Like trying to catch the station, reentry is equally complicated.

If we miss the window, we could find ourselves in the Pacific thousands of miles away from the nearest rescue, or worse, in hostile territory.

Ideally, we hit the window at the right time and come back down over Canaveral where we use the landing rockets to bring us down to the pad – which could mean I'm home in time to grab dinner at Outback Steakhouse and get to sleep in my own bed.

The alternative is a prison cell in North Korea or burning to death in the upper atmosphere.

"Reentry profiles loaded, Commander."

"Hold your horses, Dixon. Let's see what the folks at Nashville have to say."

"Are you that bored of space already?" asks Peterson from the seat behind me.

She's joking, but there's something cold in her voice, like it was forced. She can't be scared, can she?

"Unicorn 22, this is Nashville. We just spoke to the US/iC commander and she says they think there may be a sensor alignment issue and they won't know until they do a space walk. And even then it could be days. Please load up the reentry profiles and we'll tell you when to proceed. Over."

"Affirmative, Nashville. Doing a systems check now. Over," says Bennet. "Dixon, what's our ETA to a Canaveral window?"

I'd already done the math. "In 34 minutes we'll need to start our reentry burn."

He nods then starts going through screens on his console. Out of the corner of my eye I see him digging through directories of all the onboard sensors. I'd never seen him do that in the simulator – but we've never been in this kind of situation before.

"Nashville, this is Unicorn 22. It looks like we've got our own sensor issue on our heat shield. Over."

Suddenly a bright red box starts flashing on my console telling me there's a heat shield malfunction.

I start to flip through sensor readouts and scan for anything that looks out of line and then my screen goes blank.

Confused, I turn to Bennet. "I've lost my display."

He relays this back to Earth. "Nashville, this is Unicorn 22. My co-pilot appears to have lost his display. I'm giving Dr. Peterson redundant controls. Over."

"Roger that, Unicorn 22. We'd suggest a reset, but if you're experiencing a shield sensor issue, we advise against that. Over."

"Affirmative, Nashville."

I reach out to touch my display, to see if it was just a video issue. Bennet stops me with a sharp look. "Dixon, keep your hands off it. Peterson and I have this."

"I have control," says Peterson. "Checking heat shield sensors. Nashville, I can confirm we have a sensor problem of our own. We'd need to make visual confirmation to verify. Over."

"Unicorn 22, please stand by. Over."

It's amazing how calm everyone can be when you just realize you've been fucked by the universe.

The US/iC can't let us dock and we just found out we might burn to death on reentry.

Making things worse is the fact that I think Bennet intentionally shut me out of my screen so Peterson could have access.

First the gun. Now this.

Something is not right, but I keep my mouth shut.

[4]
HOT MESS

"WELL KIDS, ANY SUGGESTIONS?" asks Bennet, while we wait to hear our fate from Nashville.

Peterson types away on the console behind me, while I stare at my own matte finish reflection in my screen. Bennet's question was rhetorical, at least in respect to me.

"ISS doesn't have a spare docking collar," says Peterson. "Checking on OPSEK. No, she's only got the Soyuz-type free. What about New Star?"

"The Chinese station?" says Bennet. "Didn't they have a rapid depressurization problem with their airlocks? I think I'll risk burning up."

She left out one option. "There's the Korolev," I point out.

"The K1?" replies Bennet. "There's a thought. Peterson, what do you see?"

"Pulling it up now. They've got a universal dock that looks free. Although they're pretty cagey about non-Russians on there. They say the K1 is for industrial research."

"I think this is an extenuating circumstance. Nashville, did you get all that?"

Even though we use a lot of "overs" and "affirmatives," our comm is always open. That's why the sting of Bennet telling me to keep my hands to myself hurts so much. It wasn't just Peterson who overheard it. Everyone I work with did.

"Affirmative, Unicorn 22. We're checking on that now and putting in a call to Roscosmos. Over."

"I'm going to put a pin on our reentry at this point until we've heard back. Over."

"Roger that, Unicorn 22."

We spend the next half hour waiting for a response from the Russian space agency. While Peterson and Bennet run through their control panels, I stare out the window for the first time since we reached orbit.

Our craft has a small spin so it doesn't get too hot as we go through the sun side over Earth.

While the stars are too hard to see through the internal glare of our displays, Earth is a bright blue and white disc that takes up the entire window when we rotate towards it.

The hard thing to understand, even if you experienced it virtually, is how big the earth is from low orbit. While we're in space, we're still only about 400 times the height of the tallest building in the world.

The distance from the ground to my window is less than the trip from Cape Canaveral to Miami – a three-hour drive for most people – half that for me.

Space, technically speaking, is the place where you can orbit the earth without running into too much atmosphere. If the earth had no atmosphere and was perfectly round, you could orbit an inch off the ground if you were going fast enough.

At our altitude of 200 miles, we're roughly just over 2% of the earth's diameter away from the surface. Which means the earth looks really fucking huge even from here.

But it's still far away.

There is 200 miles of progressively thicker atmosphere below us. If we were just dropping straight down, that would be no big deal. We wouldn't need a heat shield.

But we're traveling 17,000 miles per hour. People often get confused as to what it means to burn up in our atmosphere.

It's not that the air is a giant oven up here. Quite the opposite.

What matters is our velocity. At this speed, the friction from hitting those air molecules so fast it's hotter than an industrial furnace.

The skin on the bottom of our ship, Pica-Z, is designed to handle atmospheric reentry from even higher velocities. The problem is if one part of it gets a little too hot or there's an uneven spot.

The Unicorn has reentry thrusters and is designed to land via rocket propulsion, but if we have to use them in the upper atmosphere to slow us down, then that means we'll end up burning all our fuel and need a parachute to land nowhere near our intended zone.

The ideal situation is we get to dock with a station and check the sensors before attempting reentry.

If nobody has any room, then we're kind of screwed in the short term.

Worst case scenario; iCosmos sends up another craft on autopilot in a few days to come get us and lets the Unicorn 22 attempt an unmanned reentry.

Theoretically, it's a choice between trying to reenter with a faulty sensor and hoping iCosmos can send up an unmanned craft for us to dock and transfer to – which is a lot easier said than done. Possible, but extremely time consuming.

"Hey, guys, this is Vin here." The face of Vin Amin – the CEO whiz who started iCosmos – appears on Bennet's display. It looks like he's Skyping from his home office. "I just want you to know we're doing everything we can to figure out a solution. We're having trouble figuring out what readouts you're getting, Halsy. But Dr. Peterson says she's getting the same thing?"

"Affirmative," she replies.

"David, right? Any luck with your control panel?"

I'm not sure if telling him Bennet won't let me touch it will go over very well right now. I just say, "No, sir."

He smiles. "Vin. Save 'sir' for Commander Bennet."

"Any luck with Roscosmos?" asks Bennet.

Vin loses his smile. "Well, we're working on it. Zhirov, the head of their space agency, just gave us a flat out no."

"Sounds like that's our answer," says Bennet.

"I don't know about that. I've got a call into his boss, Radin, the head of the Russian Federation. The two have been known to disagree. Plus, there's one more thing..." Vin holds up his phone. "I just tweeted that we're asking the Russians to let us dock at the K1 because of the solar flare."

Bennet shakes his head. "You're hoping a bunch of people on Twitter will make Zhirov change his mind?"

"No. I'm counting on them to persuade Radin. He's a bit more media aware." He looks at something on his computer. "Oh good, our hashtag, 'LetThemDock' is trending!"

Jesus. Christ.

My life depends on a bunch of hipsters retweeting a plea from a man probably sitting on a Yoga ball right now.

[5]
PARTY CRASHERS

I IMAGINE SOME KIND OF HIGH-LEVEL negotiation somewhere in a huge, dark tapestry-lined Kremlin office where tsars had been poisoned, disloyal party members had their death warrants signed and pogroms were planned – all based on how high #LetThemDock is trending on Twitter right now.

"You have the post-docking reentry profiles?" Bennet asks Peterson.

It sounds a little presumptuous to me to start loading reentry profiles for departing the station when we haven't even docked yet. We could be there eight hours or a week, all depending on what our sensor inspection shows us. You don't plan a reentry profile for a departure when you don't know when that's going to be. There are thousands of variations.

Maybe Bennet is just running drills so he knows Peterson is ready to take the pilot seat?

If that's the case, then that means he has no plans for letting me sit at a working display.

Relax, David.

Peterson has been into space multiple times. She's NASA. Bennet is former NASA. She's the one he wants working with him in a crisis.

Yeah...but, she hasn't been trained in all the iCosmos procedures. Putting her in my seat is one thing when my panel goes out mid-crisis, but leaving her there after we have a chance to switch seats or fix the problem – totally not cool.

If Bennet is acting out of line, they'll say something downstairs. If I make a fuss, it'll only justify him taking me out of my role.

"Commander, let me know if there's anything I can do."

"Will do, Dixon," he replies without even looking at me.

I feel like a toddler sitting at one of those fake steering wheel consoles they put on the back of car seats. Hell, at least those did something...

"Hey guys!" says Vin as his face pops up on the display. "Man, those Russians. Whew. And I thought dealing with Chinese investment bankers was rough. Long story short, we got hold of President Radin's guy, I met him at an Aspen Summit two years ago. Oxford educated, brilliant. Anyway, he took it to the man himself. Radin, as you know, has been trying to take a more diplomatic role – in no small part because falling oil prices are making them more dependent on foreign investment, etcetera. He said, 'Sure, why not?' Which is great, but then Zhirov, I'm told, lost his shit and said something about the universal docking ring not working on the K1. Which was news to me. So I called up Lena Golov, she's the actual mission supervisor for all the Russian launches. Great woman. I had her and her husband on my yacht last summer. We're trying to get her to come work for us. Fun to hang out with when she's all loosened up. Have you guys been to the yacht? You have to come out sometime."

"Love to," says Bennet, sharply.

"Oh, right, so anyway, I called her direct. She said her boss had no idea what he was talking about and was just quote, 'Being Russian about it.' I love that. Anyway, I tell Radin's guy he should really talk to her. And he did."

"And?" asks Bennet.

"We're still working on it." His screen goes dark.

I can see the muscles tighten in Bennet's jaw. If he wants to use his gun to shoot the screen, I'd totally understand.

I love Vin Amin. What he's single-handedly done for space travel can't be measured. He's one of those people like Musk and Bezos who helped us start dreaming again. He's created three successive startups, each one worth more than the last. Then he bet everything on getting into the space business, going toe-to-toe with the upstarts and the giants. He's got balls.

But he's also the guy in a YouTube video shot at Burning Man, walking around in a silver Speedo, high out of his mind, giving a rambling talk to his iPhone about why this would be the place to meet alien chicks for interspecies sex.

I guess with that kind of brilliance comes a special kind of crazy. His crazy is what got us up here. And it's probably what it will take to get us down. I hope.

"Good news!" says Vin as he pops back up on the display.

"You got the yacht reupholstered?" asks Bennet.

Vin blinks for a moment then bursts out laughing. "Oh man, you NASA guys. Hold on. I'm tweeting that one out..."

And he honest to god picks up his phone and starts typing the tweet.

"I hope my will is in order," I mumble under my breath.

This gets me a sly grin from Bennet and a snort from Peterson. Well holy smokes, Yoga Boy finally managed to do something to get an acknowledgment that he's more than dead weight.

"Where was I?" says Vin.

"Telling us if we're going to live or die," replies Bennet.

"Right! Good news. They're going to let you dock at the K1. And listen, just so you know, there were always going to be other options. I wouldn't let you guys down."

Other options? Does he have some secret rich person's space ark?

Hell, who knows with Vin. Guys like him don't see anything as being impossible. I could almost imagine him telling us we're going to burn up on reentry but he's pretty sure his engineers have time travel figured out so he'll just make sure it all never happens.

"Zhirov is super pissed and has a bunch of conditions for docking with the K1. Apparently they're doing some research on biofilms and whole sections of the station are off limits to us because of trade secrets. Can't wait to hear what that's all about. I'm sure one of their scientists will tell me when they get drunk on my boat and come asking for a job. Oh, man. The stuff people tell you to impress you. Anyway, Mission Control has all the details. I'm going to go look at carpet samples. Later."

I think that was a joke, but I'm not certain.

[6]
AIRLOCK

IN A BORED, OFFICIOUS VOICE, a Russian mission control operator drones on to us about the rules. "No more than one American astronaut shall leave the craft at a time, and always with an escort. The American astronauts will be allowed only access to the docking pylon, the lavatory facilities adjacent to the pylon and the airlock for doing their EVA. All EVA's will be under supervision of the K1 commander or a subordinate in order to prevent damage to the K1. No American may set foot onboard the K1 without permission from the K1 commander. While Unicorn 22 is docked on the K1, it is under jurisdiction of Russian Federation. As are all astronauts and passengers. We reserve right to inspect your cargo for any hazardous materials or contraband. If the commander of the Unicorn 22 agrees to these terms, please say 'affirmative.'"

I try to suppress a chortle every time he pronounces unicorn as "you KNEE corn."

"Dah," says Bennet before turning on his microphone. "Affirmative, Roscosmos. We agree to the terms. And thanks for helping us out."

We spend the next two hours bringing our orbit into alignment with the K1. The computers mostly handle this. We've been linking up with Russian spacecraft since

1975 when Apollo and Soyuz craft docked and their crews shook hands.

That was also the last flight for Apollo. On reentry there was a problem with the air system and two astronauts had to spend weeks in the hospital recovering from lung damage.

Let's hope this one goes a little better.

After checking velocity, alignment and all the other details that go into a docking procedure, we begin our final approach.

Bennet keeps his hands near the stick, but I notice he avoids touching it at any point during the window where it's safe to do so.

Through the porthole, K1 gradually grows from a tiny white grain of sand to a space station the size of two football fields.

Built like a giant cross from bus-sized cylinders, massive blue-black solar panels fill the squares between the pylons.

The docking module is a shaft sticking out of the bottom of the station. Two Soyuz capsules are berthed on either side as escape modules – the same kind that served as an emergency lifeboat on the International Space Station. In fact, the Soyuz modules were the workhorse of manned spaceflight for decades for the US and Russia.

Until Elon Musk and Vin Amin came along, NASA wasn't too proud of the fact that after the Shuttle program shut down, if you were an American astronaut that actually wanted to go into space, it was going to be onboard a Russian space taxi.

On the flip side for me, it turned out that learning to fly a MiG gave me an upper hand in iCosmos astronaut training. Being able to understand all the switches on the spacecraft of necessity for the last two decades was a definite plus – along with my ability to not have to pee every twenty minutes.

The K1 fills the sky in front of the Unicorn. Bennet's display shows the camera view of the nose coming in to the docking ring as a computer voice calls out the distance in centimeters.

There's an occasional burst from our docking rockets as they make fine adjustments to our approach. When we finally touch the collar, it's softer than a knock at the door.

A metal ring clamps shut and there's a tiny jostle as our ship is mated to the connector.

"Unicorn 22, this is K1. We have hard lock. Prepare for atmospheric equalization and to power down."

Before we can open the hatch and slap our comrades high fives, we have to make sure air pressure is equal on both sides. Otherwise, we could pop our eardrums, or worse, shoot out of the docking ring like a champagne cork while our hatch is wide open.

Fun times.

We put on our helmets just in case.

The air begins to hiss as we equalize with the K1 and Bennet powers us down. This is to prevent us from short circuiting the K1's electrical system until their electrician has a chance to make sure our power feeds aren't acting erratically. In space there's no way to ground an electric current. If you have stray voltage, it'll find a path, no matter what.

All the lights go out for a moment.

"Dixon," whispers Bennet. "I need to know right now, can I count on you?"

"Yeah, sure." This is a little odd.

"Listen to me very closely. I need you to do everything I or Peterson says. If you do that, it will all be fine."

I get the sudden realization that he's not talking about shaking hands through the airlock.

"What's going on?"

"Just listen. If anything should happen to Peterson or me, I want you to load up the reentry profile she prepared."

Peterson leans in and taps me on the shoulder. "Be a good boy and stay on the Unicorn. Everything will be okay."

"He'll be good," says Bennet.

Jesus. Fucking. Christ.

This has to do with the gun.

"What are you two up to?" I whisper.

"Need to know basis. Robbie was supposed to be in your chair. Until that retard screwed things up."

"I think I need to know."

"You can't know. Do you trust me?"

"In this exact moment? You're freaking me out."

"Do you trust me?"

Hell of a question to ask after the gun, pulling me off the pilot seat and whispering to me in the dark.

This is Bennet, an American hero. I've relied on him countless times underwater, dangling from parachute cords and sitting inside smoke-filled capsules simulating onboard fire.

"Yeah, Bennet, I trust you."

"You're a good man. If it gets dirty, you have to bug out. Got it?"

Dirty? What the hell? "What about the heat shield sensor problem?"

"There is no problem. I can't give you specifics. It's better that you don't know. I just need to know that if Peterson or I tell you to launch that you'll do that."

"You mean without you guys?"

"Exactly."

"You mean leave you on the K1?"

"You won't be leaving us. We'll already be dead."

"What the hell?"

He puts his hand on my shoulder just like the first time he shoved me out of an airplane. "This is bigger than us. A lot more is at stake. Can I count on you?"

"Affirmative." What else could I say?

[7]
BORDER PATROL

I'M CLENCHING MY FISTS inside my gloves as the hatch swings open. Bennet's little pep talk has completely put me on edge. Now that the Russians are coming I'm about to jump off the cliff of anxiety mountain.

A round Slavic face pokes into the airlock and announces, "The American astronauts will please remain seated while Commander Yablokov conducts his inspection."

Bennet, back in his seat after opening the hatch, replies, "Permission to come aboard."

I notice that no permission was requested and as Yablokov drifts into the compartment he barely even acknowledges Bennet.

Yablokov somehow manages to look even more Russian than the guy who announced his entrance. Compact, with a shaved head, even though he's not in his military uniform, he still wears it somehow.

I guess Bennet and Peterson are the same way. There's a composure they possess that sets them apart from slack yoga boys like myself.

Yablokov rests a hand on the bar above the display consoles in front of Bennet and me, and fixes eyes on Peterson. "You are Lieutenant Peterson?"

"Retired," she replies.

She spent ten years in the Air Force. The last five on a NASA detail. She's only 31, it's weird to think of her as "retired."

Yablokov nods then turns his gaze to me. "You are not Robert Carlyle."

"No, sir. I'm David Dixon."

"Why are you here?" he asks.

While I'm pretty sure he means why am I filling in for Robbie, it kind of feels like a question about the reason for my existence.

"Carlyle had a training accident. I'm his replacement."

Yablokov fixes me with a stare. It's an intimidating, unflinching gaze – like he's waiting for me to confess something. Bennet is also watching me out of the corner of my vision.

I notice his hand is casually floating in the air a few inches above the thigh pocket that holds his gun.

I can't get Poe's *Tell-Tale Heart* out of my mind.

The gun is calling out to me. My whole world centers around the pistol. I catch myself stealing a sideways glance at the pocket. I try to make it seem like I'm looking at Bennet for instructions.

As a kid, I had a friend who did magic tricks. Whenever he tried to hide something in his hand, that whole side of his body would go stiff. He assumed that because he knew it was there, the whole world knew. When the only clue we had was his weird body language.

Right now, I'm sure my body language says, "Commander Bennet has a goddamn gun in his pocket!"

Deep breath. Yablokov is still staring. What would a less scared version of myself do?

Smile, David. The best I can do is a slightly smug grin.

"You are not military," says Yablokov.

This sounds like an on-the-spot assessment and not him recalling some fact from my profile he just looked over before drifting in.

"No sir. They didn't want me."

"I can understand why."

Damn. I just got zinged in space.

"Your face," he says, "you wear everything on it. Your first mission into space, your ship malfunctions and now you have to come to the scary Russians for help. Do not be afraid. Everything will be made okay."

He gives me what may be a smile, but looks more like something you'd do in the frozen wastes of Siberia to prevent your mouth from freezing.

Yablokov pulls himself over to Bennet. "Commander, you were given instructions by Roscosmos? I expect you will follow them? I hold you personally responsible for the actions of your crew."

"Affirmative," says Bennet. He's trying not to show how much this chafes him to have the Russian treat him like a lost tourist.

Yablokov slides over to the space between Bennet's seat and the wall of the capsule. For a split second I think he's going to pat him down.

He motions towards the storage lockers behind us. Those and a trunk under the capsule are where we carry cargo.

"What is your cargo?"

"I can resend the manifest if you like. Resupplies for US/iC and Peterson's equipment."

Yablokov drifts behind us and unlatches one of the panels without asking. "No unsecured gas cylinders or other hazardous materials?"

Other than the several hundreds of pounds of monomethylhydrazine fuel and nitrogen tetroxide oxidizer that will explode upon contact we have sitting in tanks underneath us for landing, and a pistol in Bennet's pocket that could poke a hole through the tanks in a split second – blowing up the Unicorn and rapidly depressurizing the entire K1 station causing it to lose orbital stability and crash into our atmosphere where it will only imperfectly burn up, leaving a debris field a thousand miles long – no, nothing to worry about here.

"None of our cargo is dangerous," says Bennet, simplifying things.

Yablokov pulls himself back to the nose of the capsule. "Only one of you will be allowed out of the capsule at a time."

"That's not going to work, Commander," says Bennet. "We're required to do all of our EVAs in two-man configurations. In order for us to inspect the sensor I need two of us."

"You will have a cosmonaut escort."

"I understand that. But it's a two-person operation, not a precaution. I thought they explained this to Roscosmos?"

"They did. But this is at my discretion."

Even though our suits have gyros for keeping you balanced and emergency jets if you somehow detached from the tether, a space walk can be a terrifying experience – especially on something unfamiliar like the K1.

The technology has advanced some since the first time men drifted out of their capsules. It's now NASA and iCosmos's standard procedure to carry a small rescue drone that can retrieve an astronaut that drifts too far away. Thankfully, this has never had to be used on an iCosmos mission.

But I'm sure as the rapid pace of orbital construction continues, that will come in handy.

For now, we try to keep one person focused on the task and another to watch them, making sure they don't get tangled up or disoriented.

Yablokov stares at Bennet, trying to read the man. Bennet does a lot better at not flinching than I do.

He has that confident trait of making his point, then not arguing; ready to wait the other out.

"Fine," says Yablokov. "Which astronaut would you use?"

"Peterson," replies Bennet.

Peterson? She's not even an iCosmos employee.

Stay cool, David.

"Alright." Yablokov points to me. "He waits here during EVA."

Why do I get the feeling I'm a hostage in something I don't understand?

[8]
BABYSITTER

AFTER CHECKING THEIR SUITS and grabbing some tools from the trunk under Yablokov's watchful eye, Peterson and Bennet glide out of the hatch.

As he passes me, Bennet gives me a quick glance that says a thousand words, none of which are answers to the burning questions in my mind.

I wait for the sound of them going through the docking module airlock, then slide over to Bennet's console, ostensibly to watch the camera feeds from their helmets as they do the totally fake inspection.

When I try to pull up the signal there's nothing. Neither of them is transmitting.

That's just odd. There's no way you'd pull this kind of thing off without someone at Mission Control monitoring everything from what you're doing to solar flare activity and foreign object paths.

Granted, our suit computers track every lost lug nut and wrecked satellite in orbit, giving us a 3D display of where everything is, plus monitor space weather, but you still want a set of eyes and ears on the ground checking on you every few minutes.

Should I radio Bennet and ask?

No. This is intentional. He shut their cameras down for a reason. He might put them on during the space walk, but I doubt that.

He asked if I trusted him. The answer is "yes," I trust Bennet. I'm not so sure about the guy I've been around for the last few hours. Especially now that I know he's up to something.

Whenever you hear about a workplace tragedy where a coworker flips out and starts killing people with an AR-15 they brought to the office, the survivors often describe the tragedy as coming out of nowhere.

After the fact, the signs of erratic behavior are everywhere. "Yeah, it did seem a little odd that he brought a gun with him. Well, yes, he did seem a little erratic that morning."

I'm starting to freak myself out. Peterson is part of this or knows something is up. Is there a little thing between them that's about to erupt onboard the Russian space station?

See something, say something, David.

I'm not about to start blurting this out over our comm system; even the secure line. I have no way of knowing who else at Mission Control will be listening in. All I need is someone to report it right back to Bennet. It's not even a question of who they'll trust between us.

However...we have a text-based communication system that's basically instant messaging for talking between the Unicorn and Earth or any of the other iCosmos properties.

I could direct message Renata through here with something innocuous, like, "Bennet seems tense. Is there anything I should know?"

If she knows what he's up to, then all she has to say is, "It's okay," or something like that. Then I can relax and casually mention his gun discreetly.

When I try to access the messaging window, I get an alert that say, "iComm unavailable at this terminal."

Bennet shut down the system?

I slide out of the seat and try Peterson's panel. Same message.

Jesus. They've locked me out of both systems!

Alright, enough is enough.

We keep a set of laptops in the trunk in the event our displays stop working or we need extra terminals.

I float over to the trunk and remove one. The minute it takes to boot up feels like a year. I'm afraid Bennet is going to come back and find me hunched over the thing, trying to send my secret message.

Fuck him. I'll just tell him flat out I was trying to work around the message system lock out.

I pull up the iComm window and type in my credentials. A second later I get a different error message: Channel offline.

He shut down all outward access for the messaging system. Hell, is my microphone even live?

"Nashville, this is Unicorn 22, can I get a time check? Over."

Nothing.

I pull up a command line and type in crew/channel/status=

Comm01: Active
Comm02: Disabled
Comm03: Active
Comm04: Disabled
Comm05: Disabled
Comm06: Disabled
Comm07: Disabled
Comm08: Disabled
Bio01: Active

Bio02: Active
Bio03: Active
Bio04: Disabled
Bio05: Disabled
Bio06: Disabled
Bio07: Disabled
Bio08: Disabled

Jesus. Bennet disabled all the microphones except his and Peterson's while leaving my suit's biosensors live. The only way I can talk to ground control is if I have a heart attack in Morse code.

"Are you checking Facebook?" asks a female Russian voice from the hatch.

I'd jump out of my seat if I wasn't already floating a foot over it.

I look up and see a young woman staring at me from the nose cone. Large cheekbones and short red hair, she kind of reminds me of Peterson, only Russian.

"Just doing a routine check," I say, sounding like someone who only says "routine" when he's doing something very much not part of a routine.

"You are Pilot David Dixon?"

"Yes."

"I'm Flight Engineer Sonin. I am here to babysit you." She says this in what sounds close to a friendly tone – at least the most friendly I've heard since launch.

"Do they pay you by the hour or the orbit?" I reply, trying to sound totally not stressed out.

"This is funny," she says without a trace of laughter. "Commander Yablokov said you were not military."

"No, ma'am. Just a slack-jawed civilian that wants to be a space man."

"I see. What did you do before working for iCosmos?"

"Me? I was a school teacher for about three weeks."

"You weren't very good at it?"

"Probably not. I wanted to be an astronaut even more."

"But you are a pilot? Yes?"

Why did I feel like everyone here is very interested in my résumé? Don't they have LinkedIn in Russia?

Peterson and Bennet are the interesting ones. But maybe that's it; they've both got full Wikipedia pages with their entire life story. I'm a line of red text with nothing to link to on a page listing all of the current iCosmos astronauts.

When the Russians found out that we were coming and that I was a last-minute fill-in, I looked like the suspicious one.

"Yes. I'm a pilot." In the interest of international conversation, I'm about to point out that I'd even flown MiGs in Russian and learned a little of the language.

But I don't, because all hell is breaking loose.

There's a loud bang and an alarm goes off, filling the air with deafening noise.

"This is not good!" shouts Sonin.

You don't say...

[9]
BLOOD STAINS

"MICROMETEORITE?" Sonin asks.

As if I would know.

She gives me a confused look then pushes off the airlock hatch and flies away to investigate the alarm.

Micrometeorites are a real thing. The Space Shuttle came back to Earth twice with dings in the windshield. One went halfway through. They started orbiting the craft upside down and backwards so the engines, not needed for reentry, would take the brunt of the damage instead of the part that held the people. Not the most reassuring solution.

The popping sound could have been one striking the K1, but I can think of something else that can make that sound...

I call into my comm, "Commander Bennet? Peterson?"

Nothing.

The local ship-wide comm should at least be working. They're either choosing not to respond or can't.

Procedure is for me to wait onboard the capsule until further notice and get the ship ready for launch. But nothing is going according to that book, so I'm just going to throw it out the window.

I pull myself through the hatch into the docking module. We're at the base of the pylon where three other tunnels lead to airlocks. At the top of this junction is the long module that leads to the main junction that forms the nexus of the K1.

I drift into the pylon and look up. Red warning lights splash across the walls of the station accompanying the siren. There's also a buzzer and a few other alarms sounding.

This isn't like movies where you get just one general alert sound. Every important system has its own alert. The most critical ones involve fire and air supply. They're either telling you we have a fire, a depressurization event going on, or something is affecting the air supply like a material fire that could release toxic fumes.

I pull myself up the module and spot a cabinet with air masks for use in case of an air quality issue. I notice that Sonin already opened it and removed one. I do the same.

As I pull myself closer to the junction I can see that one module is completely dark. The one across from it has a blinking fluorescent light. Fluorescents in the age of LED lighting? The Russians are weird.

Directly above me is the module that leads to the command section and the airlock where the EVA would take place. It's empty.

I push myself into the dark tunnel. Tiny systems lights shine like green and red stars on the walls. At the far end there's a partially opened airlock door leading to another dark section.

I drift towards there and something wet splashes me on my cheek above the mask. Even in the darkness I can tell what it is when I wipe it away – my fingertips are covered in blood.

Fuck.

"Hello?" I repeat the word in Russian, "Zdravstvuyte?"

Nothing. However, under all the noise I think I can hear the sound of someone yelling.

I glide towards the next module, pulling myself along by handrails and trying to dodge the floating drops of blood.

Through the gap in the door there's flashes of light.

"Anybody there? Yest' kto tam?"

Still no response.

I pull myself into the next hatch. The air is colder here. There's a small breeze whistling through the gap.

A beam of light flashes across my face, blinding me for a moment. When my eyes adjust, I can see the disc of light as it spins around the module. At the end of it is a small penlight floating by itself.

"Hello?"

Suddenly all the alarms are silenced and the flashing lights in the other modules go dark.

Maybe the crisis is over?

If so, where is everybody?

I drift forward into the darkness, looking for any sign of life.

If there had been a depressurization event I should feel a breeze – unless they sealed the hatch in time.

In that case, everyone on the other side is either trying to patch a hole, unconscious or dead.

CLUNK!

Something bangs the wall in the next darkened section.

"Hello?" I give up on translating myself.

I reach the hatch at the end of the module. At first I think it's sealed, but notice that it's cracked slightly. If there was a hole in the station this thing would have closed up. This tells me the explosion I heard was something from inside – possibly from someone I know.

My mind races through all kinds of possibilities.

Bennet's talk before he and Peterson went aboard pretty much told me that some bad stuff was about to go down.

He was also pretty specific that I wasn't supposed to leave the ship. And here I am.

I push the hatch open so I can slip through.

A blinding light races towards me and I hear a scream.

[10]
EMERGENCY LAUNCH

A FLASHLIGHT SLAMS INTO THE HATCH next to me, spins in the air then catches Peterson as she flies towards me.

Her eyes widen when she spots me. "Dixon!"

She's out of her spacesuit and holding her hand to her side as blood pours from a wound, leaving globules behind her.

"BACK TO THE SHIP!!!" she screams.

I don't hesitate. I don't question.

I flip myself over in the air and pull at the handles, hurtling myself through the airlock, checking back just once to make sure she's following me.

When I reach the main junction, I yank myself into the pylon leading to the docking module like a dolphin diving into the ocean.

As I fly towards the nexus, I steal a look behind me again. Peterson is twenty feet away, still holding her side. In the light of the module I can see her face is pale, real pale. She's lost a lot of blood.

I slide into the Unicorn's hatch and maneuver over the seats to get to the first aid kit.

Peterson reaches the airlock and stops there. She throws a small black square covered in blood at me. "Take it!"

It wobbles towards me and I pluck it from the air without thinking.

"Let me help you!" I go to assist her through the airlock.

She pushes my hand away and shakes her head. "No time!"

She starts to swing the hatch closed.

"Wait! Where's Bennet?"

"Bennet's dead." She slams the metal door before I can stop her.

Through the small window I can see as she looks behind her. She grabs an emergency handle and pulls it.

The interior locking mechanism automatically disengages.

"Wait!" I yell.

She hasn't shut the K1 docking hatch.

Without that...

BOOM!!!

The capsule hull lurches at me, slamming the hatch into my head, making me see stars.

I float there, dazed for a few seconds.

When I come to my senses, I realize that she disengaged the docking collar while the other hatch was open.

The explosion was the sound of the air popping the capsule out like a BB from an air rifle – ejecting the Unicorn and killing her.

Seconds ago she was alive...

No time to overthink. I can only react.

I slide myself into Bennet's chair and try to stabilize the ship.

The controls are now responsive. Did he have them triggered to come back after some kind of event?

"Nashville, this is Unicorn 22, we have an emergency." My voice is calm, just like Bennet trained me.

"Nashville, can you read me?"

Nothing.

The comm is still down.

Something catches my eye from the side porthole.

It's Peterson.

Her arms over her head, red crystals of blood staining her white uniform; she looks as if she's diving into a pool of black.

The Unicorn tumbles away from her while I sit stunned.

Time goes by, Earth flashes past the window dozens of times. I finally stabilize the ship when I come to my senses slightly.

There's a crackle on the short range ship-to-ship radio and a Russian accent commands, "American vessel, return to the K1."

I ignore it.

Christ. Peterson is dead. Bennet too.

There was blood. Lots of blood.

My space suit is still speckled with it.

I realize I'm still clenching the black square and shove it into my thigh pocket then yank the Russian air mask off and slide on my space helmet.

"American vessel, return to the K1."

I'm not in a talkative mood right now. And I'm pretty sure I won't like what they have to say.

"American vessel, return to the K1. Now!"

I shut the radio off.

This situation is so fucked, I don't even know how much. It could have been some bizarre accident or a damn international incident.

I'm so lost in it I don't even notice at first there's a phone ringing from under Bennet's seat.

Something went down. Something serious enough for Peterson to sacrifice her life.

Ring.

And now the Russians are yelling at me to return to the K1.

Ring.

Bennet told me something was going to happen. But this?

Ring.

Peterson's face as she drifted past the window. My god.

Ring.

All my training and nothing prepares me for this.

Ring.

What would Bennet do? Forget the crazy Bennet that may have just got himself killed. What would the guy that taught me everything about being an astronaut do?

Ring.

Be present. Focus.

Ring.

I unstrap and reach into the small tray under the cushion.

It's an iPhone with a satellite antenna case.

The display says "Unknown caller."

I decide to answer it, rather than deal with the angry Russians. "Hello?"

An electronic voice responds, "If you want to survive, do exactly what I say."

[11]
GROUND CONTROL

"WHO THE HELL IS THIS?" I shout at the phone as if it will help. "What the fuck is going on?"

"I'm the guy that's going to save your life. Pull up reentry profile eight."

I load the eighth profile Peterson had programmed into the system. The tracking is all wrong.

It has the ship coming down over Brazil.

"What the..."

"Why can't I just go back to Canaveral or Mojave?"

"Take a look at the S.O.T."

I pull up the Space Object Tracking map; a 3-dimensional model of all the different objects currently in orbit. Each one has a dot and ghostly outline tracing its orbit.

"See those two dots that just moved from their orbital paths?"

Two specks in Low Earth Orbit have moved away out of their tracks.

"Those are Russian satellite killers. Each one is armed with a chemical laser that will burn a hole in your hull at the moment of reentry. If you try to land anywhere on US ground, you'll be a pile of ash before you hit the surface."

"Why can't I talk to Mission Control?"

"Right now Roscosmos is telling them that you went berserk and used a smuggled gun to kill Bennet and Peterson before almost destroying the K1."

"What? That's bullshit! I'll tell them I don't know what happened! They'll have to believe me."

"Do you want to take that chance? And not everyone with an American flag on their lapel is your friend."

"What's that supposed to mean?"

"Part of the reason Bennet and Peterson died is because not everyone can be trusted."

"Why are they dead?" I remember the black square in my pocket. "What did Peterson give me?"

"You'll live longer if you don't know."

"Fuck you!"

"Rotate your heat shield towards the K1 now!"

"What?" I reflexively spin the Unicorn so the nose is towards Earth and the heat shield is facing the station.

There's a flash on the heat shield sensor display. A portion of the underside is getting ridiculously hot.

"What the hell is that?"

"The K1 just fired a laser at your ship. Start your reentry now if you want to live."

"Let me get a message to Nashville."

"They can't help you."

I watch the temperature climb on the heat shield. There's a red line point at which they can do permanent damage and I won't be able to land.

If I hadn't turned when the voice told me, I'd already have a hole in the hull. If I survived the explosive decompression long enough to get my visor down, I'd still be stranded in space and my only chance of rescue would be the Russians who just shot at me.

"Do it now, David." The electronic voice somehow conveys the sense of urgency.

Fuck it. My life is over either way. I punch the button on the screen and the ship's rockets begin to fire.

The K1 recedes behind me but the heat shield sensor stays steady.

My trajectory still keeps my heat shield towards the station. At this altitude, I need about three minutes before the station is beyond the horizon and its laser is out of reach.

After four minutes the reading goes back to normal and I rotate the ship towards atmospheric reentry.

They tried to kill me. The damn Russians tried to kill me!

The reentry profile has me doing an aggressive loop around the earth, slowing down in the upper atmosphere before beginning a steep drop over the Southern hemisphere, landing somewhere around the southern part of Brazil.

"Brazil? What the hell?"

"Would you prefer Africa or India?"

"I'd prefer Cape Canaveral."

"You won't make it to the ground. And if you do, through some small miracle, you'll never make it out of an interrogation room."

"Jesus Christ."

"David. I need you to follow my instructions very carefully. We only have a few minutes before we'll lose signal. First, give that chip to Wallman. Only him. Nobody else can be trusted."

"Who the hell is he?"

"He'll find you. What matters most right now is your survival. Go to the trunk and pull out Peterson's bag."

I tuck the phone into my helmet, unhook my harness and drift over to the cabinet. There's a large black duffle bag inside.

I place it into my old seat under the harness and take Bennet's console. "Now what?"

"The Russians are going to figure out that you're taking a different reentry path. They won't be able to re-task the kill-sats fast enough, but they will be able to send long-range MiGs to intercept you in the air. They will fire upon you if you're over the ocean or an uninhabited area."

"Well, fuck."

"We have to land the Unicorn in a bay."

"Jesus Christ."

"If you're out to sea you'll never make it. They'll have a ground team en route. We can't let them get you or the package."

"Wonderful. How about I just radio them that I surrender?"

"You can't do that, David. Lives other than your own are at stake."

"And you can't tell me why..."

"I'm just one part of this. My job is to get you to the ground safely."

"So I land in some Brazilian city?"

"The trajectory touchdown is Rio de Janeiro."

"Wonderful."

"But when the Unicorn lands you won't be in there."

"Come again?"

"Bennet said you could pull this off."

"And what happened to him?"

"He died for a reason. Pull this off, and you'll make it. Lots of people will."

"Pull what off?"

"We're going to use the ship's emergency parachute to slow the descent of the Unicorn in the upper atmosphere instead of the retro rocket. We're then going to jettison the drogue chute and let the ship free fall for 10,000 meters so the MiG's can't get to you."

"We?" I stare the phone in disbelief. "Great. Just great."

"At 1,000 meters you're going to engage the thrusters at full throttle and then tilt the Unicorn at a twenty degree inclination."

"Lord almighty. Why?"

"Reach inside Peterson's bag."

I unzip the duffle and see what's inside.

"No fucking way."

"David, it's the only way you survive."

"Nobody has ever done this before."

"Which is why the Russians and everybody else won't see it coming."

[12]
CRASH DUMMY

WHY AM I GOING ALONG WITH THIS? Because a drowning man will cling to anything, even the tail of a great white shark if it happens to swim by.

Right now there's only one voice trying to steer me through this crisis. Although it very likely belongs to the person who instigated the entire situation.

If I hadn't spun the ship when the mysterious robot voice told me to, I would either be dead or strapped down in K1 as the prisoner of a bunch of angry Russians.

Now the voice on the sat phone is telling me I have to do a hybrid landing in the middle of a crowded tourist destination – but not actually land the thing. Oh, no, it gets better.

When Elon Musk first proposed landing all the parts of a rocket back on Earth using propulsion instead of parachutes, everyone said he was crazy. When SpaceX finally pulled it off, everyone said it was the most obvious idea in the world. All the public and private space programs rushed to develop their own propulsive landing systems.

The end result is that modern spacecraft like the Unicorn are designed to land back on Earth by doing two controlled burns. The first one in the upper atmosphere is intended to slow the ship down from 17,000 miles per hour to something just over the speed of sound, letting atmospheric drag then bring the Unicorn to terminal velocity around 200 mph. The second burn is the landing burn, gradually slowing the ship down so that it can nicely touch down with pin-point accuracy.

If you wanted, you could land the Unicorn on the helipad of a skyscraper – assuming the top was covered in asbestos.

That is a long way away from the days when you hit the upper atmosphere with enough uncertainty your splashdown zone was several thousand square miles of the Pacific.

If you were just dropping from a stationary point above the earth, you could narrow that area down considerably, but since you're hitting the atmosphere angled at an incredible velocity, the place where you're going to land is on the other side of the horizon. And between you and that spot, there are all kinds of thermal variations, wind currents and other factors; including the fact that a one degree variation in your approach angle can affect your drag enough to widen the landing area.

Computers helped a lot to narrow that zone. The Space Shuttle was also a big improvement. Because it was a controllable glider, you could fine tune its flight path and bring it down on a runway.

However, powered landings were the real game changer. They meant a crew could touch down and look out the window and see their car in the parking lot – a far cry from waiting for an aircraft carrier to retrieve you from shark-infested waters.

The key to a powered landing is letting the onboard system do all the work. The computer can do precisely timed engine bursts, sometimes lasting milliseconds, to finely adjust the landing path with minute precision.

Out of all the times you want to have a human handle the controls, this is not it. Nobody has reactions fast enough to make that work. Sure, a good pilot could land the thing without making a crater, but trying to hit the X on the pad – and not the cafeteria skylight – is a different matter.

And Mr. Mysterious just told me he wants me to take the stick at this most critical phase.

But it gets even better...

Even though this ship can launch and land entirely on rocket power, it has two backup parachute systems in the event there's an engine failure. The first one is opened in the upper atmosphere and serves as a drag chute to slow the ship down to a less ridiculous velocity. After that's jettisoned, a second one is opened to bring the ship to a more graceful landing over who knows where.

Around iCosmos, we call this landing "caveman" style.

But this isn't what the voice has planned for me...

He's telling me to open the ship's emergency parachute at a high altitude instead of doing a reentry burn to slow my descent. This means that I'll actually be dropping a lot faster initially – theoretically to avoid those MiGs he says are waiting to catch me.

However, when the Unicorn is at its most vulnerable, dangling from the second parachute, as easy a target as there is in the sky, he says don't use the chute. Instead, he wants me to have the ship free fall to Earth for a few miles, you know, no big whoop, then, THEN, at the point of no return, use all that fuel we didn't use on the reentry, to TAKE OFF AGAIN.

Now, it's not like there's an infinite amount of fuel on this thing. It'll only take the ship so high, about 10,000 feet or so. But for anyone watching where I'm about to land, won't that be a surprise...

They'll see the Unicorn drop down over the sunny bay – I think it'll be day there – then shoot up into the sky like a meteor in reverse – only not straight up.

Of course not. That would mean it would come right back down where it almost landed.

No sir. By tilting the ascent by 20 degrees, the Unicorn is going to shoot like a missile over Rio, the beaches, the Jesus statue and all the beautiful people in one giant arc, bringing the ship down in some monkey-infested jungle.

Here's the really, really good part. When the Unicorn lands, probably on some lost temple, I won't be there.

My mysterious friend wants me to do the unthinkable.

Shortly after the Unicorn starts its fake-out relaunch, and at some point when I'm conscious and able to actually move, I'm supposed to pop the hatch and jump out with a parachute of my own, conveniently packed in Peterson's duffle bag.

The burning question in my mind – other than will I live past the next few minutes – is why are there three chutes? Was this the plan all along?

[13]
BAILOUT

"ARE YOU READY, DAVID?" asks the voice on the speakerphone.

"Define, "ready" for me. What are my other options?"

"There are no other options. We'll probably lose contact when you get to ground. You need to find Wallman and bring him the chip."

"Yeah, about that. How?"

"I'll tell you when it's time to know."

"What if I lose this phone?"

"Don't lose it."

"Yeah, but let's assume for a moment I do. Then what?"

There's a very long pause that's disconcerting. Among all the planning for dramatic reentry burns and take-offs, my unseen friend forgot to account for the most basic situation – what happens if we lose contact?

Besides what happens on the ground – assuming I make it there in one living piece – there's the question of the next several minutes. I'm not getting any telemetry from Nashville. This is flying blind at its worst.

In the olden days, when a space capsule returned to Earth, it lost communication with Earth for several minutes because all the ionized air from the heat shield formed a kind of Faraday cage blocking radio signals.

Reentry had to be carefully planned in advance and it was the pilot's job to make sure everything was on course.

Since the Space Shuttle had such a large surface area, there was actually a gap in the ionized bubble above it where they could send and receive communications via satellite, get telemetry and carry on conversations all the way down.

For smaller craft, like the Unicorn and the Soyuz, this problem persisted until the development of a laser-based system. It doesn't allow for huge data streams, but it's enough to get by. Having another set of eyes tell you everything looks fine is rather reassuring.

In the simulator you train for all kinds of situations, including having no support from ground control.

Theoretically, the Unicorn and Alicorn, the rocket that launches the Unicorn into orbit, can run entirely by themselves. If one second after liftoff a lightning strike took out mission control, the automatic systems would take the Unicorn to orbit and the Alicorn's two stages would either land on the pad if there was an okay to proceed signal, or dump themselves in the ocean.

So, yeah, I don't have to have anybody on Earth in order to land, but it would be kind of nice.

"David, we will lose contact during reentry. But I'm confident you'll know how to handle this. Put your parachute on now before reentry begins. Things will get bumpy."

I reluctantly slide the harness over me. The straps are wide enough to go over my suit. Peterson, or whoever packed her bag put a little more thought into this than the voice on the phone.

To make this work, I'm going to have to have my hand on the stick as I watch the altimeter and squeeze the throttle at the right moment, tilting the craft at an angle.

So I don't drop the side hatch on a schoolyard filled with children, I'll have to blow it right when I'm over the bay – a bay I don't even know the name of.

"Okay, I have your contact point. Once you land, go to the train station by the Maracanã football stadium. Someone will meet you there."

"Did you just decide this now?"

"We're trying to adjust to the situation."

"What if there's a problem?" Bennet taught me to always have a backup.

"Hold on...okay, if we lose contact on the ground look for more information from this Twitter handle..."

A text message pops up saying "@CapricornZero."

"Seriously? I'm trusting my life to someone who just decided to create a Twitter account based on an OJ Simpson movie?"

"Focus on reentry, David. That's all you need to worry about now. Once you make it to the station, everything will be fine."

I'm not sure if I like the totality of "fine." But there's no point in arguing that point right now. I'm about to dip down into the atmosphere and experience some severe turbulence.

If I hit it wrong, I can bounce back up and miss my intended landing zone, so I keep a careful eye on the display panel.

It starts to shimmy, then begins to jostle the craft like a speedboat crashing through waves – if the waves were hitting your hull at 17,000 miles an hour.

Below me, the heat shield is starting to absorb all that energy. I pray that the Russians didn't poke a hole in the surface. One tiny gap is all it takes and the whole ship is lost.

While the new Pica-Z material is self-healing and can fill in gaps created by micrometeorite strikes, I'm not sure if it has been tested for mad Russian lasers yet. I'll have to ask the iCosmos engineers if they really thought of every contingency...

The first part of reentry feels like an airplane trying to slow down after a landing – pressing me into my seat as my body's inertia pushes against the spaceship which is now being slowed down by the thin air it's slamming into.

Outside the window I can see the coronal glow of the ionized air. Technically speaking, the air is so hot the electrons leap out of their orbits and fly around like some kind of electric swinger party. Which means basically, I'm a giant neon sign right now.

Now is a good time to close my helmet in the event of a hull puncture that could instantly incinerate me.

I leave the phone next to my ear, although I haven't heard anything from my helper.

Whatever system he was using to communicate with me, ain't going to work during this period. So if I want to mutiny and choose my own path, now is the time.

I scan the options on my control panel and contemplate it.

I could still adjust my reentry and bring myself down somewhere where I speak the language.

It's crunch time, David. Yes, he probably saved me from the Russians, but that doesn't mean he's my pal.

While I trust he doesn't want me to die before getting to the ground, he seems very adamant that I don't link back up with iCosmos or US authorities. And that, my friend, is a tiny bit suspicious.

You have seconds to decide if you're going to say "Olá" or whatever the Brazilian-Portuguese version of hello is supposed to be, or try to land on US soil and pray the kill-sats are imaginary and the Russian ground teams don't reach you in time.

Screw it. Let's see if the senhoras are wearing their string bikinis this time of year.

If I don't die, it'll give me something to think about when I'm in Federal prison or locked up in some Siberian gulag.

[14]
FLY BY WIRE

AS THE UNICORN BASHES AROUND like a golf ball in a dryer, I keep my heavy hand near the control stick and watch the altimeter, waiting to manually release the drogue chute. Do it too soon and it'll shred itself apart. Wait too long and I'll still be burning the retro rockets as I crater myself in Guanabara Bay – that's the name my satellite map is showing me where my trajectory is taking me.

Flying a spacecraft like the Unicorn isn't quite like anything else. Maybe the closest analogy is a helicopter, but even then the comparisons kind of end beyond up and down controls.

At the root level, all fast-moving vehicles have their similarities – whether it's a Lamborghini or a high-altitude glider. You need to use finely tuned instincts to keep yourself from making a split-second mistake that can end your life.

The first time I ever took control of a flying machine I was seventeen. The end of that summer, a few weeks after I had my eye surgery, I took a bike ride to the local airport on my one day off.

Looking through the chainlink fence I saw an old guy in a windbreaker wiping the windshield of a white and blue twin engine Cessna 310.

"You fly?" he asked me when he saw me watching.

Man, I can't tell you what that question meant to me in that moment. Here I was, a teenager on a rusty beach cruiser who couldn't even afford a car and this guy asked if I was a pilot. For a brief second I could have been a peer – not some Air Force and Navy recruitment office reject.

"No," I replied.

"You want to?" he said, dropping the wash rag into a bucket.

I got my first good look at him. He was tall, tan and in his seventies but looked like a healthy fifty-year-old. There was a confidence about him you see in pro football coaches and generals.

"Yeah. Some day."

"How about today?"

Today? "You mean right now?"

He checked his watch. "A couple more hours of daylight. Why not?"

Up until that moment I had been a bookish kid who played flight simulators and toyed with the idea of being a pilot, but the only ambitious thing I had done was make enough money to get my eyes fixed. Beyond that, it was a kind of "some day" dream.

To be a pilot, not just the Saturday morning kind, but a guy who goes out there and pushes the envelope and tries to make the machine do things it wasn't supposed to, means having something in you that says, "Fuck it. Let's do it."

Getting into an airplane with a stranger ranks right up there with accepting rides from creepers with vans and eating strange candy from the dude down the street who still lives with his mother and watches you through the window.

Even worse, it's not like therapy can help you deal with the kind of fatal trauma you get when you're killed in a crash.

I knew the sky was my destiny when my mouth said, "Yes," before my brain even processed the information.

Mr. Sterner, that was his name, was breaking all kinds of rules when he casually asked me if I wanted to take flight in his plane.

Sterner couldn't have cared less. He'd flown sorties in Vietnam, trained pilots in the Navy then left the service to go run an insurance business with his brother.

He could give zero fucks what anybody told him was right or wrong.

In a split second he'd sized me up and decided that I was okay – that I wasn't going to go run my mouth off about the crazy guy at the airport that took me up in his airplane.

He treated me like an adult when he asked me if I wanted to fly.

Ten minutes after take-off he leaned back and folded his hands behind his head and told me to take the controls, just like that.

Where I'd been trusting him not to kill me in the air or try to grab my dick, he just sat back and said, "She's yours now," putting his life in my hands.

That was the first time I felt like a pilot. That was the first time I *was* a pilot.

I was nervous and scared, but that was just a small dull roar, like the sound of the shower running in another room. Yeah, I was aware of my anxiety, but it didn't affect me one bit.

I knew all the gauges and levers and switches from my simulators. But I didn't know the gut rolling feeling when you changed your pitch or brought the plane into a steep curve.

Where others feel motion sickness, for me it was like finding out I had a new sense.

I wasn't a pilot just because I had the balls or the stupidity to say "Yes." I was a pilot because in that moment it felt right.

Once a month I'd go fly with Sterner. Afterwards he'd buy me lunch and tell me stories about flying inches over jungle tops, scraping the trees, landing on carriers and crazy stories about his fellow pilots and trainees.

The week after I got accepted into college he died of prostate cancer. At the funeral reception his brother pulled me aside and handed me a cardboard box.

Inside was the windbreaker I met him in and a plastic display containing his Top Gun flight school cap.

The message was clear; wearing the hat was reserved for the men that actually went through that program. But taking care of Sterner's hat was being entrusted to me, his final student – a kid who never had a chance to set foot on a carrier as a pilot – but eagerly dropped his bike on the sidewalk and climbed the fence to ride shotgun with a crazy old man with a death wish.

"Save a beer for me, Sterner," I say, getting ready to hit the parachute release.

[15]
DROGUE

AS THE ATMOSPHERE SLAMS into the Unicorn, attempting to vibrate me into a jelly coating on the floor and walls of the cabin, I watch my velocity, and get ready to release the small drogue chute designed to help slow me down to a less ridiculous speed.

Astronauts who have been onboard Soyuz and the Unicorn say there's no comparison. When working properly, and not doing what I'm doing, the Unicorn is a much smoother ride down on its retro rockets. While the Soyuz is a controlled crash, that despite two parachutes and a last-second retro rocket assist, manages to hit the ground at twenty miles an hour or more and then bounce back into the air – tricking first-timers into thinking they were on Earth. Nope, they get to relive the impact again a few seconds later.

Despite the first ever Soyuz capsule launch – which after a drogue chute failure turned a heroic cosmonaut into a pancake where only his heel bone was recognizable – the craft, as terrifying as it is to ride – ended up having the best safety record of any manned spacecraft until the new generation of capsules came along.

Up until now, the Unicorn has a perfect safety record, which I'm about to ruin when I die because I'm doing everything you're not supposed to do.

I hit the drogue release and get slammed into my seat hard. I was already pulling close to 4 G's – which I was only able to cope with because of prior training and all the practice sessions I did in a mock-up cockpit with a lead-weighted suit that showed me what it's like to try to press a button when your arm weighs a hundred pounds.

With the release of the drogue, there's a shift in my center of gravity and the Unicorn not only vibrates like a mofo, it starts to fly around and spin like a piñata at a birthday party for hyperactive kids.

My display shows a stabilized image of Guanabara Bay below me as a bright blue pool. I focus on the serene waters while my brain starts to liquify.

The Unicorn gradually settles down a bit. Right now, if the voice on the phone is to be believed, Russian fighters, probably launched from Venezuela or Cuba, are plotting an intercept towards me based on what they think my altitude will be when I release the drogue and deploy the main parachute – bringing me to a more leisurely descent at around twenty miles an hour – instead of the two hundred I'm hitting right now.

Ha ha, suckers. Main parachutes are for losers.

Won't they be surprised when they see me fly past at ten times my expected velocity? Won't we all?

BANG! The Unicorn jostles when I detach the drogue. My body pushes against the seat harness as I hang in mid air like the Wile E. Coyote momentarily forgetting that gravity is a thing.

I'm back in free fall – a much slower free fall than when I hit the atmosphere. I'm going just a mere 170 miles an hour now and not the ludicrous 17,000 when I de-orbited.

Ever see what a Ferrari looks like after it crashes into a concrete wall at 170 miles an hour? A lot like a mural of what a Ferrari would look like it if crashed into a wall at 170 miles an hour.

Komarov, that's his name, Vladimir Komarov, the cosmonaut who got to be the first one to ride and die in a Soyuz – they say he knew it was doomed but went anyway, because refusing would have put Yuri Gagarin, the first man in space and a world hero, in the death seat.

And I'm doing this because? Right, some asshole with a voice disguiser says it's the only way to save my life.

My life...fuck...I watched Peterson die in front of me.

Compartmentalize, David. You have two minutes before you have to pull off the most stupid maneuver of your inevitably short life. Deal with their loss later. Stop yours now.

I put my left hand around the stick and get ready to squeeze the throttle while my right finger hovers near, but not over, the hatch release by my head.

The bay grows bigger and I can see individual crests and the long wakes of boats.

Are the people down there looking up in the sky at this missile shooting towards the water?

Hell, is this on the news? I hit the upper atmosphere long enough ago for this to be a breaking story. I doubt anyone other than the United States and Russia has figured out my trajectory well enough to narrow it down. So that means no news crews waiting to film my death. I think. Good thing, because mom had all her students watch my launch.

Well, I'm sure somebody on the beach with a telephoto lens shooting voyeuristic shots of girls in their string bikinis will manage to capture the end of my life. It won't be a total waste. He'll probably be able to sell the footage to a tabloid site within minutes. Good for him.

I suddenly realize that I'm well below the envelope where a Russian fighter could have fired on me over international waters.

So that's good to know. Either this maneuver worked or Capricorn is full of shit.

The bad news is I have ten seconds to decide whether or not after I squeeze this throttle if I'm going to yank the stick to the side and aim the Unicorn straight over a heavily populated city.

Capricorn said that's the only way I survive.

That sounds really selfish now that I can see individual apartment buildings and beaches filled with people.

He also said if this McGuffin in my pocket falls into wrong hands it could mean lots of people will die.

Okay, technically he implied that. But that was the gist of things.

Cosmonaut Komarov took one for the team. Apparently so did Bennet and Peterson. What about you, David Dixon?

I guess, technically, if I do the safe thing and just use the retro-rockets to land in the water, I'm actually acting selfishly.

What would Bennet and Peterson do?

What would Sterner do?

I start the engines, let the hypergolic propellants mix and light up a tower of fire below me.

I can hear the thunderous roar throughout the cabin.

Every single person on the beaches in Rio has to be seeing this right now. They're going to hear it in a second as the sound reaches them...

And if you think that's cool folks, wait until you see my next trick...

[16]
ESCAPE

HOLY CRAP! Is that a fucking helicopter?

Out of nowhere the thing flies in right below me on my landing display while a speedboat bounces across the waves ahead of it. What the fuck? Did they think the bright shiny thing falling from the sky is a goddamn care package?

My finger is already squeezing the throttle by the time I see them. I pray those dumb bastards had the chance to get away before I started the world's largest beachside barbecue.

Worry about them later. I've got one second before the retro rockets reverse my direction and I'm shoved into my seat.

BOOM!!! The hatch above my head blows outward when the explosive bolts fire.

Good to know my right hand is still reacting while I'm rubbernecking.

It's a strange thing when you practice stuff so much your body takes over. That kind of motor learning is what makes the difference between a skilled pilot and a smoking wreck on the ground.

Astronaut and space vehicle training is practicing for every possible contingency until you can literally sleepwalk through them. It's a lot like martial arts. You train until you don't have to think about it anymore.

The roar of the thrusters was loud before – now it's super-fucking thunder through the open hatch. The fuel mix makes a crackling popping sound that reminds me of a bunch of grenades all going off like Chinese firecrackers. And I'm on top of them.

As I fly off at an angle, I rotate the craft over so the hatch is facing the ground and I'm upside down. There's no way in hell I'll be able to get out any other way while the rockets are firing. Even then, it's dicey. The inertia is still going to be intense at the highest point of my arc where I have to jump out.

I'll probably end up tripping and falling towards the storage trunks in the back and die on impact. If I don't, the rocket plume is going to burn me to a crisp anyway.

So no matter what, it really doesn't matter.

I glance down and see the city flying by underneath. It looks rather nice. It hardly seems overrun by monkeys. The Simpsons lied to me.

I spot a stadium directly below and wonder if that's the Maracanã football arena.

If I'd timed things right, I could have just jumped out here and been done with the whole thing.

Well, there's always next time, David.

Speaking of bailouts, I check the altimeter and the fuel gauge. I'm hitting the highest point of my trajectory and can kind of sort of move my arms.

This would be a good time to hop out. If I wait any longer I'm going to be stuck in this can as it smashes into the mountains to the north of Rio.

The computer is all set to keep firing the engine then pop the primary parachute. In theory, sending the Unicorn on a thirty mile trek away from the city – and hopefully anyone looking for me.

Of course, my parachute won't exactly be inconspicuous. Which means I've got to do a last minute chute open to kill my fall. Assuming it can handle the force.

Christ, for all I know, Peterson could have packed her pole dancing class clothes in the backpack instead of a parachute. Won't that be hilarious as they find my cratered body inside a spacesuit next to a bunch of thong underwear?

I unhook my harness and grasp the edge of the seat.

The good news is that pilots have survived Mach 3 bailouts.

The bad news for me is that they were in ejection seats that did all the work.

Thankfully, I'm not going anywhere near that speed. Just a mere 300 miles per hour.

The moment the Unicorn starts to level off I reach up and grab the handrail by the hatch.

FUCK! The incoming wind is so intense it smacks my fist into my helmet.

Stop hitting yourself, David, my older sister taunts.

I try again, this time making a karate chop shape with my hand so it has less resistance. Sensei Mike would be pleased.

I grasp the handle with my left, then do the same with my right. The downward pull of gravity is still less than the inertia pulling me into my seat, but with a little bit of effort on my part, I'm able to get myself into the hatch.

BAM!!! The wind smacks my head against the edge of the hatch.

If I hadn't been wearing this fancy spaceman noggin protector I would have cracked my skull open like an egg. Even with it, I'm seeing stars.

Christ.

Literally, Christ, holy crap, I can see the Christ statue from here! That means I need to bail out now or end up in the mountains.

I stick my head and shoulders all the way through the hatch by standing upside down on the seat.

You know, it's actually kind of beautiful from here.

I pull myself free and fly away from the Unicorn.

FUCK!!!! The exhaust cloud from the rocket exhaust just swallowed me. I see goddamn flames on my visor!

Yeah, this suit is fireproof, but it's not fucking rocket exhaust proof!

Thankfully, I fall away before spontaneously combusting. I reach back and make sure the parachute didn't incinerate.

It's still there. Thank god. Peterson's laundry lives to see another day. I can't wait to tell her...fuck.

Focus, David.

See that big thing coming at you real fast? That's called the ground. While he wants to be best friends and can't wait to meet you, it's important that you play hard to get and ease into it.

First, flatten out my body so I slow down.

Thankfully I've done this dozens of times in a full spacesuit jumping out of an airplane and in one of those vertical wind tunnels at iCosmos.

While this spacesuit is mostly aerodynamically slick plastic and not a wingsuit, spreading your arms out like a flying squirrel still helps.

Okay, I'm flat and can see Mr. Ground coming right at me. Since I forgot to pack an altimeter or look at my altitude on the panel before I jumped out, hell I didn't even count the seconds since I left, I'll have to eyeball this one and treat it like a BASE jump. You know, suicide.

If my goal is to avoid calling attention to myself, then I have to release the chute at the very last second – and pray it has high-tension cords and fabric.

I just watched somebody turn a corner on a moped. A blue Vespa with a dented fender. Yep, I think I'm close enough. There's a nice empty field to shoot for.

I yank the release and the harness pulls into my arms and chest, jerking me upright.

I watch the field fly past my feet as I overshoot it.

Instead of a nice grassy plot, I'm heading for a very rundown block filled with demolished buildings and the largest garbage pile I've ever seen.

Huh, I thought they took care of that problem?

I'll take it up with the mayor later. I need to make sure I don't get impaled onto some metal rebar as I...

[17]
IMPACT

SLAM INTO THE DAMN GROUND! Oomph! I hit a mountain of trash and go face first into a pile of broken bottles, beer cans and please, God, not dirty diapers.

A cliff of garbage collapses over me. Something scratches my ear inside the helmet, but I'm too winded to move. I just need a second...

The harness pulls at me. Crap. The parachute. There's not much point to making a discreet landing if you've got a massive white billowing flag catching the wind, telling the world where you are.

I claw myself free. I'm thankful that I have a suit on and don't have to smell this place – well at least not until my onboard air supply quits in about three minutes.

I make my way through garbage bags, newspapers, and a goddamn broken sink until I see daylight. In digging myself free I manage to get the parachute cords all twisted around me.

I make it to my feet and unravel them, then start pulling the chute in to hide it before helicopters fly by or whatever they do in Brazil when they see a man in a spacesuit leap from his spaceship.

Spaceship....

I look up and see an arc of white smoke stretching across the sky like a rainbow made of dirty cotton.

In the distance, way over the mountain top, I can see the Unicorn at the end of the smoke, its thrusters still burning, followed by the echo of a dull roar. What's the count now? 227 seconds?

And it stops. There's one final puff of smoke as the last of the fuel spurts out. It's tiny from here, but I can make out the details well enough.

Three...two...please let the main chute deploy...one...

There it is, a bright orange canopy blossoming from the nose of the ship. It begins a slow descent to the earth and vanishes out of view behind the large green mountain standing between us.

Please don't land on an orphanage.

With any luck, it'll fall in a hard-to-get-to remote area and my pursuers, either real or imagined, will find the empty craft with its popped hatch and deduce I made a run for it – and I'm now totally living off the land in the monkey-infested jungle with my awesome survival skills.

In a spacesuit.

Right.

I'm the guy that can't eat a chalupa if there's no verde sauce.

The alternative to the chute opening is they find a wreck on the ground with no busted-up David Dixon and deduce right away that I bailed out somewhere between there and the bay.

Nothing I can do about that now. If I can avoid being seen, and find something less conspicuous than a quarter-million dollar spacesuit to wear, I can try to get to the football stadium and unload the McGuffin on someone more responsible.

No problem, I'm only in a foreign country surrounded by people who speak a language I don't understand.

Stealth is going to be my only way to survive.

I reel in the parachute as it balloons in the wind and get a quick glimpse beneath the canopy of a pair of legs.

There goes being unseen.

When I grasp the fabric and start packing the chute into a small package, I find myself staring at three pairs of eyes watching me in rapt fascination.

A little girl in a dirty dress, maybe eight years old, is standing next to two smaller boys wearing equally dirty pairs of shorts and nothing else. They're all staring at me.

She points to the trail of smoke in the sky.

I nod to her. I don't know what good lying to her will do.

They watch as I finish shoving the parachute into the pack. I flip up my visor and give them a smile, so they don't report me or whatever.

The oldest of the two boys points to me and says, "Homem de Ferro?" Which sounds kind of rude.

"Watch it pal," I reply, then look for some place less conspicuous to stand than on top of the tallest garbage heap in the middle of an apocalyptic urban renewal project.

"Americano?" asks the little girl as she follows me.

I say, "Si," because I have no idea how to say "yes" in Portuguese.

"Homem de Ferro!" shouts the littlest boy as he leaps in my path with his palms facing me.

He's got a big grin on his face. So I can't tell if he's trying to block me or tell me to go another way.

"Yeah, yeah, gigante homo de fairy-o. Now out of my way."

The kid's eyes go so super-wide at my admission and the cracks of dirt on his face begin to flake off. "Uhul! Homem de Ferro!"

"Wait?" I roll the words around in my head. Homem...like man? Ferro...as in ferrous or iron?

...Man of iron

Idiot, the punk didn't call you gay. He asked if you were Iron Man.

I guess the spacesuit does look a lot like Iron Man, I mean I wouldn't take it trick-or-treating and expect people to make the connection. But to this poor kid out in the middle of whatever this part of Rio is called, yeah, I guess that works.

Hell, David, they just watched you jump from a spaceship. Of course it makes sense.

I slap the hard plastic chest. "Yo soy Homem de Ferro."

The little girl looks to the street and says, "Polícia!"

She breaks into a run like a skittish cat and the others follow.

I hear the siren too.

The kids definitely seem to be running from it, not towards the sound. I've heard that street kids here don't exactly have the best relations with the local police, so I can't blame them.

They scurry down the hill and race towards some collapsed shanties.

The littlest one stops to look back and sees that I'm following them. It only takes him a second to realize that Iron Man doesn't want to get caught by the polícia either.

He waves me on and shouts, "Por aqui! Por aqui!"

I stomp along as fast as I can in a suit that was made for zero-gravity and not exploring planet garbage.

As the sirens – lots of them – grow louder, the other two children stop at a wooden fence and pull the slats open for me.

"Ir por este caminho , o homem de ferro !"

"Thanks!"

Let's hope the rest of the locals are just as helpful.

[18]
CRAWLSPACE

I SLIDE INTO THE SMALL GAP between the wooden slats and knock one of the boards loose. The littlest one picks the plank up and starts to carry it through until the girl (his sister?) makes him put it back. I think she called him Luca.

Once I'm on the other side she leans the board back over the gap, kind of hiding our tracks.

I glance around at the trash-filled alley. It's a narrow passage, four feet wide with concrete walls on either side. To the left is an unfinished house with no side wall and bare wooden struts supporting the upper floor.

Rotten plywood and dirty plastic tarps litter the interior.

I unscrew my helmet for the first time since I landed. Something hits my shoulder and falls to the dirt.

The sat phone.

I kneel down to pick it up. The screen is bashed in and non-functioning.

So much for hearing from Capricorn. Although he made it sound like his part of the mission was over.

I realize what the sharp pain was I felt on my ear when I landed. My fingers reach up and touch the blood and broken shards stuck into my lobe.

"Você está machucado?" asks tiny little Luca with a sad look on his face.

"I'll be fine." I hand him the helmet - which is half the size he is.

"Quieto!" says the girl as she peers through the gap in the fence.

Two police officers, wearing bullet proof vests, are walking to the top of the trash heap. One of them uses his hand to shield his eyes as he studies the fading contrail of my spaceship.

That didn't take them long to get here. I need to keep moving.

I take off my gloves and toss them into the helmet, then start removing the chest piece. The other boy is fascinated by this process. He inspects each part of the suit as I set it down.

When I'm finished, I'm left in the bright blue iCosmos thermal suit, which is proper attire for a micro-gravity space station, but not exactly inconspicuous.

Although, I wouldn't look entirely out of place as a goalie on a soccer field.

Speaking of which, I've got to figure out how to get to the stadium before the polícia find me.

First order of business is hiding this suit. I step into the abandoned house and look for a plastic tarp to cover the parts.

I have zero expectation that it'll last more then 45 seconds after I'm gone and the little ones here decide they want to flip the thing to their local junk dealer.

But if I can keep the authorities from finding it long enough to get away from where I am, that gives me some advantage.

I grab a paint-splattered piece of plastic and carefully pull it aside, not wanting to alert the cops who are still outside trying to decide if someone really did land via parachute or if this was just another chupacabra sighting.

The little girl taps me on the back and points to a piece of chipped plywood. "Aqui."

"What?"

She points to the board and says, "Aqui," again.

The older boy goes over to the edge and raises the plywood, revealing a small hole dug into the ground.

I look inside and see their little stash of treasure. There's a Thor action figure missing an arm, several stuffed animals in various states of disrepair and a collection of water-stained children's books.

Alright, you little con artists, get me to put this in your safe place and when I come back, it'll be gone. Just make sure the junk man gives you a good price for this thing. You could buy a whole neighborhood with what it's really worth.

I stow my suit and packed chute inside their hiding spot, and almost forget to take the square Peterson gave me right before she...

Focus, David.

I take a glance through the fence, hoping the cops have decided to go elsewhere.

Nope. There are four of them now. One is pointing in our direction.

Damn.

"Por aqui," whispers the little girl as she tugs on my arm, pulling me back into the alley. The older boy does the same.

They dart away through the choked passage, climbing under boards and over piles of broken toilets. I do my best to follow, but this was not meant for adults.

"Damn!"

I look down at my feet and see that I just stepped on a pile of rusty screws.

The bottom of my thermal is just a thick piece of fabric with some heat exchanging wires. It wasn't meant to be rugged urban wear.

I try to go a little further but have to stop when I reach a bunch of broken glass.

The kids, all of them barefoot, have no trouble. They possess the advantage of being nimble, lightweight and have callouses on their feet as thick as a baseball glove.

Luca, the slowest one, sees me struggling. "Pare!" he whispers to the others.

The girl sees me rubbing the bottom of my feet.

I point and say, "Zappos?"

This gets me a confused look, then she nods her head and replies, "Sapatos?"

Close enough. "Yes." I start digging through the rubble for something I can wrap around them, even a Tyvek plastic bag would help.

She says something to the older boy and he takes off running.

I glance back towards the entrance of the alley, worried the cops might be coming at any moment. With their thick police boots, they'll have no trouble stomping through here.

The girl squeezes past me and goes back to the wooden fence to watch what they're up to. Suddenly, she jumps back.

I duck behind a pile of concrete mix sacks. Luca, thinking this is a game, or totally understanding the stakes, slides a rotten piece of cardboard over me.

An adult voice echoes down the alley. I can only make out a few words. I'm pretty sure he said something like "pára-quedas," which sounds an awful lot like parachute.

The little girl responds, "Não, não." Which I'm pretty sure isn't Portuguese for, "The man you're looking for is cowering in the alley behind me and completely vulnerable."

The adult voice stops and the girl comes running back down the alley to my hiding spot.

When she pokes her head under the cardboard she puts a finger to her lips, which is the universal sign for keep your fat mouth shut.

She glances up at the sound of small footsteps running from the other direction.

The older boy climbs over a pile of tiles and presents a pair of rubber boots to me.

They're not exactly Nikes, but they fit.

I have no idea where he got them from, and I don't think I want to know.

There's a crashing sound from the alley entrance and the children wave for me to finishing putting the boots on and hurry my slow ass up.

[19]
STREET GANG

MY ESCORTS CLIMB and crawl through the alley, dodging piles of bricks, rusty rebar, box springs and whatever detritus people saw fit to leave here.

While Luca and his friends are quite agile at making it through the maze, I'm too slow to keep up. Thankfully, he stops periodically to make sure I don't get too far behind.

Overhead, I hear the sound of a helicopter passing by and press myself against the wall, afraid I'll stand out like a sore thumb from the air.

Luca waves me to a side alley even more narrow than this one. A tiny dark chasm between a concrete wall that's falling apart and rusted metal siding, I hesitate, not certain that I want to try to squeeze through.

When I hear the sound of lumber and other trash being knocked aside behind me, I decide to trust that Luca isn't planning to leave me stuck in an impossible situation.

Evidently, the police decided the story of a man parachuting down was credible enough to take seriously, despite the insistence of the little girl.

I have no idea how seriously they're going to take this or how far they plan to pursue, but I'm reasonably certain I'd rather follow these kids than take my chances with the Brazilian authorities.

I push myself through the narrow gap and feel my boot sink into something wet and fetid. I'm so thankful in this moment for the footwear that the other kid brought me, that I promise myself if I survive, I'll come back here with some kind of reward – and have the kids all checked for ringworm.

Who are these children? Do they belong to somebody? Do they live on the street?

They're incredibly dirty and look like they haven't had a change of clothes or a bath since their last birthday.

There's a sliver of daylight ahead of me as I make it through the darkest part of the passage.

My nostrils are assaulted and I look down and see a rotting cat.

"Gatinho morto," says Luca as he looks back, plugging his nose.

"Morto is right," I say, stepping over the foul carcass.

We reach the end of the corridor and step out onto a street. Concrete walls stretch in either direction, with sliding metal doors sealing off their yards.

I have no idea if this is a good or a bad neighborhood. Across the street, an old woman lays out rugs on a second floor metal railing, gives me a momentary glance then goes back to work.

My thermal suit isn't the weirdest thing in the world. It kind of sort of looks like something you might wear to go surfing. The only problem is the "iCosmos" logo on both sleeves.

Until I can steal something better, I need to figure out a short term solution.

In movies when you're on the run, there's always a convenient clothesline where you can steal something that's the perfect size.

People here don't seem to trust each other enough to make it that easy for me.

I'll need to figure out another way to get something that blends in.

The girl is walking down a street that leads even further away from where I landed. While I trust her instincts when it comes to avoiding the police, I have no idea where we're going.

I got a pretty good look at the city while I was free falling and could probably make it on foot to the airport by the bay, but I doubt I'd get very far looking like I do right now. And I still have no idea where this stadium is supposed to be.

"Dónde está el estadio de fútbol?" I ask her in Spanish.

"Campo de futebol?"

"Sí," I reply.

She shakes her head and says, "Sim," correcting me.

"Sim?"

She nods her head.

I nod and repeat "Sim," again. Alright, now she's taught me how to say "Yes" in Portuguese.

"Campo de futebol," she explains to the others.

They break out into a brisk run and I chase after them, hoping it doesn't look like I'm trying to run down a group of children.

"Maracanã campo de futebol?" I ask as I catch up with her.

She answers in a flurry of Portuguese I can't follow. All I pick up is the word futebol.

We turn a corner and she points to the campo de futebol and smiles, proud that she's brought Homem de Ferro to his destination.

Only I'm pretty sure this isn't the Maracanã stadium. The campo de futebol technically isn't even a soccer field, at least not one by my American standards.

It's a fenced in cement court with two soccer goals on either end and a group of six boys kicking a red ball around. Concrete tables with tile chessboards surround the court. The closest thing to a parking lot is a bubble-shaped Volkswagen car – the kind you only see outside the US – parked on the sidewalk.

"Maracanã?" I ask the little girl.

She gives me the universal shrug for "I don't know."

These kids probably have no idea what's a mile away, let alone the other end of the city. For them, their neighborhood is the world.

Imagine what they would think if they could have seen what I saw just a few minutes ago when the earth was hundreds of miles below me?

Before I can find an adult, she runs to the fence and yells in a very loud voice, interrupting the boys playing their game. "Onde está o Maracanã?"

One of the boys points to the East. "É dessa forma." He then looks at me, "Você é um jogador de futebol?"

I think he's asking if I play soccer. It's better to lie than say I'm an astronaut.

"Sim," I reply, nodding my head.

"Quer jogar com a gente?"

I laugh off the question, not sure what the hell he just asked me.

I start to walk in that direction, then realize I have three little shadows. As helpful as they've been, I can't let them go any further.

"Wait," I say, holding out my hands, telling them to stop.

Luca raises his hands, imitating me – imitating Iron Man shooting his repulsor rays.

"No. Espera aquí." I tell them to wait in Spanish and point to a table.

That seems close enough to make them stop.

Maybe they could help me out with one more thing. "Dónde hay un hotel?"

The girl thinks for a moment then yells my question to the boys back in the court.

One of them points to the south. "Cinco blocos."

That seems pretty self-explanatory.

I leave my little helpers sitting at the table, their legs dangling from the concrete benches as they watch me walk away and wave.

I pray this isn't a thing where they wait forever for their spaceman friend to come back.

[20]
INVISIBLE

SO MY BRILLIANT PLAN to blend in with the local population and vanish from my pursuers is a complete failure before I even started.

I'd asked the kids about the location of the nearest hotel because I had this fantasy that I'd walk up to the valet drop-off, grab a bag and then shout something like, "Hey, you forgot your suitcase!" and chase after a taxi that was pulling away – making it look like I was a good samaritan, when in fact I was a thieving no-good samaritan.

The Hotel Saint Moritz is a fenced in enclosure with concrete walls and a steel door you have to talk to an intercom to get through.

In fact, just about everything in this part of Rio is like that. There's no wide open windows to the stores. Every entrance has either a guard or a grim-faced shopkeeper. Everything is either nailed down or behind a locked gate.

They've made it very hard for a guy like me to steal what I need to survive.

I don't know how much further I can go in my iCosmos suit before someone realizes who I am.

If the phone Capricorn had given me was still functional, I could at least try to buy something online.

I'm sure I could Amazon Prime some Levis and sneakers to a location near me. I mean, this isn't the Dark Ages.

If I'd been expecting a pit stop before returning to Canaveral, I would have brought my wallet. Next time, David. Next time.

Every few blocks I spot a green bubble shaped payphone that says "Oi" on the side. I guess that's the Brazilian version of AT&T. I'm tempted to call somebody collect and have them wire me some money.

Of course, whoever is trying to stop me, the Russians, the Americans, the Illuminati, the Klingons or whatever, will probably be monitoring that kind of thing. So it's only a last resort.

I saw an old man sweeping his sidewalk in front of his house and briefly considered a home invasion, but I'm going to save that contingency for last resort.

What I need is – BAM!!! – something just hit me in the back of the head.

"Paneleiro!" shouts a teenager on the back of a moped as he and his friend fly past me down the street.

I don't have to know Portuguese to guess the context of the slur.

I touch the back of my head and feel where the rock hit me. There's blood.

In any other situation I'd avoid the conflict – especially given the kind of shit storm I'm in the middle of, but that little pecker may have just solved a problem for me.

He's looking back at me, grinning, at the end of the street while they wait to cross the intersection.

I grab a rock, hurl it and shout, "Big words for somebody riding bitch!"

The rock hits him in the arm as he raises his hands to protect himself. His partner guns the moped at the wrong moment, off-balancing him, and the rock thrower falls off the back of the bike.

I race towards him and kick him in the chest before he can get up. He falls back down and I put a foot so far into his balls he'll have to see an oral surgeon. "That's for being a homophobe."

His friend turns the moped around and drives it straight at me – which would be a great move if he was riding something with more horsepower than a riding lawnmower.

I grab the handle bars like they're steer horns and twist the bike to the side. He has to stick a leg outwards to keep himself from falling over.

I kick him in the knee, buckling his leg, and he falls down, with his moped landing hard on his inner thigh.

"Give me your pants!" I yell at him.

He looks up at me, terrified. I'm not sure if he understands English, but I can tell he knows the man his friend just called a homosexual is now demanding that he take off his clothes.

I'd be scared shitless too.

"Now!" I shout, shoving a foot into his chest.

He starts unbuckling his jeans and sliding them off.

"Your zappos too!" I demand.

His friend is holding his nuts and crying. I walk over and grab the hem of his soccer jersey and whip it over his head.

He raises his hands and wails, "Não mais!"

The driver starts to get up to make a run for it, but I throw an arm around his neck and slam him into the pavement before he can get three feet with his falling pants.

He takes them off and I let him run away. I put them on, then slide his shoes on my feet. They're loose-fitting Adidas, but a better fit than the rubber boots.

Rock thrower is struggling to get up, so I help him and take his wallet and phone from his pocket then kick him in the ass, sending him into a concrete wall.

I realize I'm being observed as I spot a mother holding the hand of her little girl watching the whole fracas.

I point to the crying teenager and say, "Bandidos."

The woman gives me a hesitant nod then walks the other way.

I pick the moped off the ground and take off down the street in the general direction of Maracanã stadium.

I'd feel like a bad ass if it wasn't for the fact that neither one of my assailants was older than eighteen or weighed more than 130 pounds. I just beat up children and robbed them.

Fuck it. They started this with an attempted hate crime. Better it happened to me than some poor kid who decided to dress a little different or be himself.

It just so happened that I needed a reason to steal, and those two assholes gave it to me.

[21]
PARANOIA

I DRIVE ANOTHER MILE in the general direction of the stadium then turn into a small alley so I can take a look at what I stole from the teenagers on the moped.

Both phones are crappy generics and have screen locks in place. I should have beaten their pin codes out of them. Next time. Still, on one I can spot two thick ketchup stains over the virtual buttons for 5 and 9.

When a company like iCosmos hires you to take a billion-dollar piece of technology into space, they make damn sure you're not going to screw things up by using dumb passwords or malware infected thumb drives that let the competition know vital secrets. You're forced to endure endless seminars on security from in-house specialists and researchers they bring in. Sometimes I listened.

I remember a woman explaining that 20% of four-digit pin codes were couplets – two digits that repeated. Like, 1212 or 3030.

I'm going to hazard a guess that the genius who decided to throw a rock at me immediately before coming to a stop at a busy intersection probably slept through all the security seminars they sent him to at asshole school.

5959

Nothing.

Three more attempts before lock out....

9595

Click. I'm in.

Yikes. There's a photo on his home screen that could be considered another layer of security. I can't tell if it's his mother or his girlfriend. No wonder he's throwing rocks at strangers.

Focus, David. Now that we have a working phone, what are we going to do with it?

Capricorn said something about Twitter...

Check @CapricornZero.

I manage to make my way through the Portuguese menus and pull up a browser and direct it at Twitter.com/CapricornZero.

There is one and only one tweet there:

Proceed to the destination.

Thanks for that wonderful bit of helpful advice. Nothing about enemies trying to kill me. No mention of who the hell I'm supposed to look for.

More importantly, there's nothing telling me if I can trust this mysterious voice.

Out of curiosity, I go to CNN.com to see if this made the news.

Uh, yeah.

BREAKING: Russian Officials Claim US Astronaut Shot Two Onboard K1 Station

Scattered reports indicate that a US astronaut working for iCosmos may have killed two of his crew members with a gun smuggled onboard the Russian K1 space station. Even more bizarre, reports are coming in that the astronaut, believed to be named David William Dixon, may have stolen a space capsule and killed another crew member in a rapid ejection procedure and is now in orbit or at large.

Jesus Christ! How can things possibly get any worse? And the page just refreshed...

BREAKING: Stolen iCosmos Spacecraft Spotted Making Emergency Landing in Brazil near Rio de Janeiro.

There's photo and video of the Unicorn firing the thrusters in the middle of the bay and then launching back into the sky over the city.

That was minutes ago.

I'm so screwed.

Oh lord.

I feel my stomach tightening into a knot that's about to condense into a neutron star. I want to throw up.

None of my training prepared me for this kind of crisis.

My instinct is to call a lawyer. That would be great advice if I just walked into the kitchen and saw a pool of blood and my wife was missing.

That's probably a horrible idea if Russian kill squads are out to get you and there's supposed to be some highly-placed mole in the US government that will rendition you to oblivion.

Lawyers are great for figuring out legal maneuverings. My primary concern is predator drones and snipers.

I look up at the sound of rotors and see a white helicopter flying overhead towards where I'd just came from. It's a Eurocopter EC 155 – the same make and model I saw right after I landed.

It's got to be the same one. That's not good. It means somebody is really interested in the neighborhood I just came from. I need to get going.

I do a quick count of the cash in the wallets. There's a few hundred Reals. I have no idea what that will buy me here. There's also two credit cards with different names. If they're still valid, that might be helpful.

I take the moped out of the alley and head towards the highway that will get me to the stadium as quickly as possible.

But before I get there, I need some kind of plan. Capricorn could just be waiting for me to show up with the black square and then murder me on the spot.

As much as I want to believe I'll be met with open arms and told everything is going to be okay a few minutes after the truth of the matter is told to the world, I have no reason to believe that.

I'm skeptical that Capricorn's contact is even going to let me survive the encounter. Whoever went through this much shady shit to pull this off might want to keep their tracks covered.

If this McGuffin is as important as they say it is, and could cost thousands of lives because, um, because, then maybe I need to be very careful who I hand it over to.

More important, is protecting this life. I have to ensure that David Dixon, most wanted man in the world and in space, doesn't meet a quick death in the parking lot of a soccer stadium.

I'm a guy that goes fast and lets people do stupid things to my body. I'm not a spy. I'm not a cop. All I know is from watching movies and I'm pretty sure if my life depends on doing parkour across rooftops, I'll be a bloodstain on a sidewalk before the bad guys even have to draw a weapon.

What I do know is fear and how to manage it. I know how to think on my feet and not do something stupid.

Walking into a dangerous situation, not knowing what's in store for me, is the height of stupidity.

[22]
HIGH GROUND

I DO MY FOURTH PASS down the street that runs next to the stadium. At the north end there's a small parking lot. It's nothing like the vast acres of pavement that surround most American sports complexes.

However, there's a massive walkway that connects the stadium to a train station on the other side of a highway. I assume that's what everybody uses when they go see a game.

Right now, there's not a lot of "everybody." The parking lot has a dozen school buses and I see some high school-aged kids in soccer uniforms walking back and forth, but other than that, the stadium is kind of dead.

While that should make it easier for Capricorn's contact to find me, it also makes it a cinch for anyone else. With my name and face all over the news, a thin crowd is probably worse than a dense one.

I park the moped next to a row of motorcycles at the west end of the street.

I'm getting an even more anxious feeling than my already impossibly-high level of anxiety. Walking straight into the parking lot feels like a bad idea.

I don't know who or what I should be on the lookout for or how to spot a Russian sniper from a Brazilian giving me a longing look across the street.

Survival training didn't prepare me for any of this. I can use the fishing line in the crash kit to make a rabbit snare or catch a salmon, but I don't know how to garrote someone's neck or tell if I'm about to step on a booby-trap. That's why I need to take it slow and stupid.

The guard at the west gate doesn't even ask me for a ticket and just waves me through.

I'm not quite sure what his job is, other than to keep out anything on more than two legs.

Instead of going straight to the parking lot, I get the sudden inspiration to take a look at things from higher ground.

I take an elevator all the way to the top deck, glad I don't have to make my way up or down the ramp when ten thousand soccer fans are flooding in.

The top section is a ring that opens to the outside on one side and the massive open-air stadium on the other.

The players on the huge green field look like miniatures from all the way up here, but it's still pretty easy to follow the ball as it's being kicked across the field by high school teams. The first few sections are filled with other teenagers cheering them on.

An announcer is calling the game over the PA as if it were a major sporting event, adding to the excitement.

There's a near miss and everyone is on their feet screaming and cheering like only Brazilians can do. Even from here it seems pretty thrilling.

I leave the seats and head towards the far end of the level that overlooks the parking lot. Maybe from here I can spot my contact in a trench coat pretending to read a newspaper as they look out from under their fedora.

There's a long wall in this area with a few closed food stands and some doors leading to the stadium and others to closed sections. Even out here, the announcer and the roaring kids still manage to echo all the way through the corridor.

But other than the noise from the stadium, everything is dead. The only other person is a workman on a break leaning on the railing looking at the ground below.

The announcer lets out a scream in Portuguese as something very riveting must have happened and gives an energetic play-by-play of the game in progress.

I'm kind of worried about my life right now, but he seemed to make it sound like this was the play of the millennium, causing me to turn and look towards the nearest set of doors.

Curiously, the workman doesn't move.

He doesn't even flinch at the sound of the announcer's yelling.

He keeps his gaze on the outside of the stadium.

To be more precise, he's watching the parking lot.

Sometimes you have to make a split second decision. It's better to look a fool later than not be looked upon at all.

I turn on my heel and walk the other way.

Probably too quickly.

I make a bee-line for the nearest set of doors and enter the stadium.

Okay, David, you're probably just overreacting. Don't be a racist, not everyone in South America loves soccer.

Hah, who am I kidding? Of course they do.

I walk down to the landing and make a sharp left on the next deck and keep going until I reach the ring that separates the upper and lower levels.

I drop into a chair and try to look as inconspicuous as a man can when he's the only person in a sea of eighty-thousand empty seats.

I glance back towards the entrance and see the workman – who is probably not a workman – stepping into the stadium and looking for someone.

Looking for me.

Part of me wants to think this man is Capricorn's contact and we're only minutes away from drinking a couple of cold cervejas together in a bar before calling a press conference and explaining that it was all a misunderstanding.

One look at his face tells me otherwise. It's unflinching, serious, and staring right at me.

If this was Capricorn's contact I think I would have been greeted by a smile or a wave.

Not this man. He eyes me then checks to see if there's anybody else nearby.

I'm at the lowest part of the upper deck and have nowhere to go. If the man is about to pull anything other than a sandwich or a set of binoculars out of his suspiciously tactical-looking backpack that I should have noticed before, I'm fucked. Seriously fucked.

There's no place to run.

[23]
IMPULSE CONTROL

WE LOCK EYES and then something strange happens. The man's grim expression flashes in an instant to a smile. "David!" he says, pronouncing it a little more like "Da-veed," than "Da-vid."

If he'd met me with the smile a second ago I'd think this was Capricorn's man, or Capricorn himself. Instead, he waited too long. He checked to see if I was alone and realized that even though the stadium is almost empty, the two of us stand out up here.

He starts to walk down the stairs towards me, holding up a friendly finger, telling me to give him a second.

I freeze, not because I believe him, but because I have no idea what else I should do.

His backpack slips from his shoulders and he makes an "oops" face as he kneels down to pick it up.

Your misdirection needs some serious work, pal.

I hazard a guess this is his attempt to draw a gun on me, so I don't wait to find out.

To live a long life as a pilot, sometimes you have to just go with your impulse and do the thing logic tells you is a horrible idea.

I grab the railing and leap over.

I do not look down.

I do not aim.

I don't hang there like some kitten in a motivational poster.

I jump into the fucking air over the edge.

It's a twelve foot drop to hard concrete.

I should have hung over the edge like that goddamn kitten.

BAM!!! My feet hit the ground so hard the echo reverberates across the stadium.

I'd like to thank my parachute instructor for teaching me how to not break my ankles on a hard landing. But, HOLY SHIT this hurts.

I bend into the fall and my ass touches my heels.

As painful as that was, the upside is the noise attracted everyone's attention.

I bounce back up into the air like a Whack-A-Mole that refuses to be whacked.

I don't stop to see if Workman is following me. I race towards the next set of steps and start leaping down half a floor at a time, using the railing to keep me from falling on my ass when I lose my balance.

I've attracted a bit of attention as people are starting to watch from the lower sections.

Who the hell is this maniac that just jumped an entire level and is now running towards the field?

A security guard in a yellow vest starts to jog towards the end of the row I'm leapfrogging down. He's obviously concerned that I'm about to do something stupid on the field.

And he's right.

BANG!!! I watch as the corner of a blue seat to my left disintegrates.

Workman is probably on the rail with a gun aimed at me.

On a gut impulse, I flatten myself on the steps.

BANG!!! A seat five feet away gets a hole punched straight through it.

He's behind me, firing at an angle. That means if I lay flat he can't shoot me until he changes position.

The trick is knowing when he's about to give up his sniper position to run to a new firing spot.

I watch the security guard, who for some mysterious reason, has had a sudden change of heart about trying to intercept me.

He's standing on the field, cowering a little and watching the section above me. His head moves to the right as he tracks something.

Workman is on the move.

I jet out of my cower into a slightly less-cowardly jog that probably only makes my spine that much more easy of a target.

I take row after row of steps in great leaps and get a flash of inspiration to try to jack-rabbit it by not moving in a straight line.

BANG!!! A seat shatters fifteen feet in front of me. Workman doesn't have his gun rest yet and is firing from the hip.

I reach the last row before the field and do a dive over the barrier.

BANG!!! I hear the hit of the bullet right behind me.

Referees are blowing their whistles and the announcer is somehow yelling even more excitedly into the microphone, telling the players to clear the field.

Which I guess is the smart thing to do, but doesn't really help me out all that much.

Not that I would ever use some poor kid as a human shield – sure I'll kick them in the nuts and steal their stuff if they're a violent sociopath – but having people on the field would certainly make my life a little easier.

Focus, David.

BOOM! There's an echo that sounds a lot like Workman jumping onto the lower level.

I bolt, trying to keep my body as low as I can behind the barrier that separates the field from the seats.

I pass by a row of cowering students. They're watching me with frightened eyes, not sure if this is some kind of random shooting where anyone could be a victim – only if they get close to me.

Ahead of me, there's a tunnel leading to the outside of the stadium. If I can make it there...

BANG!!! Concrete chips fly off the wall in front of me.

How the hell?

I change my direction and go diagonally. Out of the corner of my eye I spot another workman on the opposite deck, leaning on the railing with a rifle.

He'd been using the wall I was running behind to range me. Fuck.

Now I'm a wide open target in the middle of an empty soccer field. I should have climbed over the wall.

And then what? Wait for them to come get me?

No dice.

I'm not sure if I can make it to the tunnel before one of these assholes puts a bullet in my head.

I need a better way.

I need a miracle.

Holy crap. Was that thing here all along?

The stadium is so fucking huge I didn't even notice it.

Please work. Please, please...

[24]
EMT

THIS IS EITHER going to look like a master-stroke of evasive maneuvers in about two seconds or I'm going to be dead.

The stadium is so damn huge the ambulance was just one tiny detail against the wide-open expanse of bright green grass. Now it's my one chance of not getting murdered.

PING!!! A bullet whizzes past me and strikes the side of the van. The next one is going to hit me if the driver locked the door.

I mean, who the hell locks an ambulance in the middle of a soccer stadium sideline? What are the chances someone will try to steal it?

Thankfully the door opens and I slide my body inside just as a bullet shatters the left-side mirror with a CRACK!!!

PING! PING! PING! The sides of the ambulance are being battered by the Workmen firing on me from both sides. Fortunately, neither of them has a direct angle at me...yet.

Please have keys! Please have keys!

Fuck! No keys!

"Que porra você está fazendo?" screams a man from the back.

I look behind me and see an EMT getting up from a nap on the stretcher.

PING! A bullet puts a hole in the wall near his head. He reflexively ducks down.

"Keys now!" I yell at the top of my lungs. "Llaves!" I shout in Spanish, praying that's not Portuguese for abandon me.

Scared, he fishes a metal ring from his pocket and tosses it in my direction. I find the ambulance key and twist it in the ignition right as one of the Workmen runs to the far side of the upper section on the lower deck to take a new firing position.

CRACK!!! Glass shatters from my right as the other asshole also finds a new place to shoot.

I jam my foot on the accelerator and send the ambulance down the sideline, trying to keep my body below the dashboard as much as possible – which makes for some exceptionally shitty driving.

I scrape the left side against the concrete wall to the left then overcompensate and smash through a line of chairs that was holding an entire soccer team just a few seconds ago.

Seats go flying into the air and I try to keep the van from flipping.

My companion in the back lets out some Portuguese swear words and starts to pull himself towards me.

"Stay down!" I yell.

A bullet hits the back window, underscoring how serious it is for him to keep his body flat. I mean, if he'd like to let me lay down and avoid the gunfire while he drives, by all means. After all, he is the one wearing the uniform that means he's supposed to save lives.

I turn the van into a wide arc to steer it into the tunnel without smashing into the side. I'm so focused on not hitting the walls I don't even realize until the last second there's a metal gate down.

In a movie I'd be able to ram right through that thing. In real life, I'm not so willing to take that chance.

I spin the steering wheel, coming inches away from the barrier and drive straight towards where I came from – which leaves the front windshield open to the shooter.

I gauge how far I have to go then just duck down out of sight.

PING! PING! Two bullets hit the hood and the side of the windshield, but nothing actually goes through it, or more importantly, me.

Remember when all I had to worry about was a hole in my spacecraft heat shield? Good times.

I race towards the far tunnel stepping on the gas, not caring what's on the other side. If there's a gate on this one, maybe at least I'll have enough speed to tear it down.

If not, well, I don't have a seat belt on, so I'll die of a concussion real quick when I fly out the windshield. Positive thinking, David.

The EMT behind me is muttering some kind of prayer. He realizes we're being fired upon and probably thinks this is the end of his life. He can't make up his mind if I'm his savior or the devil. I vote both.

PING! PING! PING! Bullets hit the side of the van as I get closer to the tunnel exit. Nothing hits the windshield, which means the Workmen are behind me.

There's no gate blocking my exit this time, so there's that. The downside is the exit actually leads into the lobby of the arena. Wonderful.

The van blows through the tunnel and I have to turn a hard right to avoid slamming into a concrete pillar.

I'm in a food court with rows of colored signs to my right and a long wall to my left.

A few dozen people scatter as they realize the terror from outside has now come into their safe place next to their hambúrguer and cerveja stalls.

PING!!! There's a ricochet behind me as one of the Workmen has taken a new firing position, apparently from the field.

That means he's only seconds away from entering the tunnel.

I mash the gas pedal and send the ambulance flying down the corridor, hitting rows of trash bins and destroying an entire section of high-top tables.

Ahead of me, I see a group of three men who look like cops of some kind. They've got guns drawn and are standing in the middle of the court near a concrete column.

Should I bail out and ask for their help? I start to slow down.

BANG!!! BANG!!! BANG!!! They open fire on me!

I yank the wheel to the left as the windshield begins to crack from several rounds. This brings me to my closest point to them and I get a quick glimpse before I accelerate into what looks like daylight.

These guys aren't Brazilian. They all look like cousins of Commander Yablokov back on the K1.

BANG!!! BANG!!! BANG!!! BANG!!! BANG!!! BANG!!!

The back of the ambulance is assaulted by a barrage of fire. And not just any barrage – congratulations, David, you've just met your first Russian kill team!

And it gets even better...

The bright ray of light that you thought is the outdoors where there aren't any bad men trying to send you to heaven? It is! Except it's also a ramp leading to the upper section of the stadium!

Remember when you wondered how they got all those people in and out of the stadium? The answer is a huge walkway suitable for building the pyramids – and plenty wide enough for one asshole driving an ambulance the wrong way.

[25]
WALKWAY TO HEAVEN

WITH A RUSSIAN KILL TEAM CHASING ME, two snipers lurking somewhere in the stadium and a scared passenger in the back who keeps saying the same prayer over and over, I, David Dixon, master pilot and awesome driver, have not only managed to miss the damn exit to this stadium, but done the worst possible thing imaginable – I've driven my bullet-ridden stolen ambulance onto the walkway that leads to the upper level where I first encountered the snipers.

Yep, I just hit do-over, but this time all the bosses are here and ready to blow me away.

Ahead of me there's a ramp switchback. In the passenger-side mirror I can see the Russian kill team racing after me. Choices...

For a fleeting second I think about not turning the wheel and seeing what would happen if I tried to just drive straight off the ramp.

Would I burst through the wall and fly into the air and then land like The General Lee in the *Dukes of Hazzard*? Or would I smash into the steel-reinforced concrete and get thrown through the cracked windshield and have my body tumble to the earth, smashing my spine and skull as I hit the sidewalk?

I decide to make the sharp turn.

I get some nice acceleration going up the ramp but have to brake right away as it levels off and I see that beyond the shadow of the roof of the stadium, I'm about to hit a wall.

Whatever fantasy I had about driving straight down the steps and back onto the field to find another exit is destroyed by inconvenient reality. There's not just the wall, there's the fact that this upper section and the lower section are separated by a twelve foot chasm. Feel that sharp pain in your ankles, David? That's what happened last time you tried to make the jump.

The Russians are still probably running up the ramp, which gives me a spare few seconds.

I slam on the brakes after making it a quarter way around the upper deck. "Get out!" I yell at my passenger.

He bails out of the back door without even so much as a thanks and runs into the stadium. And to top it all off, the asshole left the back doors open.

BANG!!! A bullet fires from somewhere. I don't wait to stick my finger in the air and gauge windspeed and direction.

I push the gas pedal into the floor and race the ambulance down the deck, trying to find an exit before the shooters get to me.

I whiz past an entire open section that looks out into the stadium. The field is still clear and I don't see any bodies on the grass; so that's good.

I turn my head back to the path in front of me and see a Workman putting his rifle on top of a trash can and aiming it at me.

How did that asshole get up here so quickly?

My first impulse is to duck and try to swerve past him in the narrow corridor. Then something darker takes over.

Fuck him.

I aim the vehicle straight at him.

His eyes go wide and he realizes that even if he shoots me, the van is going to smash him like a bug.

His own survival instincts take over and he abandons his position and leaps into a row of seats just behind him.

Reinforcing the wisdom of his decision, the ambulance bumper bashes into the trash can and catapults it across the corridor, sending his sniper rifle into a wall.

I'm not sure how I feel about the fact that I didn't get to run him over.

I try to pay attention to the signs, looking for a way out. But I'm faced with two problems; I can't read Portuguese and it's not like I'm in a parking garage where the designers put in signage to help a van-sized vehicle navigate safely through. This was made for people, not psychopaths in stolen ambulances.

Just past the bend up ahead, I spot a wide open section leading to what I hope is another ramp like the one I drove up.

If not, my only alternative is to try to go all the way around and go back down the way I came up – which would be suicide.

I assume all the killers trying to kill me know this place better than me. If there's no other way out, then the smart thing is to just wait for the gringo to come back and ambush him with all the shooty things they have.

I slow down and turn into the open section, hoping that it's just not a cliff they were too lazy to put caution tape over.

Bingo! I'm back in sunlight and heading down another ramp. I take the turn at the switchback a little too hard and scrape the side of the van on the concrete wall.

SHIT! I almost hit a yellow-vested security guard. He jumps clear and starts screaming at me.

I know, buddy. I know. It's that kind of day.

The walkway leads back into the stadium lobby.

Fucking great.

But this is a whole new section I haven't had a chance to destroy yet.

I tear the van through a row of food kiosks and nearly come to an abrupt stop on a concrete pillar.

Seriously guys, less of those next time?

There's a huge glass wall to my right with a set of doors that opens onto a plaza.

The ambulance is too big for the doors, but I decide to take my chances.

I aim straight through the middle, grip the wheel and curse myself for not putting on a seatbelt.

SMASH!!! There's a shower of broken glass and twisted aluminum as I rip the doorway out of the building.

I take the van down the walkway and along the fence until I see a gate being opened by another yellow-vested security guard.

He waves as I pass, probably assuming that I'm trying to take some injured person to the hospital.

[26]
FUGITIVE

FLYING DOWN THE STREETS of an exotic city in a stolen ambulance is certainly one way to get around quickly, but it also attracts a lot of unwanted attention. I've also noticed that other drivers aren't as yielding to the right of way to emergency vehicles here. They seem a little indifferent to the idea that I could be carrying someone on the verge of death – Hell, I am carrying someone who is precariously balanced on that edge: Me.

I make it two blocks then realize that the back doors are still open. I turn down a side street, put the van in park and shut them.

As I crawl through the back, sunlight greets me through dozens of bullet holes punctured through the walls and cabinets. If that EMT hadn't hit the deck, he'd have been dead. More importantly, if I hadn't put the rear bulkhead between my shooters and myself, I'd be dead.

Let's not get ahead of ourselves.

Right now there's a half-dozen men in that stadium on their way to find me. They'll make that happen if they get the chance.

Were these locals hired on the spot? Or did the Russians know I'd be landing here? I'd love to ask Capricorn or Murdock these questions, but first I need to put some distance between what just happened.

I race the ambulance another several blocks, take a few more side streets then come to the realization that having a screaming siren on top of the vehicle is helping me go a little bit faster, but it's also a big huge "I'm right here!" arrow to anyone searching from the air.

I remember the white helicopter that was searching the neighborhood where I landed; that can't be too far away, plus whoever else is out there looking for me. By now, that would be all of Brazil.

After going another mile, I turn off the siren and go down a less trafficked street.

The map on my stolen phone says there's a hospital three blocks away. I figure that's a pretty good place to leave an ambulance.

I ditch it in a parking lot near the emergency room entrance, but towards the back, so the bullet holes won't get as much attention.

I step onto the asphalt and have a look at the van. Holy crap.

Even with the damage, giving it up isn't easy. Twenty minutes ago I was on a moped, riding through the streets of Rio without a care in the world – except the potential threat of Russian kill teams and spending my life in prison – now I'm a pedestrian with a real kill team after me.

Right now my biggest concern is having the cops stop me on the street or someone recognizing me from the news.

I zig-zag down several blocks away from the hospital then finally catch my breath under a tree next to a side street.

I take out a phone and check twitter for any update from Capricorn.

Nothing.

I get the feeling I'm not going to be hearing from him in a timely manner. I need to figure this out on my own.

It's getting dark and I figure I have a couple hours before people start watching TV and seeing my face. That gives me only a small window of time to make sure the guy they see on the news clips and the description of what I was wearing at the stadium don't match up with what I look like.

The phone tells me where to find a big box store that sells everything from breakfast cereal to lingerie.

I've got about six hundred Brazilian bucks on me and have no idea what that's worth. With any luck I'll be able to buy a suit and some hair products. If not, maybe a magic marker to draw a mustache and an eyepatch on my face.

[27]
SHOPPING

MAKING IT TO THE MEN'S SECTION meant running a gauntlet, getting greeted by half a dozen people eager to help me – which only makes me even more anxious.

At any moment I expect someone to make the connection and nervously back away. Nope, all the salespeople in their orange polo shirts are super-friendly.

I just nod and grin and keep the fact I can't speak the language to myself. Every time someone stops me, I point towards another section and smile.

I find a cheap dark suit and white shirt that'll take up half my money. I decide to stay with the sneakers because they're more agile than dress shoes. Although I do spring for some athletic socks. Blisters are already starting to form on my feet.

In the personal grooming section I take a look at the different hair dyes and realize I have no idea how to use them. I'm just as likely to bleach my eyebrows as I am my brown locks. I grab a razor instead.

It's a scientific fact that all well-built bald guys in sunglasses look alike.

For the last step, I find some artificial tanning spray. Brazilians come in a wide spectrum of colors and I don't really stand out all that much. But I could stand out a little less if I had a more tropical shade to my skin.

I pay for my disguise in cash and find the nearest bathroom at the other end of the mall.

My biggest regret is not getting deodorant. I can still smell Rockthrower's stench on me.

I do my best to wipe my body with toilet paper – man is it thin here – then start to use the spray tan and stop myself when I realize I should probably shave my head first. Wouldn't that be hilarious. Christ, I'm not cut out for this.

Using the razor, I shear myself over the toilet and flush my curls. The bathroom is empty for the moment, so I sneak out of the stall and have a peek in the mirror and fix a few patches.

Satisfied that I am indeed bald, I go back into my little office and use the spray tan in very light touches, checking in the mirror as I go along, making sure that I don't give myself some kind of skin disease.

The instructions say to wait for the tan to set, so I have a seat on the toilet and check my phone – I've decided the stolen one is mine now.

Somehow I manage to fumble through the settings and change the language to English.

I open up Twitter and check @CapricornZero again for any updates.

Nothing.

Fantastic.

Meanwhile, the Brazilian news is covering my landing on the front page. There's no mention of the stadium fiasco, but that was just fifteen minutes ago.

There were too many people there who weren't part of the hit squad. Sooner or later somebody is going to make a connection.

Meanwhile, THERE'S A FUCKING RUSSIAN KILL SQUAD AFTER ME.

This is the first moment I have to take a breath and let everything sink in.

Jesus. Christ.

The smart thing would be to find my way to an American embassy.

Yes...but if I were the Russians, I'd be staking that out, waiting for me to do that.

I could call them...

But @CapricornZero said that a highly-placed mole would rendition me.

What if he's lying? Maybe he's some Chinese spy trying to play the two sides against each other?

This is all very confusing.

I create a Twitter account of my own so I can follow him and send a direct message without using my own Twitter – which I'm sure newsrooms around the world are watching to see if something happens.

There's a thought...

I could post something and explain it's all a big misunderstanding.

Right, David, you'll clear this up in 140 characters. Meanwhile, you'll let the whole world know that you're alive and in Brazil.

But if I just give up the square then the problem is no longer mine.

It's tempting.

It's so god damn tempting.

Right now I'm running on the advice of an anonymous voice and Bennet's last words to me.

The choice is simple, David.

If you trust Bennet, then you keep moving.

If you don't, then you call iCosmos or the embassy and tell them you don't want to play this game anymore.

I think about it real hard.

Bennet saved my life once in a training exercise.

Would he have risked his life, Peterson's or my own if it wasn't worth it?

I have to act on faith right now. There's also the nagging suspicion that turning myself in won't be as easy as I think.

It's decided, my primary goal is to secretly get the hell out of this country before it kills me.

No passport.

No money.

Finally, this is one problem I might actually be able to solve.

[28]
THE FRAT

I SPOT MY PREY from across the street as they get out of a van laughing at some inside joke. Dressed in navy blue suits with their jackets over their arms or tucked into their small suitcases, they enter the Hotel Solara as a pack.

It's a nice place, not too touristy. It's more of an executive hotel close enough to all the good bars and restaurants. It's exactly the kind of location where I knew I would find them: An international airline flight crew.

I know their ways. I know their language.

Sometimes the pilots mingle with the flight attendants, sometimes they don't. This looks like a mixed group, which is good for me.

Infiltrating them is tricky. If you just go straight at them, they'll assume you're trying to screw the hot redhead the co-pilot has a thing for. You'll run into the alpha male, almost always the pilot, and get shut down right away.

Worst is when the most senior flight attendant, a woman who stopped getting passes before this century, decides to cock block you out of jealousy. She'll make you a pariah and signal to the group that you're some desperate loner that shouldn't be approached. Even if the redhead liked you, she doesn't want to risk fifteen hours trapped with a woman implying every way possible that she's a slut.

This takes a delicate approach. I learned this when I was an eager college student desperate to fly in the jump seat or get free travel to other parts of the world.

I learned the master approach to these tribes and how to become one of them.

It doesn't work every time, because they don't always have what you need, but when they do, it's golden. You're in.

While the alpha male and the alpha female of the pack protect them from outsiders, there's one person whose job is to bring novelty and excitement to the group: Their social secretary. The gay male flight attendant. If he's black, it's even better.

Yes, it's a cliche, but if you grow up black and gay in white circles you have to learn real quickly how to defuse prejudices and read the room.

He's the tallest one of the group. Early thirties. As he walks through the doors with the others, he exchanges a big laugh with the silver-haired captain.

This is good. Real good. It's a team that likes to fly together. One happy family. If one of them is cool with you, they will all be.

Their plan is going to be to go up to their rooms, get changed, then meet back in the hotel bar in a half hour where they're going to decide where to go to dinner. If it was earlier in the day, there would have been a high chance that they would splinter off into different groups – the flight attendants going shopping and the pilots to the beach to read.

This late, they all just want to get a drink, get something to eat, and for a couple of them, possibly get laid.

I just want a ride back to America.

I make my way to the hotel bar, check my appearance in the mirror and make sure that my tan hasn't sweated onto my collar.

I order a Diet Coke because it looks like it might be a hard drink and rehearse my story in my head. The bartender seems pretty disinterested in me as he goes about doing a bottle count.

There's a television in the corner that's playing some talk show with the volume muted all the way down. Thankfully it's not the news.

I take a sip of my drink and watch as the co-pilot – the one with less silver hair – comes into the lounge and takes a seat and checks his phone. Two flight attendants come down a few minutes later, managing to change into suitable evening wear in less time than it takes me to get a tie on straight. These ladies are world travelers.

After the pilot takes his seat, the social secretary enters the room with a bombastic laugh, wondering aloud why he's always the last one down.

The pilot comments that it takes him so long to get his hair just right – which everyone laughs at because he's bald.

I'm hoping the social secretary will take everyone's drink orders and come to the bar where he'll make a sidelong glance at me and strike a conversation.

Instead, it's the pilot. He walks up, gives me a quick nod, places his order then returns to the group.

Damn it.

Now I'm going to have to try a different approach. I can still make this work.

I just need to think of a...

"Hey look!" says the social secretary, "It's that crazy asshole that hijacked the space station!"

Shoot me now.

[29]
SELFIE

MY HEART STOPS and I feel all my blood drain from my body. One moment I'm in a bar figuring out how I'm going to use my douchey pick-up artist techniques to infiltrate a group of people – taking me back to my college days – the next, I'm punched in the face by reality as I realize I'm not playing some kind of game.

I gain control of my limbs and step away from the bar, pretending I didn't just get called out. After all, that's what a guy that was Totally-Not-Fugitive-Astronaut-David-Dixon would do.

If I run, I look suspicious. If I act casual, it's no big deal.

Out of the corner of my vision I realize they're not looking at me; they're watching the television. The talk show cut over to a news report showing aerial footage of the Unicorn in a clearing in a jungle. The orange parachute is dangling over some trees and the open hatch is facing outwards, towards the camera.

One of the flight attendants, a petite dark-haired woman, is translating the news to her friends.

"They think he may be in the jungle or could have drowned when it first landed. The police got reports that he jumped out over Guanabara Bay."

Well, thanks for unreliable witnesses.

She continues, "But there have been reports that there was a shooting at a football stadium and that he was sighted there."

"He's like the white chupacabra," says the social secretary. Then he looks up and sees me watching them watching the television. "There he is!"

FUUUUUCK.

All eyes turn on me. I'm about to drain other bodily fluids since my blood has already departed.

I manage a weak smile and hold my hands up like chupacabra claws, because that's what Totally-Not-Fugitive-Astronaut-David-Dixon would do.

Haha! We're all having fun because that would be absurd!

The group bursts into laughter. I laugh with them like a carefree guy who wasn't almost murdered by a Russian kill team an hour ago.

I let out a sigh then head for the exit, making plans to run for it as soon as nobody is watching.

"You're not going anywhere!" says the social secretary as he bounces up from his chair to intercept me.

I want to run, but that would be bad. I could say that I have an important meeting to get to, but then the conversation I leave behind me will be all about how weird it was that I left as soon as the crazy astronaut was on TV – and didn't that guy look a lot like him?

I have to do the opposite of what people would expect a fugitive to do. I turn around and smile.

The social secretary grabs me by the arm and leads me back to the group. "What's your name?" he asks.

"George," I reply. It's part of my prepared alibi. I had a friend in college, now a pilot doing charters, named George Williams. My assumed identity would be his real one. I know enough about him to pass myself off as George. Also, he's from Toronto, so I can say that I'm

Canadian, making me Totally-Not-Fugitive-Astronaut-David-Dixon.

"I'm Shawn," he replies, then puts a hand on my shoulder and presents me to the group. "Doesn't that astronaut look like George's whiter, less bald brother?"

This gets a few nods of agreement.

"I think you're better looking," says the older flight attendant.

I make a sheepish grin, trying to be Totally-Not-Fugitive-Astronaut-David-Dixon.

The co-pilot shakes his head. "I don't see it."

Thank you, sir. I hope I never have to rely on your acute vision in the cockpit.

"What do you do?" asks the captain.

A minute ago I was going to tell the group that I was a pilot, just like him. Now that David Dixon, fugitive astronaut, is the topic de jour, that seems like the dumbest idea in the world.

"I'm a pilot," says my mouth, deciding to wing it on its own without conversing with my brain on the matter.

"You wouldn't happen to have parked your ride in a jungle, by chance?" asks the co-pilot.

Play it cool, Totally-Not-Fugitive-Astronaut-David-Dixon. I jerk a thumb towards the television. "Isn't that crazy?"

"We were diverted for an hour because the bay was the landing zone," says the captain. "Almost had to land in São Paulo."

I'm too terrified to reply. All I can do is grin, which is apparently all Totally-Not-Fugitive-Astronaut-David-Dixon can do to keep up his end of a conversation.

Thankfully, Shawn interrupts us, saving me for the moment. Unfortunately, the next words out of his mouth make me feel nauseous.

"Let's all take a selfie with our celebrity friend!"

Oh, lord. I'm seconds away from having a half-dozen people tag and upload my photo to the Internet with a location stamped right on it.

Shawn is directing people before I can even protest.

"Captain Beransky, you over there. Whitcomb, you there. Adele, I'm not even letting you get close to him, you dirty cougar. Serena, I saw you watching him; you stand next to him. Connie, over here, next to me."

Faster than a Russian kill team can draw a bead on me, I'm surrounded by the flight crew and in the dead center of a selfie shot as Shawn sticks his long arm out to capture the moment.

I stare at my face on the phone screen as the camera clicks and half panic, half feel a measure of relief. Yeah, it's me. But I kind of sort of don't look exactly like me.

To be honest, it's a crappy picture and would not go on my dating profile; while the one provided to the news from my iCosmos page was shot by a fashion photographer and makes me out to be much more handsome than I am.

I fake the cheesiest, shit-eating grin I can manage because that's what Totally-Not-Fugitive-Astronaut-David-Dixon would do.

These people aren't idiots. I need to get away from them as conveniently as I can without attracting attention, because sooner or later one of them is going to wise up.

[30]
PARTY ANIMAL

I'M DRAGGED by the group into a taxi van and taken to a restaurant bar called the "Angry Turtle." I keep waiting for a convenient moment to slip away, but I can't find one or think of something to say that doesn't sound forced.

We take a group of high tops in the corner of the balcony that overlooks the street. The place has a seaside shanty look to it with surfboards on the walls.

I situate myself so I can see who comes in, but staying out of sight as much as I can. I also take note of all the entrances. To my left is a fire exit that leads to a set of stairs and the alley.

I'm ready to bolt through that door the moment the policia arrive. If they cover that exit, I can go up to the next level and get on the roof.

On Google Maps the buildings don't look too spaced apart. Not that I want to have to actually try to run across roof tops. I'm not even sure if that's a thing outside of Jason Bourne movies.

"Drink up!" says Shawn as he slams two handfuls of shot glasses on the table.

FAA rules are 8 hours from bottle to throttle, but I notice Captain Beransky abstains. Everyone else puts a glass to their lips and prepares to drink.

I leave mine on the table. Shawn is having none of this and puts it in my hand. "Are you flying?"

While I haven't had much opportunity to tell them my made up tale of woe since I got pulled into this hurricane, now's my chance.

"I'm hoping to get a jump seat back to the US," I reply. "Maybe cockpit."

"Are you stranded?" asks Whitcomb.

The way he asks that makes me feel extremely nervous. It's exactly what I am.

"I flew down to fly as a relief charter for some crazy Saudi prince. More money than common sense. Turns out he pissed off his uncle or something and had to turn around. That was my ride back to the States."

"Can't your charter company do something about that?"

Great question. And I have an answer. "They're supposed to. They say relax for the next three days. They're some new plane-sharing start up. Really disorganized."

"What are they called?"

Christ, this guy missed his calling and should have been in the Gestapo.

"Blue Air." It's a real thing, a small stealth startup you can look it up.

He nods. "I think I know somebody who flies for them."

For crying out loud.

"You know Carl O'Brien?"

This could be a trap. "I don't think so. I'm new with them. A friend just recommended them to me."

"Who?"

I almost say, "George Williams." Wouldn't that be hilarious. "Jeff Roberts."

If Whitcomb calls me out on that, I'm prepared to say that Roberts doesn't actually work for them, he just recommended them to me. And if that doesn't fly, I'll throw my drink in his face and run away.

I totally understand how cops work now. They just keep asking you questions, getting you deeper and deeper into your story and watching how long it takes for you to make something up.

That's why you should just ask for a lawyer up front. Unfortunately, that won't work too well in this situation.

Shawn slams his hand on the table. "Will you two bitches shut the hell up? We got some ladies that need to dance and I'm not going to let some gajo locals sweep them away. All the gajos are for this boy."

Adele, the cougar, grabs my hand and pulls me onto the small dance floor. She puts my hands on her hips and starts to sway.

I do my best to play along and keep my back to the door. The only other dancers are Shawn and Serena and a very awkward Whitcomb and Connie.

Captain Beransky sits at the table and watches us like we're his children.

"You're very quiet," says Adele over the sound of the Brazilian pop music.

I try to think of something to say, but she finishes the conversation.

"That's a good quality. Most pilots can't shut up."

Lady, you should see me when I'm not on the run from super powers and not dodging bullets. I'm a veritable motor mouth.

"I prefer to listen," I reply.

She does a twirl. "Oh my. That is a rare quality."

Shawn steps over with Serena and gives us a fierce look. "Time is up, cat lady. Let's let these two play."

Serena, the very attractive Portuguese speaker, is dropped into my hands. She was paying a lot more attention to the news than the others. I'm terrified of what's going through her mind.

Likewise with Whitcomb. I see him pointing to me and whispering to Connie. They peel away from the dance floor, leaving just the four of us.

Thankfully Adele and Shawn are great dancers and are attracting all the attention. I just give Serena a sheepish grin.

She leans in to whisper something to me. I get a whiff of her fragrance and I kind of forget all my problems for a moment.

"It's okay. I know your secret."

I do everything I can to keep moving and not stop cold in the dance floor, attracting everyone's attention.

I get ready to make for the bathroom then exit.

Do I threaten her first? Lord, no. I can't do that.

"You've been watching Shawn since we first saw you at the hotel."

It takes me a moment to process what she just said.

She thinks I'm gay!

Hallelujah!

I had been watching him since he stepped into the hotel. And to a careful observer it might look like I was interested in him. Hell, I was. I knew he was the key to the whole thing.

"Was I that obvious?" I reply.

She sighs. "Why are the interesting ones always gay?"

"Listen doll face, I'd go straight for you in a heart beat."

She playfully slaps me on the shoulder. Relieved that my secret is safe for another minute at least, I put a little more pep into my step.

My smile fades as I see two men in dark suits walk into the bar and go over to Whitcomb to speak with him.

[31]
JUMP SEAT

I TURN SERENA so my back is towards the men who just joined Whitcomb. "I think I need to use the restroom," I say, all smiles.

If I just flat out run for the door I'm guilty. If I casually go to the restroom and take a while to return, then I'm not as suspicious. That will give me a little bit of a head start if these people are looking for me.

I let her go and she gives me a playful pat on the ass. "Don't talk to strangers."

I force a big smile on my face and wink at her over my shoulder then head for the other side of the bar to pretend to look for the bathroom as I make my exit.

I move through a crowd and end up having to weave around a section of tables because I'm not paying attention.

"George!" I look over as Connie is grabbing me by the arm. "You have a second?"

"I was going to use the bathroom," I say feebly.

"It's the other way. But first, there are some people we want you to meet."

My stomach does a backflip. One of the men in suits is standing in the passage I just left.

He's not wearing his jacket and there doesn't appear to be a gun on him. He doesn't look Russian or Brazilian.

"Uh..."

"It'll only take a second." She pulls me over to the stranger.

Late thirties, clean cut, he could be FBI or some kind of government agent. "Are you the stranded pilot?" he asks.

At first I think he says astronaut and I feel my mouth go numb. "Maybe?" It's the dumbest possible reply.

He holds out his hand. "I'm Jeff Sigler. Gary over there and I are flying a charter to Los Angeles tonight. We're on standby, waiting for some Brazilian soccer player to get packed. Your friends said you needed a jump seat back to the States."

"Uh...that would be great."

"There's a catch. Our third man caught the flu. You'd be filling in for him."

If he asks to see my pilot certification I'm screwed. I already have to figure out how to make it through passport control – but that's doable if we go through an executive airport.

"What kind of gear?" I ask.

"G6. But don't worry. We just need you to be the inflight attendant. Our client's wife won't let him have any female crew."

I make a sound that resembles laughter but is actually my soul slipping back into my body.

"That would be great!"

"Cool. We're going to grab something to eat then go check the plane. Do you need to get your luggage from the hotel?"

Um, that. It does look rather suspicious that I don't have a suitcase or anything else besides the clothes I'm wearing.

"I can have it sent over." Whatever that means. "Thank you, you're a real life saver."

"No problem."

He and Connie go back to the tables and I find the
bathroom so I can lock myself inside a stall and let all the
nervous energy leave me.

I pull out my phone and load up Twitter. I have no new
followers. @CapricornZero has not deigned to follow me
back or send me any helpful tweets.

Should I send him a public @reply? What if he's been
compromised? The Workmen and the Russians knew
where to find me at the stadium...was there some kind of
leak?

A public response would be stupid. Somebody could
trace my tweet and figure out where I am. Sure, the
account is anonymous, but I'm sure there's all kinds of
device data and location information that can pinpoint me
– especially if I'm dealing with government intelligence
agencies.

It's enough that I followed him and he has a way to
reach me. Something must have happened.

Was Capricorn really my contact at the stadium? Did
he get killed in the shooting?

Hell, what if Capricorn was one of the Workmen or a
Russian kill team member?

Did I just mess up their attempt to assassinate me and
take the black square? Whoops.

I take the McGuffin out of my pocket and inspect it for
the first time. I've been running so much I haven't even
stopped to figure out what it is.

Two inches on each side and the thickness of several
credit cards, I can spot a row of metallic contact points
along one edge. It sort of looks like a large SD card.

I take some water from the sink and wash away the
blood. There are some faint letters and numbers in the
corner. The letters are Cyrillic. Which would make sense,
because it was stolen off a Russian space station.

But what is it? It could be some kind of proprietary memory module, although I'm not sure why they wouldn't just use something standard. Is it shielded to protect it from high-altitude cosmic rays? Or is it thick because it does something else?

A quick Google search isn't much help, so I decide this is a mystery I'll have to resolve somewhere else beside the bathroom in a Rio bar.

When I head back out to the table, Jeff and Gary are devouring their food while the rest of the group is discussing where to go for their dinner.

"You ready?" asks Jeff. "We just got the word our passenger is heading to the airport soon."

I say goodbye to my new friends and take down their Facebook info, promising to add them once I have WiFi.

I'm a little nervous as I get into a taxi with these new people, suspicious that it's some clever plot to separate me from everyone else.

If it is, then I give up. There's no way I can keep up with minds that devious or resourceful.

We arrive at the executive section of the airport where they park all the private jets. The guard at the gate takes a look at Jeff's passport and pilot's license through the window and waves us on through.

We exit the taxi, make it to the private terminal and get waved through yet another door by a military police officer.

While the word is out about the American astronaut on the run, I'm clearly just a pilot hanging out with two other pilots.

I feel a wave of relief as I step out of the building and onto the tarmac.

The scent of jet fuel smells like freedom.

Two seconds later I get cold feet when I see a third cop standing by a motorcycle, directly between us and the plane.

This third layer of security is unusual. He's actually checking people before they get on the plane.

As Jeff and Gary walk right up to him, I hover behind.

The cop looks at something on his phone – probably my photo – then miraculously waves us on.

It seems the head shave and fake tan were the smartest things I've ever done.

Jeff and Gary start to do an inspection. I stay on the opposite side of the nose, too afraid to go inside the plane and get trapped if something happens.

I make mindless banter with them as they go about their business.

I'm a little distracted and don't notice the black SUV pulling across the asphalt until it's just a few hundred feet away.

[32]
AIR SHOW

THE SUV IS CRUISING by very slowly. The windows are dark, but I can see the silhouette of two men in the front seat and two in the back as it passes in front of a light.

I move behind the fuselage of the plane and pretend to inspect the airspeed sensor on the nose. While I can't see the SUV from here, I can see its shadow on the tarmac.

And it just came to a stop...

Keep calm, David. They could just be passengers. Hell, it could be our Brazilian soccer player.

Sure, maybe they're federal police of some kind. But they're probably everywhere. Just be another pilot inspecting a plane.

Don't be a panicked guy about to go on the run at the drop of a hat. How many times was I going to do that tonight?

If I'd ran off in the hotel bar I would never be this close to getting a ride back to the United States.

This close...

The doors to the SUV open.

Beat.

Beat.

Beat.

And they don't close.

I hear footsteps from several men walking across the pavement.

I casually drift to my right so I'm blocked by the landing gear and lean down to have a look.

It's the Russians from the stadium.

Fuck my life.

They're speaking to the policeman.

One of the them spots me and knocks the policeman out of his way and starts firing.

BANG!!! BANG!!! BANG!!! Bullets ricochet off the landing gear.

"GET DOWN!!!" I scream to Steve and Gary.

They don't need my advice to drop flat. The men hit the deck as the Russians run towards me.

I've got a thousand feet of empty runway ahead of me. They'll have no trouble gunning me down out in the open.

BANG!!! BANG!!!

The closest Russian falls flat on his face and skids – blood smears the tarmac out of a head wound.

I'm confused until I see the grounded policeman aim his pistol at the other Russians and they run to the other side of the SUV.

BANG!!! BANG!!! BANG!!! They fire back as he races to rear of their car.

The hatch to the jet is right in their kill zone. I'll never make it.

But the policeman's motorcycle is only a few yards away. I can even see the key in the ignition...

I run to the bike in a hunched position.

BANG!!! BANG!!! The Russians and the policeman exchange fire through the windows.

I hop on the bike and start the engine. A bullet strikes the pavement ahead of me as somebody realizes I'm about to get the hell out of Dodge.

I gun the accelerator and peel out, flying away from them at full speed and twist around the jet, putting it between us.

Red and blue police lights flash somewhere behind me. I just keep going and take the bike across the tarmac.

Full throttle, I race down the taxi-way. Straight ahead there's a landing light of a jet as it rolls towards me.

I take the bike onto the grass island and blow past the wing tip. Stealing a glance behind me, there's three or four police cars with their lights on.

I don't know if they're after me or responding to the shooting, it really doesn't matter because there's also a pair of headlights belonging to the SUV, charging towards me.

Think, David.

You're trapped in an airport with fences all the way around. There's no way I'm going to pull a Steve McQueen and jump my way out. And there's no way this bike is going to knock down the fence.

While you might be able to evade the Russians by whizzing around in circles, the Brazilian police are going to catch you sooner than later if you can't get out.

BANG! Someone tries to shoot at me from all the way back there.

I glance behind me; all the way back there is a lot closer... That SUV is tearing it up. So are the police cars in hot pursuit.

This is going to be a god damn blood bath.

The Russians already had a gun battle with one cop.

BAP-BAP-BAP-BAP-BAP-BAP-BAP-BAP-BAP

Automatic gun fire! Shit! They're shooting machine guns now!

Two police cars appear out of nowhere in front of me and blow past, heading to intercept the SUV.

BAP-BAP-BAP-BAP-BAP-BAP-BAP-BAP-BAP

There's a crash behind me as a police cruiser smashes into the front landing gear of a plane when it gets hit by automatic gunfire.

The SUV swerves as the other police car plays chicken.

BANG!!!   BANG!!!   BAP-BAP-BAP-BAP   Christ, there's a full on gun battle behind me.

It slows the Russians down and helps me a little.

Maybe there is a way out of here...

And there it is...

I think I found a way over the fence after all.

It weighs 80,000 pounds and already has a staircase waiting for me.

[33]
PILOT

IN 1976 a University of Illinois graduate named Bruce Artwick started publishing articles on using computers for the novel application of 3D graphics. The editor of one of the magazines that published his work advised Artwick to take his ideas one step further. So he quit his job working for Hughes Aircraft and created a company called SubLOGIC.

SubLOGIC created a number of different software titles, but the one near and dear to my heart is what he sold to Microsoft in 1982 when Bill Gates came calling: *Flight Simulator*.

More than a game, *Flight Simulator* was based on actual instrumentation and flight physics. Artwick and the other programmers were pilots who endeavored to create a degree of realism unheard of in simulations until this point.

Because of Flight Simulator, I learned to fly a Boeing 777 when I was ten years old.

I'd take my plane out of LAX, land at JFK, refuel as I got another bowl of Cap'n Crunch then head on over to England and land at Heathrow – the world's busiest airport. After I ate a hotdog and microwave French fries – my approximation to bangers and mash – I'd fly to Istanbul, Tokyo and then back to LAX, having circumnavigated the world, taking off and landing at all the major airports.

I'd try landing with engine fires, no landing gear, bad rudders. I even managed to flip the plane in a barrel roll others told me was impossible.

I logged more hours flying passenger jets than I did in any class in school. Granted, it was another decade before I got to fly a real one – and even then under the watchful eye of an instructor, but all the gauges and controls were where they were supposed to be. It was like coming home.

With flashing red lights behind me and the sound of BAP-BAP-BAP-BAP-BAP-BAP-BAP-BAP-BAP gunfire echoing off the walls of the terminal and hangars, nothing sounds more soothing than the calming cockpit of a jet-airliner.

I ditch the bike, run up the stairs and race inside. Thankfully, the passenger seats are empty. Immediately to my left I spot the open cockpit door and two pilots anxiously talking to air traffic control as they try to figure out what the hell is going on.

The co-pilot spins around and sees me standing in the doorway. "Who the hell are you?" he demands with a French accent.

"Get out!" I hesitate to think of what to say next. "They are coming for this plane!"

"We'll shut the door," says the pilot.

"They're going to try to blow it up!"

"What?"

The men are clearly confused. As am I. All I can do is just keep escalating the threat until they get up and leave.

"YOU HAVE TO GO NOW!" I scream.

BAP-BAP-BAP-BAP-BAP-BAP-BAP-BAP-BAP

The distant spray of machine gun fire reinforces the urgency of the situation.

The co-pilot looks to the captain, who nods to him. They both get up and I back out of the way.

I follow them outside and go halfway down the steps. At the bottom, the two men make a run for the terminal.

When the captain stops to look back, I'm already shutting the door.

I race back to the cockpit and do a quick check of everything. It appears that they were in the process of taxiing the plane from a hangar. The fuel gauges indicate full tanks – which is what I'll need to get this bird out of South America.

Since there's no ground crew to pull the stairs out of the way, I use the plane's reverse thrust to back away.

While I can't actually see the steps, the jet is far enough away from everything else that I can do a wide spin that brings me clear.

The gun shots are a faint popping sound from the inside of the cockpit. Which I guess is good, but I have no idea if anybody is shooting at me.

Right now the pilot is probably screaming at air traffic control – having realized what just happened.

And what did just happen?

Ninety seconds ago I was waiting for a free ride back to the United States. Now I'm stealing a $400 million-dollar passenger jet.

What the hell am I doing?

BANG!!! BANG!!! BANG!!! Another police car blows by me, oblivious to the fact that I'm about to steal something kind of valuable.

From the sound of things, the Russians are more than able to hold their own.

I crane my head and spot the latest police car charging right towards another marked cruiser. At first I think it's to provide back up, then I see someone open fire on the other car.

Jesus. The Russians have got the police shooting at each other.

Let's not stick around to see who's the winner.

I push the throttle forward and take the jet across the tarmac.

There are other planes on the taxi-way, but they're not moving. Air traffic control has probably ordered everyone to stay put – and hopefully having the passengers stay clear of the windows in case of stray gunfire.

The upside is that I'm pretty sure I have the runway all to myself.

Are you going to do this, David?

Seriously?

Are you going to steal a god damn passenger jet?

I check my flaps and my gauges, making sure everything is doing what it's supposed to be doing, then nudge the throttle.

The plane taxis to the end of the runway and I turn around, lining the nose up with the stripes.

This thing in my pocket better be damn worth it. I'm about to add a 777 to the list of things I've stolen in the last twelve hours, including a spaceship.

This has got to be some kind of record.

I do a last minute check. Flashing blue and red lights are starting to race down the taxiing lane.

I think everything is fine – on the inside. Out there, not so much.

It's time to go before some macho cop or kill-crazy Russian decides to play chicken with me.

I pull back the throttle and listen to the engines roar.

It's a good sound.

A reassuring sound.

I forget the world around me and pretend I'm sitting at our old computer hutch about to take to the sky.

[34]
THE CAPTAIN

TAKING OFF in a 777 by yourself is no easy feat. Had I stumbled into a 747, I would have probably died on takeoff trying to jump between the flight engineer station behind the co-pilot seat while handling the throttle with my toes.

This still takes all my attention because I don't get a do-over if I forget a flap or something.

Besides pancaking into the ground, my other concern is smashing my plane into one of the many other jets currently in holding patterns waiting for ground control to tell them when they can land.

Ideally, I'd like to maintain radio silence, but I kind of sort of morally need to tell them to clear a path.

I'm sure the pissed off French pilots have told them by now that some asshole American stole their plane. I need to convince them that I don't plan on slamming it into a building – hijacking used to be so much easier before they were afraid terrorists were going to use the planes as weapons.

After I gain altitude I put on the headset and key in the mic to talk to air traffic control's main channel.

"Rio, this is..." I look for a label above the radio with the airplane's registration number. "...N9987IF. Please clear a path between Rio and LAX. There are hostages onboard."

I shut the radio off. It wasn't exactly the most professional radio call of my life, but they can figure out the rest.

If I stay on the channel and let them talk to me, they'll try to convince me to land or tell me that I'm about to be shot down, blah blah blah.

I did enough flight training to know that the worst situation on the ground is when you have no idea what their intentions are.

Right now they're panicking because someone on this jet said there are hostages and then shut off the radio.

Sooner than later I'm going to have an escort of Brazilian, then Colombian and Mexican jets. Ultimately, at some point before I enter US airspace, I'm going to meet the most highly trained fighters in the world while somebody from the Pentagon makes a case to the President for or against shooting me down.

I really don't have much of a plan for that right now. Los Angeles is at the furthest limit of this plane's range. If I'd said New York City, I'd probably get shot down without a blink.

That may still happen. I can make up destinations all I want, but at some point I'm going to actually have to land. If they haven't killed me by then, I'm going to have one hell of a welcome reception on the ground that's going to be a little more focused than the fiasco I just left in Rio.

Strangely, I'm the calmest I've been since this whole thing began. Or maybe it's not so strange. Flying is the one thing I'm good at. Worrying about all the little details like cabin pressure, fuel lines and did I retract the – FUCK! – landing gear.

Focus, David.

If I make it back to America, they probably won't extradite me to Russia. Our two countries have never seen eye to eye about that. I'll just spend the rest of my life in a Federal penitentiary if Capricorn's boogeymen don't kill me first.

If child molesters are the lowest of the low in prison, where does a guy who stole a spaceship and a passenger jet in one day rank? That'll have to give me some street cred, right? If that can't keep me from being someone's bitch, what else can a guy do?

I reach a cruising altitude of 33,000 feet. It'd be no problem to take this thing higher because there's nobody onboard, but that might signal the fact that there ain't no hostages.

I'm sure the airline already has their lawyers arguing with the insurance company over coverage in the event I get brought down.

Speaking of hostages...

I put the plane on autopilot and climb out of the cockpit – basically the dumbest thing you can do when you're flying an airplane like this by yourself – short of flying an airplane like this yourself.

I run down the aisle and start closing window shades in the front, then race to the back and close some at the rear. There are 100 windows on this thing. I'll be over San Diego by the time I close them all. I just shut enough to make it look like I'm hiding hostages.

All I need is one hotshot Brazilian pilot to fly next to the plane and notice there's nobody in the back and just one jerk in the front and the math problem of whether or not to shoot me down will get a lot easier.

Would that be an easier question if they knew who was flying? An hour ago there was a rumor that I was involved in the stadium shooting, but my actual whereabouts was unknown.

The fact that a jet just got stolen from the runway in the middle of a gun battle in the same city where David Dixon, astronaut-pirate, tried to land his spaceship, couldn't have gone unnoticed by the entire planet.

I can imagine some talking head on television news pointing out that, "Well, he is a pilot..."

Wonderful. I wish this bird had satellite television so they can explain to me why the Russian kill team and the Brazilian cops decided to shoot at each other.

Was it friendly fire? Or are there two kinds of Russians after me? The ones that just want to arrest me and kill me and ones that want to kill me before the ones who want to arrest me can kill me?

This is kind of stressful. Flying a 777 by myself I can cope with. Figuring international conspiracies is above my pay grade.

I poke my head into the cockpit to make sure that I'm not about to run right into a mountain then stick my nose in the galley because food is my drug of choice.

Holy cow! There he is, saluting me!

He may be called Capitaine on this French plane, but he was always an imposter wearing commander stripes anyway. It doesn't matter. He's an old friend whether you call him Capitaine Crounchie or Cap'n Crunch and I've got a dozen boxes of his sugary treasure.

Besides flying a 777 by yourself and leaving the cockpit, you should also never take a large bowl of milk and cereal and eat it over the controls – but hey, that's how I roll.

[35]
CO-PILOT

AS I EAT MY FIFTH SERVING of Cap'n Crunch, a JAS 39 Gripen, a delta-wing attack and reconnaissance plane made by Saab, flies about a hundred feet to the port side of my cockpit and the navigator aims a huge camera lens right at me.

I'd been expecting this. It was only a matter of time before the Brazilians sent the air force to intercept me.

Right now the only way I can keep anything resembling an upper hand is by manipulating their uncertainty. I took a flight attendant's apron from the galley and made it into an improvised balaclava. It appears real enough, but smells like burnt coffee.

I just don't want them looking through the window and seeing dumb old David Dixon flying a plane all by his lonesome.

While I can ignore the radio, if the pilot of the Gripen decides to start flashing me Morse code, they would expect David Dixon to be able to figure out what they're saying.

Commercial airline pilots don't have to know it – they just use a manual – an astronaut pilot like myself is expected to understand a variety of low-bandwidth communications methods.

Once they know they can talk to me, they'll start getting into my head. If I had to bet on me or some terrorist negotiator who has dealt with dozens of high-stakes situations, my money is on him. I'm not cut out for this.

All they have to do is get my mom on the phone and have her yell at me that I'm grounded and I'm done for.

Oh, god. My mother. She's the principal of a middle school. I called her on the way to the base, waking her up, and told her that I was finally going into space.

That's when she said she'd have the whole school watch the launch.

Jesus.

What do you think of your hero now, kids? What do you think of your son, mom?

You know what? Let's not worry about that right now. My primary concern is the Brazilian jet next to the cockpit and the two far off blinking lights on either side that have started shadowing me.

Russian MiGs? I'm still too far out of range of their Venezuelan air base, but they have access out of Bolivia...

Capricorn said they would try to shoot me down when I was in the spaceship. Would they do the same to a French passenger jet ostensibly loaded with people?

I'm real glad I took the time to close some of the windows. My claim of hostages won't stand up to the claim of the pilot whom I stole the plane from.

I hope that while he's insisting the plane is empty, the authorities are nervous that the hijacker may have snuck some onboard – hell they have to know it's me by now, the pilots would have pointed to my photo and said that's the asshole.

All the more reason not to talk to them. I'd crumble if they asked to speak to a hostage.

"Well...um...they're in the bathroom right now..."

BOOM! And they shoot me from the sky.

"What would you do, Cap'n?" I ask the smiling face I tore from the cereal box and stuck to the co-pilot's chair.

Oh crap, they probably got a photo of him too.

Wonderful. Maybe I should find some Rice Crispies and recruit Snap, Crackle and Pop into my terrorist organization?

Let them figure out the political significance of that.

I ignore my escorts and decide to worry about how I'm going to land and not die or spend my life in prison.

Although I told them my destination was LAX – realizing the panic that's probably causing, I now think that was a mistake, um, oh well, next time I'll figure out a better solution. I can't actually land there unless I have some brilliant master plan to evade the most highly trained terrorist response teams in the world.

Fun fact: The Los Angeles Police Department actually invented SWAT. And I chose there of all places.

Of course, it'll be the FBI team that probably launches the assault. They have actual airplane fuselages that they train on practicing these scenarios. But they won't even need to board the plane. One sniper in an elevated position will be able to fire an armor piercing round straight through the cockpit window before I even power down the engines.

Nope. There's no good outcome in that situation unless I get on the radio and announce that I'm ready to surrender.

And that will lead to another scenario without a good outcome.

What's my story? That some guy on a broken sat phone told me to do this? The plastic square with the Russian letters? What will that prove, other than the fact that I stole something from the K1 space station?

That's all assuming I can trust the government folks that handle this. I'm not a conspiracy theorist, but Capricorn's warning that there's someone very highly placed working with the Russians isn't out of the question. All it takes is one CIA chief to make something up and nobody will believe me. I mean clearly I'm a lunatic.

I take the pilot charts out and start considering my options. Obviously LAX is out of the question if I'm going to try to avoid arrest or a rapid lead injection.

Bailing out of the airplane would be an option if I had a parachute and was willing to smash $400 million-dollars-worth of aircraft into some hopefully uninhabited area – only to find out the black square in my pocket contained evidence of some really minor infraction, like stealing satellite television on the K1.

So...no jumping out.

I have to land this thing in a place where the cops can't get to me quickly.

I run my finger along South and Central America searching for a potentially friendly country that might give me asylum. All I realize is that I know next to nothing about international politics.

I need some other option besides a diplomatic one.

A little spot on the map catches my eye.

There's a thought...

But to make it work I'll have to crash this plane.

[36]
DEEP SIX

LOOKING AT THE CHARTS and tracing my route to my presumed destination of Los Angeles, I have a very scary realization and inspiration. Whether or not those twinkling lights in the distance are Russian MiGs flying out of Bolivia, I know for sure I'm going to get a real Ruskie escort when I pass over international water by Bolivia and Venezuela. I'll be well within range of anything flying out of Caracas and Cuba.

They're probably not going to bring me down over land – even the Amazonian jungle, but open water is a different matter.

The Russians haven't been shy about doing that kind of thing in the past. I'll never make it to Mexican airspace if I keep this course.

I need to get them off my back and hopefully out of range. And out of range may not even be a possibility if they have a Tupolev Tu-160 long-range bomber anywhere near Central America. That can go further than I can and carries cruise missiles that adds another 1,500 miles to its striking distance.

To get them off my back, I have to do something really, really stupid.

The upside is that if it works, they'll think I'm dead, as will the American and Mexican authorities.

I don't know how long the ruse will work, but it might be enough to get me onto a different path and confuse the situation enough that I get past their air defenses.

I check the autopilot and set a timer so I can steal a nap. Thankfully, this bird has enough alarms and alerts that I'm able to sleep reasonably confident that I'm not about to smash into a mountain.

I wake up two hours later as the plane begins to jostle from some turbulence. Nothing major, but probably a good time to get up.

Once I'm through it, I let myself use the bathroom, although I leave the door open in the event I have to run to the controls.

We're heading towards the Colombian border and I'm sure they're going to want to send their own planes to greet me.

The Brazilian Gripen left a while ago – as did the twinkling lights. My radar doesn't show anything close, but a military jet flying at a high altitude could shadow me without my knowledge. This thing is more useful for collision avoidance and weather.

It'll take me less than an hour to fly over Colombia. After that, I'm over the ocean and fair game to anyone that wants to shoot me down.

I run through my hare-brained scheme one more time. Yep, it's a dumb plan. Yep, I'm going to go through with it.

Two minutes before I reach the coast I turn the plane almost due north.

To everyone tracking me this has to have come as some kind of surprise. For some random reason I'm now heading away from my stated course.

For the Russians who are on an intercept path, this complicates things.

They'll be able to reroute, but this buys me a few extra minutes to get over international waters and do my really stupid thing...

I cut almost all my thrust and push the nose towards the sea.

I'm at 33,000 feet...

Now 32,000...

30,000...

25,000...

20,000...

15,000...

This is where it gets tricky.

Full throttle...

5,000...

I can see waves in the moonlight.

I'm probably going to die.

Pull out of the dive...wait for it...bank port!

I'm flying less than a hundred feet above the ocean and the plane is shaking like crazy.

This is not an optimum altitude but I keep going and keep turning.

I'm now heading south over Colombia, down an inlet.

If they're tracking me, I just dropped out of their radar right over the ocean. If this was any other commercial flight, the assumption would be that I just had some kind of disaster and the plane is now sinking into the waves.

However, that only buys me some confusion. While they're frantically trying to figure out where I went, I need to get out of their target zone.

This means flying ridiculously low over the Rio Atrata and then banking back north once I'm on the other side of the continent – which will be very shortly.

I check my radar to see if anything is following me; everything looks clear. If I have any Russian escorts, their onboard radar would have lost me by now.

Satellite tracking would have been lost the moment I changed altitude and course. They can find me again if they have some idea where to look – that's why I plan to complicate things a bit for them.

After I cross Colombia at a ridiculously low altitude, sticking to the jungle, I take the plane north once I'm near the coast and go back to a slightly more respectable height.

Right now there are hundreds of passenger jets in the skies between here and the United States. To avoid crashing into them or having a bunch of panicked pilots report my position, I have to keep my jet out of their airspace.

While I can only stay low for so long on land before I start tripping all sorts of radar, if I do it over the ocean I'm less likely to raise any warning flags – but also equally likely to lose the plane in bad weather.

There's a very good reason pilots like to keep these things as high up as they can. Besides better fuel efficiency, the closer you are to ground the more difficult a plane is to control when the weather is less than perfect.

That means lots of turbulence for me and no more cereal breaks for a while.

I check the weather radar and spot a mildly nasty storm and steer right for it.

Controlling the plane is a bit of a bitch, but after an hour of stormy weather and wanting to throw up, I come out into some nice conditions near El Salvador.

Assuming everything worked – big assumption – I'm a thousand miles away from where they thought I was going to be at this point.

I should be able to cross Mexican airspace without too much trouble if I stay clear of the airports and the cities; basically acting like a drug smuggler.

Which is what I'm going to have to do if I want to enter the United States.

[37]
ESCORTS

WE PROTECT OUR NATION'S BORDER through a variety of methods. There's our early warning systems – long range radar designed to see if there are enemy bombers heading their way. Some of these radar installations are ground-based, but our modern air defense relies heavily on airborne radar carried aloft by jets like the AWACS.

Airborne systems offer you the advantage of letting you know if some sneaky bastard is trying to fly low enough to the terrain to avoid any ground based line-of-sight installations.

Our biggest concentration of these planes is in Alaska, because it neighbors Russia. But we keep all our borders under surveillance.

The simple truth is you can't sneak an airplane of this size in undetected. The upside is that thousands of airplanes cross our borders everyday and get ignored because they're routine flight traffic.

My goal is to behave like one of those airplanes, following a flight path out of Mexico City, and only change my path at the last minute.

The Pentagon has prepared for every possible trick our enemies could try. I'm not about to fool them. However, the one thing I have going for me is that I don't have the same objective as a hypothetical Russian strategic bomber trying to penetrate American airspace.

I don't want to go near a heavily-populated city – and protecting those and military bases is the primary purpose of our defense.

While there are hundreds of places I can land that are far enough away from civilization, I don't want to land somewhere too off the beaten path only to die of dehydration or get quickly spotted from the air.

I considered a few decommissioned Air Force bases, but they're too far away from any kind of town. A small municipal airport is an option, but they'll undoubtedly have police – or will have by the time I hop to the ground.

I need a third way; a place to land close enough to a city where I can hide, but not so populated that there's a squadron of fighter jets ready to take me down before I even lower my landing gear.

In iCosmos astronaut training we spend weeks in seminars where they try to teach us unconventional problem solving. You never want to be in an Apollo 13 scenario where you have to improvise an air filtration system using spare parts found in a tiny capsule, but you need to be prepared for any contingency.

My first thought was a water landing, but there aren't a whole lot of options near the US-Mexico border. The major bodies of water are right on the coast and have Border Patrol agents in boats waiting for someone to cross.

Landing a 777 in the middle of one of those lakes might attract a little attention – unless it's spring break.

I started by looking on the map for dry lake beds. The best ones are a little further inside the States. The Mojave would be awesome. That was even a backup landing site for the Space Shuttle and one of the places we're taught to bring down our spaceships in case of a mechanical problem and need a wide area to avoid crashing into people on the ground.

The problem with the Mojave and the other good locations, besides being a little too far from civilization, is that they're all near Air Force bases. And those are the people I want to avoid.

Landing on a highway is an option, but there's a very high chance I'll hit a car. Which would be really bad for us both.

Scanning the charts inch by inch I came across a solution that's probably a horrible idea and made my stomach hurt thinking about how the airline would salvage the plane, but is way better than parking it in a lake.

I'm going to try to land this in the Rio Grande river – which at this time of year near El Paso is a dried up riverbed.

On the map I spotted a long straight path in a suburb just north of the city. The really good news is that it's less than two miles from a shopping mall.

If I don't turn into a fireball on landing, I can pop the hatch, take a fun ride down the slide and be off and running before the cops are called to the scene.

By the time they make it to the plane, I can be eating orange chicken in the mall food court and figuring out what the hell I'm going to do next.

And there's probably free wifi in the mall, which means I can use my stolen Brazilian phone to see if CapricornZero has any helpful advice for me on Twitter. Maybe he can help me figure out how I'm going to pay for my orange chicken too? Ugh. Landing is just one of many problems I have to deal with.

Focus, David. Don't start cracking open that fortune cookie just yet.

It's time to try our last bit of deception. I put the plane on a course that roughly lines up with El Paso, Texas but doesn't look like I'm heading there.

My plan is to go there way faster than I should and do a maneuver to kill my speed at the last moment and spiral down into a landing. It's something you'd never try with passengers, but should keep everyone guessing.

The sun is just coming up over the horizon. Man, it's been that long already?

BOOM!!! Suddenly the entire plane rattles and I almost jump out of my seat.

At first I think I've been hit then I see two F-35 jets blow past my window on either side.

That explosion was the sound of them breaking the sound barrier – meant to get my attention.

Christ. I wasn't expecting to be intercepted this soon.

The F-35s slow down and take a position on port and starboard less than a hundred feet away.

One of them starts blinking a light at me.

It's Morse code.

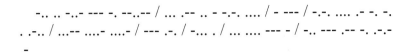

My brain translates it automatically for me:

DIXON SWITCH TO CHANNEL 344 OR BE SHOT DOWN.

Yeah, yeah. They're bluffing. I pretend to not be able to read what they said and make sure my balaclava is firmly around my head.

.-- . / -.- -. --- .-- / -.-- --- ..- / -.-. .- -. / ..- -. -.. . .-. ... - .-
-. -.. / - ....

WE KNOW YOU CAN UNDERSTAND THIS.

Damn it.

[38]
POINT OF ENTRY

LET'S ASSUME FOR A MOMENT that they're bluffing. I still have the very real problem that I now have a fighter escort. While I've got more fuel left than they have range, there will be others to replace them. Plus the fact that this means I'm definitely being tracked from the air.

Dang it. I'll bet they're using some DEA anti-drug AWACS plane to track me. It's all part of the Department of Homeland Security. They were probably able to task one of those planes to look for me.

Well, congratulations, guys, your inter-agency international collaboration worked.

I'll sleep well at night on my prison bunk, knowing that a terrorist will have a hard time pulling off this particular trick.

The moment I open my radio channel and talk to them I'm going to confirm their suspicion. I'm also going to give them the opportunity to tell me where to land unless I want to be shot down.

Let's think this through. I'm still over Mexican airspace. While my escorts have permission to intercept me, I'm assuming their ground coordination isn't exactly going to be topnotch. A lot of the desert I'm flying over is lawless territory controlled by the cartels.

The pilots onboard the F-35s are telling their commander that they were able to flash me the Morse code signal.

They have to decide if they follow through with their threat or just wait and see where I land. I've got less than two hours of fuel left.

I reach down to check another chart and the cockpit is bathed with intense green light.

Holy crap! They're trying to blind me with a laser!

If I hadn't been looking down I'd be crashing!

The light vanishes and I hear the roar of the two escorts as they pull away.

What the hell was that about?

The light bathes the cockpit again. I keep my eyes shut and fumble around for a visor.

I find a folded up reflective sun shade and put it in the window. The green light goes away, but I leave the visor anyway.

What was that? It didn't appear to be coming from the F-35s. In fact, they left before the second burst.

Was that from a satellite? Do the Russians have some kind of space laser they can blind pilots with?

Hell...why not? The ones on the K1 almost poked a hole in my heat shield. It would be even less difficult to have a space-based laser that could bathe a window in blinding light if you could track the object.

Man, I'm learning all kinds of fascinating facts about Russian weaponry. I should write a book about it in my next life.

Okay, so the Russians really, really don't want me landing where the F-35s were about to tell me.

The upside is the F-35 pilots had to have seen that laser light. So maybe they're entertaining the idea that I'm not just one lone wacko who decided to go on the most epic joyride ever.

That still doesn't change the fact that I've got an AWACS tracking me and the American military ready to meet me on the ground.

FLASH! There's the green light again.

Okay, I get it! The Russians really want to blind me and see me crash.

Maybe that's the solution...

As much as I had my heart set on orange chicken, I don't think I'm going to make it to El Paso.

I wait for another flash of light then tilt the stick towards the ground, making it look like I totally lost control. Which I kind of sort of have.

This is a very stupid dive. Right now my trackers have got to be wondering what the hell is going on. So do I.

I'm counting on the notion that the Russians only knew where to look once they saw the fighters escorting the passenger jet. Until then they were afraid to use their laser, lest they blind the wrong plane.

The ground is coming up fairly fast. I'm only a few miles from the border. What happens if I crash right on the middle?

Let's not crash. Instead, focus on that tiny patch of highway directly below me. I doubt there's anybody there right now. Let's land this thing and get as far away as possible before anyone shows up.

I level out my descent just enough to make it possible for me to actually land the plane instead of use it to dig a bunker.

I lower my landing gear and get ready for one bumpy ride.

As I count off the seconds, I adjust my wing flaps and get ready for a reverse thrust to limit how much road I have to take up.

5

4

3

Is that a god damn bus!???

What the hell, people!

I pull up and to the left. My wing tip almost scrapes into the ground. Christ! Now I'm flying over open desert filled with shrubs.

Damnit.

I have to land this thing.

BOOM!!! The back wheels hit the earth.

Full reverse thrust!

This thing is bucking like crazy.

Keep it steady!

BAM!!! My front wheels hit the ground and I see stars.

Watch your rudder!

BANG!!! My front gear hits something large and the nose bounces into the air.

SLAM!!! I feel my harness yank into me as I'm pulled back into my seat.

Don't let this thing tip!

I hold the stick steady and keep an eye on my rudder and flaps, mindful of overreacting and sending the plane into a death spiral.

I'm decelerating...

It's shaking a little less...

A cloud of dust passes the cockpit window as the wind overtakes me.

And I've stopped.

I wait a few tense seconds in case something is about to explode. Not that I can do anything about it.

CRACK!!!

The nose drops ten feet and I'm looking at the desert from a totally different angle.

The front gear must have snapped right off. At least it waited until after I came to a stop.

Wait? Is that a metal fence wrapped around the nose?

Holy crap.

I not only crossed the border, I took the fence with me.

At least I'm on American soil.

I undo the latch on the cockpit window and slide it to the side.

The wind is cool on my face as I take in a breath of fresh air. The sun, climbing over the horizon, looks spectacular.

You're not dead yet, David.

Look at that view.... If we find our way out of here, we'll be home free...sort of.

Wait, is that a siren?

[39]
BORDER PATROL

SERIOUSLY? My moment of freedom is ruined before I even get one lungful of fresh desert air. In the distance, kicking up a dusty tornado as it races along the furrow I dug in the ground, is a sand-colored Humvee.

It's coming at me from the Mexican side of the border and the whoop-whoop sound of its siren is vaguely different than a US civilian or military one. I mean, it's not blaring La Cucaracha, but I'm petty sure this is Mexican military or border police.

Did they see me attempt to land and come to help? Or were they warned I'm coming? The former means I might have a chance to slip away. The latter means I'll be slapped into handcuffs the moment they get inside.

The truck comes to a halt by the tail of the plane and starts to slowly drive around the wing towards the front.

I spot four men with rifles. Okay, not exactly a rescue team.

Since I lost the front landing gear, the forward hatch is just a few feet above ground. All they have to do is back their Humvee up to the plane and they'll be able to open the door and get to me.

I pull my head in and slam the window shut. I've only got seconds before they figure out how to work the door from the outside.

The mere fact that they're not waiting for backup is all the evidence I need that their intentions don't have my own best interests in mind.

I've heard that some of these regions are controlled by the military who often have some shady dealings with the cartels. I guess it's possible the Russians may have made them an offer. Also just as likely, these four bozos want to be the first to arrest the fugitive American astronaut.

Only seconds to go, David. Think of something...

There are several other doors I can escape from, but that won't matter if they shoot me. I need to slow them down so I can get away.

With what? Throw honey-roasted almonds in their faces?

I can hear their voices from outside. They're backing their truck up to the door.

KNOCK KNOCK KNOCK It's not a patient sound.

I think about how I planned to leave the plane if I'd been able to land in some place a little more sane. What are all the things they tell you to never ever do?

Well, I could...

Oh, this is stupid.

Just do it, David.

I pop open the overhead luggage compartment door in the first class section and pull myself inside then try to keep it as close to looking shut as possible.

This is idiocy, David.

When it doesn't work and they start laughing at you, maybe you can try to escape then...

THUNK...goes the door.

SSSSSSS...the almost properly pressurized cabin hisses.

BANG! The door hits the exterior of the plane as they slide it open.

STOMP STOMP STOMP STOMP They all pile inside. First they run to the cockpit and find it empty – well, empty except for Cap'n Crunch.

There's a bunch of chatter in Spanish. I can barely make out any of it.

CREAK They shout and yank open the forward bathroom doors.

STOMP STOMP STOMP STOMP

Four pairs of boots run past me. As soon as they're in the middle of the plane I swing my door open and drop down into the aisle.

The man in the back, closest to me, stops and turns around.

"Mira!" he shouts.

All the others spin around and point their rifles at my head.

My right hand is in the air and my left is still on the ledge of the overhead compartment.

They start walking towards me.

Wait for it...

3...

2...

1...

I pull the cord attached to the rolled up bundle in the compartment.

And...nothing.

They give me a confused look. I shrug.

SSSSSSSSSSSSSSBOOM!

The emergency exit slide belatedly inflates and shoots down the aisle, knocking the men down, then pinning them to the ground as it keeps filling with compressed air.

That will hold them until they try slicing it with a knife. I've got maybe a thirty second head start.

That's thirty seconds to figure out how to disable their Humvee and make a run for it before the helicopters show up.

I jump through the door and land on top of their vehicle then leap onto the hood before hitting the ground.

The driver left his door open. I peer inside for some way to disable their ride.

Trying to pop those tires is impossible. I could mess with the engine...

I look under the dashboard for a release, then remember that you get access through two latches on the hood.

There's a lot of screaming from inside the plane. Sooner than later one of them is going to crawl out and try another exit and come shoot me.

I'm about to raise the hood when something occurs to me...

They left the keys in the ignition. In fact, this thing is still running.

You would think with as much recent experience as I've had stealing things lately, I'd be really keen to notice little details like that.

I blame the jet lag.

I run around the Humvee and climb inside, slam the door, pop the shifter out of park and send up a cloud of dirt as I press the accelerator into the floor.

POP! POP! POP!

And they're shooting at me.

Wonderful, David.

You've been in Mexico all of two minutes and you've already got the Mexican army after you.

Wait, I crashed through the border fence...this is US territory.

The Mexicans invaded to get you. Well, that's some kind of achievement.

POP! POP! Crack! They just put a bullet hole in the passenger mirror.

I keep my head low and my foot on the gas as I bounce over the desert, north, hopefully towards a highway and something resembling civilization where I can hide before all hell breaks loose around here.

[40]
CONVENIENCE

EVERYBODY HAS TO KNOW that I've managed to crash land the plane. But how many steps ahead of the US authorities am I?

The first thing they'll do is send a reconnaissance plane to do a flyover. If there's a helicopter within range they'll send that out as well. Most likely it'll be Border Patrol on both counts.

Will my Mexican friends stick around and wait inside the border? Or will they pull back? I have no idea how those kinds of jurisdictional things work.

I suspect that since they were responding to a plane crash, crossing the border to provide "help" is probably okay to do.

That means they'll tell Border Patrol to be on the lookout for a stolen Humvee with the Mexican flag painted on the side. So maybe I should ditch this thing first chance I get...

I see a straight patch of unpaved road and turn onto it. The desert is criss-crossed with these kinds of paths. My hope is that this one will take me to one covered in asphalt with helpful signs telling me which way to go.

Thirty minutes later my wish is granted. I pull onto the blacktop and feel like I just time-travelled to the present.

A sign marker says "Ranch Road 92." Whatever that means. I just keep going north.

Odds are, if I head south I'll run into a border town that might have what I need, but that will also be the first place they look. I'm sure all the sheriffs around here have already been warned that I might be nearby.

Lock your doors, folks.

I drive for another half hour, constantly on the lookout for circling Black Hawk helicopters or highway patrol hiding behind cacti. I don't see any, but civilization slowly creeps up on me.

First it's metal cattle guards lining the road. Then it's aluminum sheds and the signs of ranches. When I start to see green fields and irrigation, I know I have to be close to some kind of town.

Agriculture means produce. Produce means trucks. Trucks mean truck stops. All of that hopefully indicates a farm community of some kind.

I pass a small collection of double-wide trailers and a faded billboard that says "Historic Hotel El Monte Restaurant and Bar 1.9 miles."

I love that they shaved off that one tenth of mile in case that was a deal breaker for some starving weary traveler.

At some point I pass the historic hotel because I'm not watching my odometer, being more focused on the town of Van Clark.

It's tiny, filled with box-shaped buildings that look half abandoned. But there are also signs of life as pickup trucks pass me on the street. I even drive past a school bus and get a few stares from kids in baseball uniforms.

For a moment I think about the children in Rio that helped me out – the ones I left sitting by the concrete soccer court.

I feel a twinge of guilt. They were sweet kids that only wanted to help their strange friend. Dirty, poor children that were only going to keep being victimized by life. And I left them there.

Hell, what was I supposed to do? Adopt them and take them on the run with me?

Focus, David. Maybe you can do something for them later. You have to get to later, first.

Wow. All the crazy shit I've done in the last twenty-four hours and that's what I feel the most guilty about?

There's a deserted RV park up ahead.

I assume it's deserted because it's missing the "V" and there are no actual RVs parked there.

I pull into the lot because it's got a line of trees at the back that look like a great place to hide a Humvee you stole from the Mexican army.

After making sure I can't be seen from the road, I do a search for anything that might be useful.

Inside the center console I find a pistol. No thanks. I also find a wallet belonging to a Sergio Flores. The grim-faced man on the driver's license vaguely resembles one of the soldiers I unleashed the whoopee cushion of doom upon.

I also recognize several US presidents and a few people from Mexican history printed on the bills. I shove them and the credit cards into my pocket – promising that I'll pay him back later.

Unlike the jerk who threw the rock at me in Rio, Senor Flores was just doing his job. I think.

I take the keys and lock up my stolen Humvee in the event I need to come back to it. Hopefully, I'll get ahold of Capricorn and he can pull me out of this mess.

Not sure if there is a center of town, I walk away from the deserted part and head towards the highest concentration of buildings that look like they haven't had a coat of paint since the Zimmerman Telegram.

I pass a defunct gas station and a few machine shops, then come to a street with more traffic. There's a truck stop with a Subway sandwich shop next door.

"Morning," says the friendly girl behind the counter with a slight Texas drawl. Red hair and freckles, she's as All-American as you can get – meaning her ancestors are 100% from somewhere else.

Don't get me wrong; I loved my eight-hour stay in Brazil, without a doubt. And the six seconds I spent skidding across the Mexican desert was a memory I'll cherish for the rest of my life, but to hear someone in English greet me– even the Texas-grilled version of it, is something I can't describe.

Sure, my flight crew friends spoke my native tongue, but I was pretending around them and afraid to say the wrong thing.

Here, I'm just a guy walking into a convenience store about to get a cup of coffee.

"How you doing?" I say with a smile. "You know where I can get wifi?"

"Smile," she replies.

"Pardon me?" I say, grinning, but confused.

"That's the password for here. It'll be the only wireless network."

Smile. How adorable. "Thanks." I fumble with my stolen phone, getting it online while I pour myself a cup of coffee.

I pay for it with my stolen cash then have a seat on a bench outside.

There's still nothing from CapricornZero on Twitter.

Damn. I need an alternate plan. I was hoping he could get me out of this, but if something happened...I'm screwed.

I spend the next half hour sipping my coffee and checking the internet. When the battery on the phone goes, I buy a charge pack in the station.

"You still here?" asks the girl.

"Yeah. Waiting to hear from a friend."

She looks past me and waves. On the security monitor over her head I see two sheriff's deputies getting out of their car.

[41]
SANDLOT

I SET A PACK of gum next to the charger and pay, trying to act like Totally-Not-Fugitive-Astronaut-David-Dixon as I watch the deputies enter the station.

"Thank you," I say as she slides my change across the counter.

Keep cool, David. The cops walk past me and straight to the coffee machine.

"How you doing, Renee?" says one of them as he takes two cups from the holder.

"Same old same old, Frank."

I head towards the door with a smile on my face, because I'm totally ONE HUNDRED PERCENT CHILL.

"You hear about that plane crash on the border?" Renee asks the deputies as I step through the door.

It takes all my will power not to lose control of my limbs and go face first into the glass. I just keep moving, like a carefree man who is oblivious to things like planes crashing in the desert.

Sure, I'd love to stay and hear what the cops have to say, but the longer I stick around, the more likely I am to get asked inconvenient questions.

I veer left and pause for a moment, catching my breath. There's the very real possibility I will get picked up at any moment. I'm on foot and an all-points bulletin is about to be sent everywhere.

If I'm arrested, I need some kind of leverage – especially if I can't trust anyone. I unwrap a piece of gum and start furiously chewing, then stop at a row of newspaper machines on the side of the store and drop a couple quarters into the Texas Journal.

My stomach does somersaults as I stick the gum to the black square then squish it to the inside corner of the newspaper machine. The cops will be leaving the market at any moment.

While I don't think they're on to me yet, I can't wait around for that to happen. I have to keep moving.

I can tell Capricorn where to find his damn square and be done with it.

I let the door close, then stop it before it slams shut entirely. It would make sense if I had a newspaper. It'll give me something to do when I'm trying not to act like I'm intentionally loitering.

With the paper tucked under my arm, I head down the main street, where I spot a few other people going about their business. Walking down here seems less conspicuous than overtly avoiding populated areas.

If I'm walking down a desolate road in an empty part of town, that will just increase my chances of getting stopped.

Eyes on the ground, I keep heading towards the newer buildings. The sun is already rising in the east and the streets are more crowded with people as they go about their business.

I pass a Post Office and a row of cafés and coffee shops. It's tempting to step inside one and try to just have a normal moment, but I don't want to invite any more awkward questions.

I hear the crack of a baseball bat and the cheers of a crowd a few blocks away. It sounds like there's a baseball game going on. Maybe I should hang out there until I know what to do?

The field is in a small community park where the grass is mostly brown and half the lot is dry earth. A few dozen people are spread out across three bleachers as they root for two teams of middle school-aged kids.

I take a seat at the furthest bleacher, near a few older couples and some loners like myself.

This is probably the only thing that's going on at this time of day out here.

An electronic scoreboard shows the home team, the Rattlers, are up two runs against the visitors, the Mustangs. Let's hear it for the predictability of Texan sports team names.

A young girl, maybe twelve, but small for her age, goes up to bat for the Mustangs. She's got a ponytail with purple ribbons tied in knots. I notice her shoelaces also match.

There's a determined look on her face as she gets ready to swing at the ball.

The pitcher is a serious-faced boy who looks like he has a glandular disorder. He winds up and sends the ball so fast over home plate the sound of it hitting the catcher's mitt makes us all jump back a little.

I guess out here there aren't enough kids to divide the league into humans and Neanderthals.

The girl, someone shouts the name Veronica, isn't fazed. She takes the strike and waits for the next pitch.

Captain Caveman unleashes a leather meteor that's in the batter's box faster than a blink.

CRACK!!!

Veronica's bat hits the ball and sends it flying into the air. We all watch as it soars over the outfield and lands in a dusty lot behind the baseball field – which I notice for the first time is a cemetery.

Everyone is on their feet cheering the little slugger. Even me. I drop my paper and start clapping.

She runs the bases with a professional determination then bursts into smiles the moment she sets foot in the dugout and gets hugged by her teammates.

I lose myself in the game until someone speaks to me.

"Do you have a kid playing?" asks a man wearing a baseball cap and sunglasses sitting next to me.

I try to think of an answer that doesn't make me sound like a weirdo. "Not here. Back home in Florida. I had an hour to kill before a meeting." I do my best to sound nonchalant. "How about you?"

"Nope." He doesn't say anything else.

I return my attention to the game and get ready to leave.

"Can I borrow your paper?" asks the man.

I get a glimpse of him out of the corner of my eye. He's in his late thirties, wearing a dark blue polo shirt and khakis.

"Help yourself." I slide the paper over to him. "I was just heading out."

"Thanks, David."

My blood turns to ice in my veins.

[42]
BLACK BOX

I KEEP MOVING. The man in the sunglasses reaches out and grabs me by the arm. It's not a forceful touch, but meant to get my attention.

He points to a black SUV parked across the field with a tall whip antenna. There are two others just like it at the other ends of the field.

I'm surrounded on three sides.

The man taps the aluminum bench with his hand, telling me to sit down. I look down and notice a bulge on his ankle where he's wearing a gun.

I get an itchy feeling.

What does my gut say?

I bolt down the bleachers, hop the mini-fence and run straight across the field. People yell at me and surly kids curse with their Texas twangs as I sprint over the dry grass.

I hop the outfield fence and land in the dusty cemetery – praying the SUVs can't reach me here.

Dodging tombstones and concrete crosses, I go as fast as I can up the gradual incline leading to the stone wall at the opposite end of the graveyard.

After hopping that barrier, it's a steeper climb as I scrambl up the hill.

I reach the crest and don't look back. Jumping, skidding and sliding, I make my way down, trying not to trip over the clumps of hearty desert brush.

WHUP WHUP WHUP WHUP

I know the sound, but I try to ignore it.

Just keep running.

WHUP WHUP WHUP WHUP

Dust flies into the air and I have to cover my face.

WHUP WHUP WHUP WHUP

I'm trapped in a whirlwind and start to lose my way.

The helicopter ascends and the cloud begins to settle.

The three SUVs are in front of me. The man from the bench climbs out of the one at the end – still holding the newspaper.

For the first time since I took it from the bin, I can see the headline.

SUSPECTED ASTRONAUT-TERRORIST HIJACKS PLANE

"Is this you, David?" asks the man as he walks towards me, the wind rustling the pages.

At first I think he's asking if I'm David Dixon. Then I realize he's asking if this is the real me. Am I what the news is calling me?

"No," I reply, head low, no place to run.

"I didn't think so. Let's go somewhere where you tell me everything that happened." He points towards the helicopter landing on a hillside.

I keep my mouth shut, afraid of saying something that will implicate me.

"We found the Humvee from the air. That's how we knew where to look. In case you were wondering."

I was curious, but not about to ask. It's not really important right now.

Two men in black assault gear holding Heckler & Koch UMPs are standing next to the chopper. Neither one has any identifying patches on the shoulders. Both are wearing sunglasses that make their faces inscrutable.

I climb inside the Black Hawk and realize that nobody has put handcuffs on me. I'd ask about that, but I'm afraid that it's an oversight that will be quickly corrected.

"My name is Vaughn," says the man as we buckle ourselves in. "I'm going to help you clear this up. How does that sound?"

It sounds like a dream come true. But I have to be careful. I know cops like to pretend they're your friends then get you to confess.

I have no idea what rights I have in an instance like this. If the newspapers are calling me a terrorist, then there's a good chance I don't have any.

We fly west over wide open desert and brown-colored cattle ranches – away from civilization. I was expecting us to go towards a city; this is in the middle of nowhere.

Vaughn doesn't ask me any questions. He sits in his seat across from me and works on a laptop. After over an hour of flying, the pilot takes us over a small airstrip with several hangars. One thin road leads from here to a spot on the horizon.

We come to a landing on the tarmac and I spot a shiny new fuel truck parked in one of the open hangars.

In another, there's an all black C-130J cargo plane.

Crap. This is one of those CIA black-ops sites I've heard about. Rumor has it that they do all kinds of legal maneuvering to avoid breaking the law – like deeding land to a friendly government so it technically counts as a foreign embassy.

Once we set foot here, I could be under Qatar jurisdiction and have no rights whatsoever.

It may look like Texas, but my rights came to an abrupt stop once the skids hit the asphalt.

Vaughn pats me on the knee as the helicopter's engines begin to rev down. "Let's go get a beer and sort this out before all hell breaks loose."

I follow him into a hangar. Nobody else is escorting us inside. The guards with the submachine guns head to a different hangar.

Vaughn holds the metal door open for me. I step inside a cavernous interior. Several portable trailers fill up the interior. It's like an RV park set inside a Costco.

As we walk down a row, I spot people through the windows working at computers, having meetings and standing in front of whiteboards with long acronyms written across the top.

It's just another business day for them.

Vaughn climbs up a set of metal stairs and holds the trailer door open for me.

Inside is a conference table and refrigerator.

"Have a seat," says Vaughn as he walks over to the fridge and pulls out two beers.

He pops the top and sets one in front of me then takes the opposite seat and places his sunglasses and phone on the table as a flurry of messages fly across the screen.

He takes a long sip. "I like helicopters, but there's something about being in one out in the desert for too long."

I stare at the sweaty bottle in front of me, confused and afraid.

"Go ahead. Drink up." He sees my hesitation. "Don't worry. If I wanted to drug you I'd have strapped you to a gurney and pumped you full of drugs by now. But I don't need to. You're not in trouble. You're not a bad guy. As soon as we can clear this up, I can get you home."

I reach out for the bottle and take a small drink. To be honest, I wasn't even thinking about truth serums until he mentioned it. I was just so full of anxiety I don't think I could even handle alcohol at the moment.

It tastes good. It's relaxing.

Vaughn keeps treating me like an old pal. "I don't know if you had a chance to see the news, but oh, man, David." He shakes his head. "People can't shut up about you."

"Who are you?" I finally ask.

"I'm the guy who finds people."

"What kind of people?"

"Enemy agents. Spies. That kind of thing."

"That's how you found me?"

"You're not a spy, David. You're a victim. No offense, a patsy. You got played. Granted, you took your shitty hand and ran with it. Hand to God. I don't think anyone expected you to get as far as you did. Of course, if Peterson and Bennet's little plot had worked, you never would have been pulled into this."

"Plot?" I reply.

He makes a face. "David, haven't you figured it out? You're an astronaut. Aren't you supposed to be a genius?"

"I chose a line of work where my job is to sit on a million pounds of explosives and press a button to light them. How smart do you think I am?"

"Peterson and Bennet were working with the Chinese. This whole thing was an attempt to steal a Russian decoder. It's espionage that went way out of control." He whistles. "I thought you might have figured that out by now."

He can see the shocked reaction on my face.

Peterson and Bennet, spies? All this time I've been working for the bad guys?

[43]
RED AGENTS

"LET ME BACK UP a bit. I can see the look all over your face. Peterson and Bennet weren't sleeper agents doing dead drops and knowingly conspiring with the enemy. It's a bit more subtle than that. Something I see all the time." Vaughn moves his chair back and sets his feet on the conference room table, like he's some kind of Texas wildcatter showing his disdain for the establishment.

"It starts like this; you're at a conference; for Peterson it was an aerospace technology transfer symposium in New Orleans two years ago. Someone approaches you from a company, in this case it was a Canadian firm – secretly owned by the Chinese. They say they're a satellite communications and security company. You Google them and find out they're real, holding patents and employing people from Stanford and the like. They tell you they'd love to get you to work for them. They talk about IPOs, huge growth and how you'd be a perfect fit.

"In Peterson's case, she politely declines and says she's happy at NASA. But they stay in contact. This company's liaison was a friendly woman who happened to be in Houston and a few other places where Peterson was working and they struck up a friendship. Coffee, shopping, wine tasting, all that chick stuff.

"Meanwhile, this woman has been recruiting Bennet. Now he's a much harder nut to crack. We're talking Bennet, right? All men have their weaknesses – their ego. I don't need to get into details but we end up with two astronauts and this woman – actually a trained Chinese Army intelligence officer in bed together. Figuratively and literally.

"So here we have two heroes compromised. But outright blackmail isn't going to work on people who offer to put their lives on the line as part of the job. Another person approaches them and says he's going to go to the press with what happened. It's a fait accompli. Nobody asks for a shakedown. Nobody offers them a deal – at least not overtly.

"Peterson and Bennet get a call from their little red friend, who they still think is just some recruiter for a Canadian tech company. She asks about some quantum entanglement processor the Russians have. She alludes to the idea the NSA or the NRO is interested in this and that there could be a fat contract for her company and two jobs for astronauts who might be soon out of work.

"Bennet being Bennet and not doing anything half-assed, and also having no love for the Russians – you know he lost a friend to an undisclosed recon mission? He found out later NKVD captured him and held the man for over a year torturing him for information about avionics. Anyhow, let's just say he doesn't care for Russians whether they're capitalists or communists. He sees the mission as a matter of freelance national security. Anyhow, David, those are the broad strokes."

I try to reconcile this with what I know about Bennet and Peterson. "So...you're saying this is because they had some three-way with a Canadian chick?"

"Do you know how many times I get called in because somebody stuck their dick where they weren't supposed to?" He rolls his eyes. "Here's a fun fact, we're in the same state as two high school students who have no idea their father is a top Chinese official. Their mother was an operative of ours. We play the game too. But I like to think we're the good guys."

He takes a drink and shakes his head. "Peterson and Bennet thought they were the good guys too." He points the top of his bottle at me. "And then there's you. You weren't doing this out of financial gain or trying to cover up some sex thing. Were you?" He raises an eyebrow.

"No...Jesus, I had no idea what the hell was going on."

He waves his hand in the air. "I know that, David. The problem is that my bosses don't quite see it that way. The Russians are calling for your head. They're demanding that when you're found you get extradited back to Russia. Russian television is calling you a terrorist. Actually, so is our media after the stunt with the airplane. Wow. That was some Jason Bourne-level shit."

I feebly try to explain. "There was a shoot out. A Russian kill team was trying to...um, kill me."

"Oh, we know. That's because you took a decryption wafer they use to communicate with their nuclear subs, airplanes and everything else that underlies their defenses. That one chip compromises their entire military. Of course they were trying to kill you. Here's the upside for you. As mad as they are, you're lucky that you have something we really, really want. We can make all of this – or a lot of this at least – go away. That wafer is your get out of jail free card."

Everything he's saying is what I want to hear. But there's something making me anxious I can't quite put my finger on.

Someone knocks on the door. A man dressed in a black polo shirt like Vaughn pokes his head inside the door. A little younger, fresh-faced, he's got the same ex-military bearing that Vaughn possesses.

"Hey Vaughnster, we need you in ComStak in twenty. Director is screaming for you-know-who." He throws me a glance and grins. "When we clear up this shitshow, how about you come work for us? These assholes could learn a thing or two."

"I'll be there in a second, Cardwell. We taking the jet to Vegas tonight? There's a new steak place at Aria I'm dying to try." He looks to me. "You want to go?"

I'm confused. "Vegas? Tonight?"

"Yeah. We won't have all this cleared up. But I think I can appease the folks at Langley and get the FBI off all our backs. We'll have some agency issue a statement that you're in US custody and that'll call off the dogs."

"And then we go get steaks in Vegas?" I ask.

"Unless you have a better place in mind."

It was Cardwell poking his head in the door that finally put the last piece in place for me.

When I was a kid my parents brought me along to some housing development pitch on the edge of a grassy lot in a trailer a lot like this. I watched a man with a casual, friendly demeanor tell my parents all about the development and how it was a great investment opportunity.

One of his co-workers even poked his head in with a friendly word and a comment about time running out. While they didn't offer us a trip to Vegas to eat at a steak restaurant – instead it was an investor's barbecue they were holding in a few weeks.

Mom and dad's weak credit didn't bother them. The man was all about "handshake deals" and "trust." Dad wanted to do it, but mom pulled him out before he could commit.

As we drove off in our beat up minivan, I remember mom saying something that always stuck with me, "You can't cheat an honest man."

The housing development was a scam. After they collected their deposits and skipped town, the lot they'd only been leasing month-to-month became an overgrown field.

This man, Vaughn, is trying to work me. I just don't know his angle.

I'm sure he could make a jet materialize and get us a table at the fanciest restaurant in Vegas if he had to. But right now, he's going to try to get me to turn over the McGuffin for just a beer.

The moment I tell him where it is, there are no guarantees.

I still have no idea who he is or what this place is supposed to be. Once they have it, the expedient thing to do is to put a bullet in my head and send my body to the Russians, minus the wafer – or whatever it really is.

If he's telling me the truth; great. If not, that thing is the only reason I'm alive.

"So what do you say?" he asks, flashing teeth that are too white. "You got it on you?"

[44]
EXAMINATION

I'M BEING PLAYED by an expert. I have to watch myself. I could end up in a steel drum buried in the desert. This whole facility is some kind of clandestine, non-existent operation that probably disappears people all the time.

Maybe he's genuine and they only rendition people who speak Arabic.

Maybe not.

The best way to avoid questions is to be the one asking them.

"Who are you?"

"I thought I made that clear. I'm the guy that finds people."

"Great, so does a bloodhound. That doesn't give it authority to do anything. Who do you work for?"

"The US government. Who else can afford all these toys?"

"Are you CIA, NSA, Pentagon? Or are you some private contractor working between the law. Are we even on US soil?"

He holds his hands up. "Okay, settle down, David. I understand that a little bit of paranoia has kept you alive. No, I'm not a private contractor or a freelancer. I work for an agency with a three-letter acronym."

"DIA?"

He taps the side of his nose. "Winner-winner."

The Defense Intelligence Agency is an under-the-radar intelligence organization that focuses on the tactical capabilities of our enemies. Its illustrious founder was Robert McNamara, architect of the War in Vietnam under Kennedy and Johnson.

One of the chief differences with the CIA is the degree that they provide combat support. These guys are usually in the shit – if not starting it.

When I graduated from college I got letters of interest from a variety of three letter agencies. I don't recall the DIA trying to recruit me, but I seriously considered the NRO, another shadowy organization that handles satellite espionage and was known to have a few pilots and astronauts on staff. But what good was going into space if you couldn't tell anyone about it?

I'm in a difficult position. Capricorn – whom I also don't trust – told me that some highly placed individual in the US government would try to catch me and kill me for the square.

And now here I am, sitting in front of a highly-placed individual in the US government that I don't trust.

Vaughn is a cocky son-of-a-bitch who's used to doing whatever the hell he wants. I have no problem with covert ops and the occasional dirty job, if necessary, but I'm also a big believer in checks and balances. Is anyone checking this guy?

"I want to speak to your supervisor," I reply.

"What? Is the beer too warm? You want to file a complaint?"

"I was told not to trust anyone."

"Good advice. Who told you that?"

Crap, I already said too much. Right now he has no idea about Capricorn or the sat phone – which is still on me. I'm kind of surprised he didn't have me frisked. Maybe that was part of his trust-building exercise?

"I'm not comfortable talking to just you."

"Want me to bring Cardwell back in here?"

"I mean here. This is all a bit...scary."

"Dude, you should only be scared if your name is Muhammed and you've decided to pack some C4 up your ass. You have nothing to be afraid of from me. I'm the guy who's going to clear this up."

"Okay...so why are we in a Black Site in the middle of nowhere?"

"Land is cheap. And don't believe everything you see in movies. This is just a remote airbase. If I flew you into Austin I would have FBI, CIA, DHS, USPS and everyone else in our faces trying to slap bracelets on you. And I don't know if you're familiar with the way they treat spies, but you'd be talking to your attorneys through a tin can with no string."

"Okay. Let me talk to your boss."

"He's busy in the Oval Office dealing with the international uproar you caused."

"I mean the head of the DIA."

"Oh, Bruce? He knows you're here."

"Could I meet with him?"

"David, you're hurting my feelings. You have to understand, he's one of the people yelling at me to arrest you. I take you into his office and you'll leave under arrest." Vaughn lifts up his phone to show me a list of voicemail and text messages, making a dramatic point.

I notice something on his screen I don't think he intended for me to see.

It's a Russian area code, specifically the number for Moscow Oblast, where the Russian space agency is based.

And how the hell would I know this? Because for two years while I was doing launch assist for all the other lucky jerks who got to ride the Unicorn before me, my job was to call Roscosmos and tell them six hours before a launch what our window was.

I'd speak to some Russian bureaucrat on the other end who would say, "Dah," repeat the time back to me, then hang up.

The purpose was to keep from bumping our rockets into each other and starting World War III. No big deal.

But I had their switchboard burned into my brain. And right now, that same number is on Vaughn's phone.

While I can understand him talking to people in Russia; operatives, colleagues, obstetricians, that number seems peculiar.

"How do I know you're not talking to the Russians?"

He's fast. Real fast. He glances at his phone. "Oh, the area code? I've got a friend in the Federal Security Service I'm trying to convince to settle things down a notch."

"Even though he knows you're after this wafer-thing?"

"He doesn't need to know that we recovered it. So can I see it?"

I shrug. "I don't even know what it looks like. I never saw anything."

His words are slow and measured. "And that's your official story?"

He just switched gears from frat pal to intense in a flash.

"Yeah..." I say hesitantly.

Vaughn closes his eyes and shakes his head. "Dumb ass. Now we have to do it the hard way. Well, hard for you."

He knocks on the table three times and two men in black armor with machine guns step into the room and point their muzzles at my head.

Another man grabs my wrist and a woman in doctor's scrubs enters and jabs a needle in my arm.

Everything goes dark.

[45]
THE HOLE

I WAKE UP in a dark room. When I say "dark," I mean it's painted black with some weird kind of noise-dampening stuff on the walls. The only light is behind me. I'm strapped to a gurney with my head fixed into place and there's an intravenous drip stuck into both arms. Everything is woozy. My head feels like it's made of a cloud.

Vaughn leans over me. "How do you feel?"

"Confused...scared..." The words slip out of my mouth before I can stop them. "Is this some kind of truth serum?"

"You know, they used to say those things were impossible. But you'd be amazed by the kind of drugs you can develop with a billion dollars of anti-terrorism funding and the public outcry over waterboarding."

"This isn't right..."

"Neither is lying to me." He points towards the corner. "We went through your clothes and I had the doctors go over every inch of your body – inside and out." He checks his watch. "In case you were wondering, that was less than forty minutes ago. We've gotten very efficient at this kind of thing."

"You're an asshole."

"Hey pal, you only have to speak what's on your mind when I ask you a question. Let's start with something simple. How old were you when you got your first taste of pussy?"

I try to resist. My mouth starts to form the words as if I have two brains – one totally detached from the other. "Fifteen."

"Fifteen? All in or just your fingers?"

Resist. Don't let him do this. You've been a medical guinea pig.

Hell, they may have even tried this drug on you.

My mouth wants to say something. I visualize myself going down on April Cassidy, the hot cheerleader a year ahead of me. "My tongue..."

"Tongue? Your first time at bat? I'm impressed. You must be a real lady pleaser. What was the occasion?"

"...Pool party. We were in the hot tub by the side of the house. We both were drunk."

Vaughn grins at me as if we were two guys swapping stories in a bar. "See, this isn't so hard."

No. It's not. I just think of someone else's story, in this case, a buddy of mine who actually did go down on April and visualize it in my mind – something I'd imagined many, many times.

"Okay, pal." He leans on the rail, lowering himself to my eye level. "You know, there's a division in the DIA where we try to get important people to sleep with our assets. Remember those Chinese Premier bastards I mentioned? That kind of thing. But you know, not all the people we go after swing like you and me. Sometimes you have to take one for the team. You ever do that?"

"...Homosexuality?" I say in drawn-out syllables.

"It's deep secret time. You can tell me."

"Are you a gay?" I ask drunkenly.

"David, the question is if you've ever done that kind of thing."

My voice is slow, like a tape played at half speed. "I...once got drunk with a friend...and held his cock while he peed...but there were girls there."

"Of course. That made it okay. So...was it thick?"

"Yellow..."

Vaughn lets out a loud laugh. "I meant his dick."

"...I don't remember..."

"How about the square? So you remember that?"

"Yes..."

Resisting is impossible. All I can do is overload my brain with other thoughts.

"I knew you would. Where is it?"

"...In the conference room......"

"You dropped it there?"

"...That's where you mentioned it....."

"Oh, got it. You're being a little too literal."

Damn straight. I can only lie about what I can see and describe.

"Is that the only time you heard about it?"

"No....the man on the sat phone talked about it."

"What did you say?"

Think of the sat phone. "I don't know where it is."

"Did Peterson or Bennet give it to you?"

I just found the sat phone under the seat. "No..."

"Do you know what happened to it?"

"I broke it."

"The square?"

Damn it. I can't stop myself. "The sat phone."

His voice grows sharp. "David, we're talking about the square. Where is it?"

Resist. You are dead the moment he finds it. Visualize something else!

Anything!

"...Inside April Cassidy's pussy..."

Vaughn slaps me across the face. "You motherfucker."

My cheek stings from the slap and I feel a little more alert.

"Let me guess, did your little astronaut training help you resist that? You think you're really fucking clever, don't you? Let me show you how clever I can be."

He starts unbuckling the belts across my chest and rips the IVs out of my arms.

"Cardwell!" he shouts to the door. "Get Stilton and Hayes in here. We're taking this little asshole for a ride."

Light bursts into the room as the two armored men come in and grab me by my arms and drag me off the table. For the first time I realize I'm just wearing a hospital gown.

I try to resist by dragging my feet, but I barely have enough muscular control to support myself, let alone fight off two trained men who spend all day moving uncooperative prisoners.

They drag me down a set of steps and out of the room, which was just another box in the small city of portable trailers in the hangar.

It's fully lit with people going about their business, walking back and forth like it's a Costco.

I'm slid past an open window, my ass bare to all the world, as a woman leans over a desk and points to a computer screen as a man laughs and makes a note of what she said. Neither even bother to look my way. I'm a ghost to them. A non-person.

It's goddamn casual Friday around here and nobody seems to care that some half-naked man is being carried away against his will.

"...Vaughn is a traitor," I try to say as loud as I can.

He's a pace behind me, typing away on his phone. "Let it out, pal."

"...He's working for the Russians. Check his caller ID...."

"Keep talking. Nobody cares."

Cardwell holds open a door and bright sunlight blinds me as I'm yanked through the threshold.

The guards carry me across the tarmac and throw me on the ground.

"Maybe your astronaut training gave you some kind of resistance to that. I got other drugs, but time is really important. One more time, where is the square?"

"Dantooine," I reply.

"Dantooine?" He looks at Cardwell. "Where the fuck is that?"

"The Outer Rim."

"What?"

"It's a Star Wars thing."

"Jesus-Fucking-Christ! You goddamn Star Wars nerds." Vaughn starts kicking me in the stomach. "For fuck sake!"

Every blow feels like a distant thunderclap – but each one also helps me wake up.

Just lay limp, David. Don't let him know you're more alert than he thinks.

Vaughn kneels down and squeezes my chin, tilting my face towards his. "Anything?"

"...My stomach hurts."

"Guess what, asshole, that's going to be the least of your worries as I put you through my own astronaut training. Load him on the chopper!"

The rough asphalt scrapes my bare legs as they drag me across the landing pad to a Black Hawk powering up.

[46]
AIRDROP

AS WE ASCEND into the air one of Vaughn's men puts a black hood over my head. My hands and legs are still free and I get the sense that this isn't done to keep our destination a secret as much as a surprise.

His masked-goons grasp me by the shoulders with my back towards the open door. The wind is really, really cold as it blows through my open gown.

We fly for about twenty minutes then Vaughn calls to the pilot to hover.

"David! Where is the square?" he shouts over the sound of the rotors.

My head is clear and I don't need to visualize anything to help me lie. "I don't know!" Right now my motivation is pure self-preservation. "Let me talk to your boss!"

"You're in no position to be asking for anything. Last chance. Where is the square?"

"Do they know you're working for the Ru..." I'm caught off guard by a kick to my chest.

I fall backwards and out the door.

Holy sh–

OOOOOOMPH! My shoulders hit the ground and all the wind is knocked out of me.

That had to be about five feet.

I feel the downwash of the rotors and pull the hood off. It blows away in the wind.

I start to pick myself up to make a feeble run for it, but the helicopter lowers and the guards jump out and pull me back in.

"Where's the hood?" asks Vaughn.

"He threw it away. Want me to go get it?" replies one of the masked men.

"Nah. I want him to see this. David, that was barely off the ground. Let's try ten feet? How does that sound?"

"Fuck you."

"I can take this all the way up to 15,000 feet if you like."

"19,000," I reply.

"What?"

"The service ceiling is officially 19,000 but you can probably go another two thousand." I sound cocky, but I'm scared as hell.

"Good to know. Maybe we try that with you?"

I see the ground drop a few feet through the window on the other side.

"Well?" he asks.

"I don't know."

"Fine." He stands up and braces himself between the seats and lets out another kick to my chest.

BAM!

I hit the ground and see stars. Man, this is hard Texas dirt and doesn't give very much.

The helicopter begins to descend. I try to get up but I can barely feel my feet. As I try to pull myself away my right hand touches a sharp rock.

Thank god I didn't land on that...

I pull my fist into my body as the men retrieve me.

"Okay." Vaughn puts his face right in mine. "We're going to fifteen feet. There's a fifty-fifty chance you'll break something. My money is that you won't. At twenty, it's a guarantee. Thirty and you'll never walk again and you'll tell me anything I want to know as you beg me for another spoonful of apple sauce. What do you say I just save you the trouble?"

"I don't know! Maybe they left it on the station?"

Vaughn shakes his head. "You're a shitty liar."

He begins to lean back to kick again. I try to swing the rock in my hand at his face but the guard on my right grabs my wrist.

Vaughn pries it from my fingers and waves it under my nose. "What the hell is this, David? Did you think you were going to hit me and spill my brains?" He smashes it against my mouth. "Open!"

I don't move.

"I said open your goddamn mouth!"

He nods to his men.

They let go of my arms, grab my head and shove their gloved fingers into my lips to pry open my jaws.

Vaughn puts a foot into my balls, leaving his shoe in my crotch. He smacks my teeth with the rock. "Open your mouth or I'm going to break every goddamn tooth in your head!"

BANG!!!

I can see his eyes go wide behind his sunglasses as he tries to make sense of what happened.

The two armored guards start looking around for the source of the noise.

BANG!!! BANG!!!

Before they can figure out what just happened, I shoot them both in the stomach with Vaughn's ankle pistol.

The pilot is starting to set us on the ground.

I climb over a screaming Vaughn and put my gun to the back of the pilot's head. "Get them and get the fuck out."

"I can't leave this aircraft." He raises his hands off the controls in protest.

I put the pistol near his helmet and fire, shooting a hole through the window inches away.

"Get the fuck out and take those assholes with you!"

He slides out of the cockpit and runs around to the side door. I keep my gun aimed at him in case he tries to pull a sidearm.

He drags Vaughn and the other two men to the ground then raises his hands above his head.

I realize I'm still wearing the hospital gown. "Give me your clothes and your helmet! Kick their weapons away then give me whatever cash they have!"

Out of misplaced pity, I throw bullet wound bandages to him – basically tampons – from the first aid kit as he drags the men to the front of the chopper.

I make him keep his hands in the air as I familiarize myself with the controls.

I've flown helicopters and simulations of the Black Hawk UH-60, but never the actual thing.

This is going to be one hell of a ride.

I finally grab the stick and gradually take to the air. The pilot sees my wobbly ascent and quickly ducks down out of the way to avoid decapitation.

Once I'm airborne, I get a compass reading and try to figure out what the hell I'm supposed to do next.

[47]
INSIDER

VAUGHN ISN'T EVEN HIS NAME. I realize this as I hand the girl at the rental car desk his driver's license and credit card. Both the ID and the black AmEx say Sean Flagler.

I almost don't feel like the worst person in the world for leaving him and his cronies bleeding out in the middle of the desert. Almost.

Yeah, it was a matter of survival, but hell, I still feel awful. I was minutes away from a broken neck no matter what I said, yet I can't just get rid of this guilt. Maybe that's why guys like him are good at his job and guys like me aren't.

Hell. I never thought I would have killed anybody a day ago. Now I may have killed three because I felt justified.

Is that what he thought? Did the assholes helping push me out of the helicopter think they were doing their duty and protecting America?

Were they? I wanted to believe he was on my side. Then he lied about the Moscow phone call – or at least I think he lied. And things escalated from there.

Fuck him. I didn't ask to get thrown out of the helicopter and tortured. Maybe he was just following orders for someone else and had no idea what was really going on, but it doesn't matter. They wanted me to think they were going to kill me. I'm pretty sure that in the state of Texas what I did was not only legal – it was encouraged.

"Would you like insurance on the vehicle?" asks the girl.

"Yeah, sure. Max it out."

She goes back to her keyboard and starts typing away. I figure I've got another hour or so before Vaughn/Flagler's card is no longer good and trying to use it will result in the Texas Rangers showing up.

I chose Eazy-Kar, because of their immaculate spelling and the fact that their cars are several years old and not likely to have any tracking transponders inside of them.

"Thank you, Mr. Flagler," the girl says sweetly as she hands me my keys.

I drive my nondescript Toyota Camry across the street to a Walmart to get groceries while Vaughn's card is still good.

In the hardware section I pick up some random tools with no idea if I'll need any of them. Better safe than sorry.

After I load up my car in the parking lot, I swap license plates with another Camry so I can get a little off the grid. I'll need to do this again when I'm further away to keep covering my tracks.

Although I landed the helicopter in an empty lot on the far side of a shopping mall, and none of the passing cars seemed to be all that interested, I can only count on that lasting for so long.

Vaughn's people have to know something is up and an abandoned Black Hawk helicopter sitting in the middle of El Paso isn't very discreet.

My only hope is that the lines of communication between his quasi-legal Black Site operation and the local authorities aren't exactly streamlined.

Before leaving here for good, I stop at an Arby's drive-thru, load up on sandwiches, then take the 10 east towards Austin.

While I bite into soothing mouthfuls of roast beef, I consider my predicament. I'm in a classic, nowhere-to-go-nobody-to-trust situation.

Considering the last US government employee I dealt with tried to break my spine presumably on the orders of his Russian masters, I'm a little distrustful of going to the cops.

Vaughn may be out of commission, but I don't know if he was acting alone. Capricorn said a highly-placed intelligence official was working with the Russians. Vaughn seemed more like the operations guy working with somebody sitting in an office in DC.

That means that there could be more people out there like him. I really can't trust anyone.

And I can't stay on the run forever. If Capricorn never reaches out to me again, I'm screwed. I need another option.

Who do I trust?

Lots of people.

Who can help me?

None of them.

My parents would just tell me to turn myself in and try to convince me that the government has my best interests in mind. I can imagine what it would be like trying to explain to my father what just happened with the helicopter drop-falls.

"Did you maybe fall out and misunderstand what happened? Could they have been trying to help you?"

I love my parents, but they're a no-go.

I just don't know any powerful, influential people. My boss, Vin Amin, the CEO of iCosmos is connected, but I can only guess what kind of clusterfuck he's trying to deal with right now. He probably wants me dead more than anybody else.

So Vin is a no-go.

That leaves nobody.

I'm screwed.

Stop that, David. Focus.

Who would want to help you? Who is connected to this?

Peterson and Bennet's families probably hate me. They think I murdered them.

If only I could tell them...

Wait, Bennet's son, Tyler, is a US Senator. He and his husband have a home in Austin. I remember Bennet talking about spending Christmas there with his grandkids.

I've met Tyler a couple times. Nice enough guy. He's got a bit of a libertarian streak and not the type I think would go for the black ops bullshit that Vaughn was pulling. At least I don't think he would. He once did a forty-eight hour filibuster against the overreach of government surveillance.

If I could reach out to him, maybe he could help me sort things out...yeah, if only I could explain to him what was really going on.

I have to give it a shot. The worst that could happen is that we have a very awkward and short conversation. Well, that and the spooks track my phone call and blow me up with an airborne drone before I hang up. But other than that...

I buy a burner phone at a gas station using cash I stole from the men on the helicopter. I avoid using Vaughn's credit card so it can't trace back to the number.

After a few more miles, I pull over to a truck stop and take the phone out of the package. Too nervous to sit still, I step outside the car and onto a sidewalk away from the road.

Thankfully, as a government representative, Tyler Bennet's office number is pretty easy to find.

An older woman answers, "Senator Bennet's office. How may I direct your call?"

I really didn't have a plan for this situation. "Uh, hello? I would like to speak with the Senator."

"I'm sorry, he's not taking any calls right now. Would you like to leave a message for one of his assistants?"

Think of a lie, David. "Yeah...Well, I'm calling from iCosmos. We found a note from his father addressed to Tyler."

There's a long pause. "Hold on one second."

A moment later Tyler answers the phone, "This better not be a joke."

"It's not, Senator. This is David Dixon."

His voice explodes in my ear. "Alright, asshole! You got a lot of fucking nerve calling me!"

"Tyler, it's me! Remember when..."

"Even if it was you, you're the last person I'd ever want to talk to!"

"Wait...I can explain!" I protest.

"Next time you call this number I'm having the call traced, you fucking murderer!"

Oh, Christ. "I didn't...wait...don't hang up!"

Click.

Shit! Shit! Shit!

My one goddamn lifeline in all this just threatened to call the cops on me.

I collapse on the curb, my head in my hands. For the first time I begin to feel suicidal.

There is no end to this nightmare.

I should have let Vaughn push me out.

I should have burned up in the atmosphere.

It should have been me that died and not Peterson and Bennet.

I'm so lost in my thoughts it takes me a while to realize the phone is ringing in my hand.

It could be Vaughn, all patched up, or one of his cronies...

I don't care. Come get me. I'll tell you anything.

"Yeah..." I say weakly.

"David, it's Tyler," his voice is calm and not the tornado of rage that he was a minute ago. "There's not much time to explain. You need to get another phone and call me at the number I'm about to give you. They're listening to everything."

"I didn't kill your father," I say, my voice distant.

"I know that, David." He takes a long breath. "I did."

[48]
DEAD DROP

TYLER TELLS ME WHEN and how to call him back then hangs up before I can ask him what the hell is going on. What does he mean that he killed his father?

So far he's the only person who seems to understand anything and he just cut me off.

I run inside the gas station, nearly causing a panic.

I'm about to cut in line as some hayseed takes his time buying his cigarettes and scratch-off lottery tickets. I want to blurt out that he doesn't have to die an early death and also be bad at math, but I bite my tongue.

Finally, the elderly clerk sells me a phone, trying to figure out what all the fuss is about. I take a deep breath, trying to stop attracting too much attention to myself.

My goddamn face is on the news rack five feet away.

Man, I suck at this kind of thing.

I get back in my rental car and drive another five miles. I think to myself that all Texas towns seem to look alike. Then I realize I'm back in Van Clark.

Crap.

There's no way around it unless I go off-roading.

I remember this is also where I left the square...

I roll through an intersection and see a group of police cars and a crime scene van parked in the RV lot where I hid the Humvee.

Keep calm.

The convenience store is just up ahead and the newspaper bin is only a few feet from the street.

Do I get the square?

Is it being watched?

How long before somebody else finds it?

Damnit. Damnit. Damnit.

I pull over on the street next to the store. Trying to act relaxed, and failing, I make sure nobody is immediately around me and there are no visible snipers on the roof.

The square is just ten feet away...

Don't hesitate. Just do it.

I get out of the car and walk over to the newspaper machine, pretending I'm calm and collected.

Hours ago I was dressed in a sweat-stained jacket and shirt, now I'm wearing a dark blue polo and Vaughn's hat and sunglasses. I'm a totally different dude.

Dressed like this, I look like any of the other spooks on the hunt for me.

I grab the handle on the front of the bin and pull.

It doesn't move.

Waves of panic shoot through my body.

Of course it doesn't open. I haven't put any change in. It's a fundamental concept of our economy, dumbass.

I pat down my pockets and come up empty.

Jesus. This is a horrible idea.

Do I just leave?

What if someone already spotted me near the machine? If I take off and come back later, there's no telling if the square is going to be here.

The square. What the hell is that thing? I'm not sure if I buy Vaughn's explanation that it's some kind of crypto chip. There might be something to that, but I'm sure it's not the whole story.

Christ. I have to get the thing now. If Tyler wants it, trying to come back here is going to be suicidal.

I go inside the convenience store. The same girl with red hair and freckles is behind the counter. Renee, I think that was her name.

I stand in front of the counter looking stupid for a moment.

"Hi there! Are you with them fellas?" she says, pointing to the back.

Two men dressed in FBI jackets are standing by the door to a small office with a monitor playing security camera footage.

Keep.

Fucking.

Calm.

"I'm...with a different agency." I fumble for a pack of gum to set on the counter and pray she doesn't recognize my face from earlier.

One of the FBI agents turns to look at me.

I nod my head like I'm one cop saluting another.

He returns the gesture then goes back to looking at the monitor.

"Any luck catching that boy so far?" asks Renee.

"No ma'am, not yet."

Renee lowers her voice and whispers. "He was right in here. Face to face with me." She shakes her head. "To think that just an hour earlier he'd murdered those poor Mexicans."

My lips start to move, but I stop myself from saying, "Murdered?"

Fucking, Vaughn.

What did they do? Shoot the Mexican army unit?

Why? What did that accomplish?

"We'll get him," I say firmly, keeping my eye on the men in back.

She hands me my change and I head for the door before the FBI men get a good look at me.

I drop my coins in the slot, reach inside and freeze. It's not there...

My heart stops and I suddenly get paranoid that I'm about to be surrounded by a dozen cops and a SWAT team.

Breathe, David. Breathe.

I exhale, then kneel down and look inside the machine. The square is wedged into a corner. It just fell. That's all.

I pocket it and return to my car. Paranoid that someone might pay attention to which way I left, I do a U-turn and go back a block, then cut through a side road before getting back to the 10.

I don't know if it fooled anybody, but if they're watching footage of the security camera and see which way I left, I want them thinking the opposite of where I'm going – even if it just buys me a few extra minutes.

Finally, with Van Clark in the distance and nothing but scrub brush on either side of me, I take the new phone out of the package and call the number Tyler gave me.

"Do you have it?" he asks.

I'm too cagey to trust anyone at this point. "I know where it is."

[49]
RALLY

TYLER IS STANDING to the side of a grilled cheese truck in the parking lot of the University of Texas at Austin stadium. Board shorts, t-shirt and sunglasses, he blends right in with all the alumni at the rally. What strikes me is how much he resembles his father. I already knew this, having met him before, but the likeness is all the more painful because his dad is now dead.

He waves me over to a standing table under the shade of a tree.

"If we have to run, go in different directions," he says under his breath. A police officer walks through the crowd. "That's campus police. Remember the uniform. If you see something different, we quietly go our own separate ways."

"Tyler..." I don't know where to begin.

He shakes his head. "Drop it. There's more important stuff to deal with right now."

More important than the death of his father?

"I don't want to know if you have the square. Just tell me that it's safe."

I just nod my head. I placed it under the spare tire next to a can of mace. It was the best I could think of.

He cautiously looks around. "Okay, I'm going to give you as much of the story as I can, so you understand what's at stake. Got it?"

"Yeah."

"Okay. Okay. Right. I'm on an intelligence committee in the senate. It's not the senate intelligence one, but another more obscure committee. The reason it exists is because there are so many leaks in the regular senate intelligence committee that the major agencies asked for some other group to take things they didn't want leaked to congressional staffers and all the way back to Moscow and Beijing.

"You'd be amazed at how idiotic some of the people I work with in the senate are. We had a senior senator giving all of her intelligence briefings to a Chinese foreign exchange student to blow up on a photocopier because she couldn't read the small print. This exchange student's father is a party boss.

"When we confronted the senator about the breach she insisted that her assistant would never actually read the briefings because quote, 'Her people were honor bound to never do something like that.' Stupid things like that happen all the time.

"Anyway. A year ago we get a briefing about a possible mole in the intelligence community. A highly placed one. This comes to us from the NRO, you know them, right? Of course. They're concerned that the DIA and possibly another organization has been compromised."

"I just had a run in with the DIA."

"Really?" Tyler's eyes widen. "And you got away?"

"Barely."

"I need to know more, but hold on to that. So I get this briefing that says there's a Russian agent in the DIA, possibly working with others. Two days later I get a briefing from the DIA telling us that they think the NRO is compromised. Both of them are asking for authority to arrest a senior intelligence official codenamed Silverback.

"Here I am, I've got two agencies pitted against each other, swearing the other has a leak and wanting permission to investigate the other. Imagine that headache."

"Is that what this is about?" I ask, trying to follow along.

"Indirectly. That's what my world looked like before an analyst from the NRO shows up in my office in DC, too afraid to go to his boss, because he's not sure who to trust.

"His job was to monitor Russian satellites for transmissions. One day he's listening to the K1 and realizes they left an onboard intercom open that was leaking part of their communications. Short-range, but we've got some very good tricks for picking that kind of thing up we modified from Naval Intelligence."

"You bounce a laser off the surface and pick the voices out of the vibrations..." I reply.

"Uh, yeah? How did you know?"

"A friend in college worked on that for her masters. Sorry, didn't mean to interrupt you."

"It's okay... Anyway, this NRO analyst shows me the transcript of what's being said. Long story short, the senior commanders of the space station were having a secret conversation away from the other crew about a special payload being sent to them from Roscosmos."

"What is it?"

"That's the million-dollar question. The square is the answer. We know what we think it is, but we aren't positive. The analyst was concerned because if he was right and Silverback was real, this would have huge repercussions. The moment word leaked about it, we'd be in a worst case scenario."

"And what's that?"

"Right now there's a power struggle in Moscow. If the current president gets reelected he's going to consolidate his power and remove any opposition. His biggest nemesis is Valentin Zhirov."

"Head of the Russian space agency."

"Correct. Do you know what he did before that? He was Colonel General of the Russian Air Force. I got a report about an audit that was done after he left. Five nuclear warheads went missing. The Russians won't even acknowledge this audit took place."

I feel my stomach tightening as everything comes together. "Wait...is that what this is about?"

"Yes. Essentially. I asked Peterson and my father to risk their lives to find out if it was true."

"If there was a nuclear weapon onboard the K1?"

Tyler stops acting casual and stares at me. "Correct. A weapon the Russian government doesn't even know about."

"Why would he put it there?"

"At first we thought it was some kind of bargaining chip, then we started getting scattered intelligence about something called the Black Curtain. Zhirov's plan is to detonate this thing in orbit and let the blame fall on Radin.

"It's not to attack us, although when that goes off, depending on what part of the world it's over, it'll disrupt communications for billions and potentially kill tens of thousands from the aftermath. And bring us to the brink of World War III."

"Wait...what's the square? Vaughn, the DIA guy, said it was some kind of encryption chip."

"That's partly true. That's what the Russians think you stole. It's actually the trigger for the bomb."

"Holy shit." And it's in my rental car right now. "Good thing we got it."

"Yeah. The problem is they're sending up another."

[50]
SECRET OPS

TYLER SURVEYS THE CROWD while I just stand here, leaning on the table, numb. In the past few hours I've had two men tell me stories about what this is about. While Vaughn was working hard to convince me and put me at ease, Tyler just scared the shit out of me.

I kept hoping all this would be worth it. But I didn't mean like this. A nuclear weapon in Low Earth Orbit would be more than a pretty light show. It would destroy half the satellites in space and send thousands of airplanes dropping from the sky. Not to mention the effect it could have on power grids, causing blackouts and plunging cities into chaos.

"You okay?" he asks.

"Still processing."

"Hell of an info dump. You're here because I asked my father and Peterson to find out if the K1 had a nuclear weapon onboard. And it would appear that it does..."

"What about Capricorn?"

"Someone whose job was to make sure you got to ground safely."

"And the person I was supposed to meet in Brazil?"

"In the hospital right now. Hit by crossfire at the stadium."

"Jesus Christ. Maybe if you told me more."

"Maybe if a lot of things were different."

I'm alive and he lost his father. "We should tell the world about this."

He shakes his head. "It's complicated. Zhirov controls the entire Russian space program. If we say this is about a nuclear weapon onboard the K1 the Russians will call us liars and Zhirov will make sure there's nothing to be found if the Russian president somehow gets access."

"But we could stop him from getting the next trigger."

"No. If we call Zhirov out on this right now and the Russian President shuts down their next launch, the K1 commanders will be able to improvise a trigger."

"What good would that do if their president knows that it was Zhirov's plot all long?"

"Politically? Nothing. But strategically, Zhirov could then resort to using it as a threat. If he detonates the bomb over the US or China, there's going to be hell to pay for Radin."

"That's insane." What madness is this?

"That's Russia. Zhirov knows once the shit hits the fan he's a dead man. That's why he's playing this for all he can. He already assumes that if Radin gets reelected and sweeps with his party, he'll be seeing the inside of a Russian prison, no matter what. He's got nothing to lose."

"Okay. I get it. The Russians are nuts. What's our play?"

Tyler stares down at his hands on the table. "I don't know. Silverback, the spy, we think he's controlled by Zhirov. And to be honest, there are people in our government who would be okay with this playing out if the detonation happens over a part of the world that doesn't speak English."

"China?"

"A Russian EMP could set back their industrial base a few years – at least their telecommunications. While that might be bad for iPhone factories, plenty of people in the Pentagon wouldn't cry over that."

"It could also start a war."

"Yes, but the aggrieved party would be severely handicapped. And the moment that bomb goes off, Zhirov or one of his pals will storm into Radin's office, place him under arrest and make peace with the rest of the world before the shooting starts."

"Christ. How do we fix this?"

"We're not totally alone. Peterson and my father had some help. I've got a trusted contact in the NRO. A few in the CIA and even a couple friendly Russians."

"Can I give you the square, so at least I'm out of the picture?"

"The moment I take possession of that they could come get me."

"You're a senator."

"With a husband and kids. Right now there's a black SUV parked at the end of my block. It's been there since the moment you guys docked at the K1 – before dad..." His voice falters for a moment. "I contacted the Secret Service about it and they tell me that they have no idea who it is, but they have government plates."

"You're being spied on?"

"I figure that I'm about to be served any moment with a warrant accusing me of espionage. It'll be bullshit. The DIA or somebody else will say I gave secrets to some ex-lover – chances are they've already paid one off. My name won't mean anything."

I nervously look around, afraid that he may have brought more trouble to me.

"Relax. I've got some friends with local law enforcement. There's a perimeter here."

"These guys kill cops."

"I know. That's why I have to ask you to take it a little further."

"I'm a wanted man. I might not be the best courier. Why not ask one of your cop friends?"

"I don't trust anyone that much. I need you to take it to a man who might be able to do something about it."

"The President?"

"No. Somebody with real power. His name is Markov."

"Sounds Russian."

"It is. But he's one of ours. He defected in the 70's. Since then he's been one of the most sought after analysts in the intelligence community. He's also probably one of the smartest people on the planet."

"And you trust him?"

"If Markov wanted to take over the world, I'd defect to his side.

"When he came over to us the Soviets put his family on a train and sent them off to Siberia to use as a bargaining chip. They died of cholera a month later in a gulag. The Russians fucked up big time on that one. They turned a mildly motivated defector into their worst enemy.

"Legend has it after the Berlin Wall came down Gorbachev called up Markov and said, 'You win.'"

"And you need me to bring the square to him?"

"This is a game I don't know how to play. I'm not sure anybody does. Markov is the only one who stands a chance."

"What the hell? What was your plan? Your dad is dead, so is Peterson. How did you see this playing out?"

He stares at me for a moment without blinking. "Dixon, go fuck yourself. My dad is dead because he believed in things more important than himself. We didn't have a plan. We had an opportunity we had to take. Dad knew it. Peterson knew it. If we waited, a lot more people were going to die. And they may still...I know this has been a rough..."

"Rough? You act like this is a fucking road trip."

"Well, you may see the end of this and live. Dad won't. Peterson won't."

Christ. "Don't lay that guilt on me. I didn't ask for this. I wasn't even supposed to be on that rocket."

People turn to look at us as my voice rises.

Tyler keeps his low. "No. You weren't. Robbie was."

"This should have been his problem," I say exasperated.

"It was going to be. Until dad changed his mind."

"Wait, what?"

"Robbie was in on it. But dad decided he didn't have what it took to see things through if it went to hell. He called me up and told me he was going to have Robbie back out so you could fly. Dad thought that even though you weren't military, you'd be the man to count on."

I shake my head. "Well, he chose wrong on that one."

"Are you kidding?" He stares me in the eye. "Are you seriously kidding me, David? Dad said you were the best pilot he ever met. Dad said you were the quickest thinker in a fix he ever met. Dad thought so much of you, holy shit, I wanted to be you."

"I never knew." This was a very different side of Bennet than the one I worked with.

"Of course not. The man could have given stone-face lessons to the Sphinx. You're more like dad than you realize. And you're the only person I trust to get it to Markov."

"Can't he come to me?"

"He's older than Yoda."

"Fuck." I groan. I'm in this too deep. I get it. "Fine. Where does he live?"

"Well, there's that. It was a condition of his defection. He wanted some place secure but not on government property...it's a private community inside Disney World."

"Seriously?"

"Seriously."

[51]
DETOUR

THE DRIVE TO FLORIDA has made me complacent. I stayed at the speed limit, did my best to blend in and made sure to take my naps in places far enough away from the gas stations and rest stops where I assumed the police would be looking for someone on the run.

In case of an emergency, I had Vaughn a.k.a. Flagler's driver's license, which kind of sort of could pass for me at a midnight stop. There's no way I'd get through airport security or something more thorough with it.

Between what I stole from Vaughn and his men, there was over two thousand dollars in cash. I have no idea what they needed that for, other than throwing at strippers in Vegas after a hard day dropping suspected terrorists out of helicopters.

When I had to go into a convenience store to use the bathroom, I made sure to get in and out pretty quickly so nobody could compare my face to the guy on the news.

Blending in isn't too difficult if you wear the Southern "regular guy" uniform of khaki shorts, baseball cap and fisherman sunglasses with a strap running around the back.

I also changed my license plate in a movie theater parking lot when I got into Louisiana and again in Florida. This time I didn't put my stolen plate on another car – that would establish my trail. Instead, I stole two plates, swapped one and kept the other.

The person whose plate is on my car will probably never realize their's has been stolen because I put some other poor schmo's plate on their car.

All of this is great and all, but may be for naught.

Five miles after I take the exit off the I-10 to I-75 I stop inside a convenience store for a cup of coffee and a pee break.

As I'm heading towards the back, avoiding contact, I overhear a heavyset woman complaining to the cashier. "It took us a god damn hour to get through that check point! Sobriety check, my ass. It's all about that asshole on the news...No, the other Virginia Slims."

Check point?

I watch as she waddles out to her car and leaves the gas station going north bound.

"Is there one going north?" a mustached man in a slightly beat up t-shirt asks the cashier.

I follow all of this with great interest.

"I don't know," says the clerk. "But I saw about twelve state troopers heading north."

Shit. They're locking down the highway.

Did I do something to tip them off? Or is it the fact that I'm getting close to Cape Canaveral and iCosmos?

The launch feels like a distant memory, but that was just two days ago. I landed the plane in the desert yesterday – so if they thought I was heading home, now would be the right time to try to lock down the roads.

Damn.

I pay for my coffee and go back to my car to look for some other option using the map on my phone.

Other than some small streets, I-75 and everything connected to it is cut off.

Do I risk driving through a smaller town, trying to find another route?

I crane my neck and look up as a helicopter flies south. It's got FBI written on the side in big bold letters.

Yep. This is about me.

I take a moment to read the latest online news.

There's nothing saying that the manhunt is focusing on Florida, but they've definitely announced that I'm the guy that crashed the plane on the border. They've also said that they think I killed the Mexican army soldiers. Wonderful.

Meanwhile, there's nothing on any of the Texas websites about Vaughn or his men. So maybe the DIA is keeping that under wraps – I guess that would be harder to explain?

I still need to get to Markov. He's the magic man who can solve all my problems.

The trouble is that there are a bunch of police between us who are convinced I'm some kind of violent-terrorist cop killer. Plus, there are probably people from the DIA and maybe a few Russians who will kill me on sight as well.

And...everybody I know is probably being watched. I can't ask them for help.

I could take a side road and risk it. Chances are I'll get stopped by some county police – maybe then...

I stop scrolling through the news when I see an article about Tyler Bennet:

BREAKING: US Senator Tyler Bennet reportedly killed in domestic disturbance.

Fuck! I feel my lungs seize up.

They killed him.

They goddamn killed him.

Tyler was worried that they would serve him with some kind of warrant, instead, they shot him and made it look like an ex-lover did it.

It's a sloppy way to silence him, but they're not worried about the long term. They needed to stop him now. And they did.

Christ.

Focus, David. You need to get to Markov. If you don't, you'll get killed too. It doesn't matter if the state or local police stop you, Silverback, whoever the hell he is, will find you and kill you.

All that matters is getting to Markov.

I need help.

Who do I know that they don't know I know?

I'm drawing blanks.

Okay, who do I know that has as much interest in this as I do?

Still nothing.

I fumble with my phone as I try to think of someone, anyone I could go to.

The third item down on Google News catches my eye.

Why do some bloggers insist Astronaut David Dixon is being framed?

What the?

I read the WIRED post twice. The short answer is that some space enthusiasts claim they overheard Russian chatter that contradicts what happened and uploaded it to the internet. But then intelligence officials debunked the YouTube video of the audio as a hoax.

One name stands out in the article, Laney Washburn. Where do I know her from?

Of course.

The Glitter Menace.

I do a search and realize she only lives eight miles away.

Can I trust her?

Do I have a choice?

[52]
MENACE

I'M NOT SURE where I expected the Glitter Menace to live. But a trailer park, admittedly a well-kept one, wasn't in the equation.

Blue Water Cove is eight streets of double-wides with tiny yards. It's the kind of place retirees in the snowbound north dream about moving to. It's modest, but defies the stereotypical description my elitist friends tend to have about who lives in these homes.

The yards are filled with gnomes, flamingos and painted plywood caricatures of grandmothers tending to vegetable patches and cartoony animals.

Laney Washburn's address is towards the back. When I get there, the driveway is empty. It's already dusk, so I feel comfortable enough to sneak around the side and peek in the windows.

I'm afraid to knock on the door and find out her boyfriend is a policeman getting ready to go on duty.

Through an open window in the back, I spot a room full of race car posters. The next window reveals a room with pictures of planets and spacecraft. There's a desk in the corner with an old MacBook covered in glitter. A pair of crutches lays against the wall next to the chair.

This is where the tyrant blogger who helped kill a quarter-billion in government pork sleeps? The disconnect takes a moment to sink in.

There's a flash of headlights in the grass as a car drives down the street. I take a peek around the corner as a van pulls into the driveway.

Laney is behind the wheel with two boys, maybe 8 and 10, jumping around. There seems to be some kind of argument.

She opens the door and puts her crutches on the ground. Dressed in a hoodie and jeans, there's less flash than I saw at the press conference. She looks like a grad student ready to pull an all-nighter in the library. The boys pile out, ignoring her, and head for the porch.

"No video games until your homework is done," she says, trying to keep up.

"Whatever," says the youngest as he slams the door behind him, leaving Laney outside.

I watch as she hops up the porch and balances a crutch so she can open the door.

Maybe now isn't the right time to approach her.

I still don't know if I can trust her. I sure as hell know I can't trust those little jerks.

I go back to the side of the window and wait, trying to keep to the shadows, hoping that I don't get arrested as a peeping tom.

The home is filled with yelling about picking things up and who said what to who. A light flicks on in the race car room and the loud shrieks of a video game begin to emanate from a television as the little jerks start to play a game.

A door slams and a light flicks on in Laney's room. Through a reflection in the wall mirror I see her lean against the wall and let the crutches fall away as she puts her head into her hands.

She wipes her nose with her sleeve then goes over to her computer.

I think I'm starting to understand now.

I watch her for a few minutes, trying to think of the right thing to say. I'd call her, but I don't have her number.

Maybe there's another way...

I open up the browser on my crappy phone and pull up Twitter. Using the account I created to talk to Capricorn I @reply her.

Do you think Dixon is innocent?

There's a bubble sound from her computer as the message goes through. A second later I can hear her type a response.

I think it looks suspicious.

I type my reply.

Follow my account. I have something to tell you.

A few seconds later she sends a direct message.

This better be good.

Would you help him if he asked for it?

Probably.

Would you listen to what he had to say and not call the cops?

I'd do the right thing. You figure out what that means.

I need your help.

Who are you?

David.

Bullshit.

Promise me you won't scream?

Why?

I take a deep breath then type:

Look out your window.

Laney does a very slow motion turn. When she sees me she lets out a scream anyway that echoes off the aluminum walls of the trailer park.

"Shut up!" yells one of the boys from the next room.

She sits there staring at me. Eyes wide, not sure what to say.

After collecting her thoughts, she asks, "What happened to your hair?"

"I had a Brazilian. I thought you weren't going to scream?"

"I thought you were lying." She gets out of her chair and finds her way to the window and looks around the yard.

"Come on, get inside." She slides the window all the way open and pulls at my shoulder.

"Maybe I should use the front door?"

"I don't want my brothers seeing you. They won't shut up about it."

I pull myself over the ledge and land in a room decorated with unicorns and spaceships.

"How old are you?" I say, picking myself up off the floor.

She has me sit on her bed then shuts the window and closes her blinds. "Twenty-three. Oh, this?" She looks around. "Infantilization often goes hand-in-hand in dealing with a handicap."

"Oh..."

"I'm not a virgin," she awkwardly volunteers.

"Um, I wasn't asking. I was just worried if your parents were here."

"I'm sorry. That was weird of me. I just never thought I'd have an astronaut with an AFI of 8 say that to me."

"An AFI?"

Her face goes red. "Um...it's a thing space groupies came up with. I'm not one of them, but some of my friends are. AFI means Astronaut Fuckability Index. A five is solid. An eight is exceptional. Elevens are reserved for Neil Armstrong and Yuri Gagarin."

"Good luck with them."

"Elon Musk is a ten." She pauses. "Bennet was a nine. So was Peterson. I'm sorry. This is horrible." She wipes away at her eye. "What the hell happened? Why the hell are you here? I mean, what the hell?"

[53]
SUPPORT CREW

LANEY STARES AT ME like I'm a ghost. I'm having serious second thoughts about coming here. As she sits under a shelf of model rockets and glass unicorns, I feel like I've just brought an innocent into something very dangerous.

Peterson and Bennet are dead. So is Bennet's son, Tyler. This is a bad idea.

I stand up. "This was a mistake. Give me a head start if you're going to call the police."

"Sit down," she says, rising to her own feet.

There's something about the complete conviction in her voice despite the fact I can see her legs are about to betray her.

"There are some bad people who could be here any minute."

She puts a hand on my shoulder. "Sit down. I have a gun." She pauses, "I mean, I'm not going to shoot you. But if they come..."

I fall back on the bed. "This could be very bad." I nod to the room next door where her brothers are loudly playing their game.

"Understood. Tell me what's going on and we'll figure it out."

I give a nervous glance towards the window, trying to decide if I should run.

"I knew something weird was going on at the Korolev station," she says.

"How do you mean?"

"Before you even docked with them. They have an open channel and a secure one. There has been almost nothing on the open one. They use it for talking to school kids and stuff. The place was on some kind of lockdown before you even got there."

"Yes..."

I don't know what I should tell her. I notice a tall bookcase in her corner filled with binders. I walk over and take one down and start flipping through. It's a schematic of the Soviet N1 heavy launch system. Not just outlines, but detailed drawings.

I take down another one. It's filled with specs of the X-20 Dyna-Soar, an Air Force space plane that never made it past testing.

"Are all of these rocket schematics?"

"Communications systems. Space suits. I have them all on my computer but I like the physical copies best."

"And you've read them?"

"No. They're just there to impress guys. Yeah, dumbass. I've been collecting them since I was a kid. I couldn't decide if I wanted to fly them or build them."

"Why not both?" I reply, sitting back down.

"Yeah..." Her eyes drift off to the side. "Peterson and Bennet? Are they really dead?"

The image of Peterson's dead body floating by the window is still in my mind. "Yes."

Laney wipes at her eye. "I'd talked to Peterson several times. Did you know that? She was always nice. And Bennet, oh my god, he's a legend. What it must have been like to have learned from him. He knew Armstrong and Musgrave."

"Bennet was something else...So was Peterson."

Laney puts a hand to her mouth. "I'm so sorry. I can't imagine what it must be like for you."

"It's fine. To be honest, I'm still a little numb. There's time for that later."

These were people I worked with. For Laney, they were heroes. In some way, maybe she even feels more strongly. Peterson wasn't just some cool person she could fawn over. Peterson may have been a role model, a version of Laney in a different universe.

Laney uses her wrist to wipe away a tear. "Why are you here?"

"Why aren't you calling the police?"

"Because nothing makes sense. The Russians are lying and I get the impression you had nobody to turn to."

I nod. "Pretty much."

"So what the hell is going on?"

I make a flash judgement to trust her. "There's a nuclear weapon onboard the Korolev. The head of the Russian space agency is planning to detonate it in order to stage a coup."

"Holy shit. Zhirov?"

"Yeah, him."

"He's an asshole. You know that he's been trying to militarize their space agency into another army?"

"I don't think Radin is going to let that happen."

She sits there for a moment processing everything. "Why isn't our government doing something about it?"

"Zhirov has a spy inside our intelligence community. They already had a rendition team torture me."

"Oh my god!"

"I...got away." I prefer to gloss over that episode. "Anyway, apparently we're worried if it gets out there's a nuke on the K1, Zhirov will go ahead and pull the trigger."

"Who is we?"

"As far as I know, it was Bennet, his son, Peterson and someone else. You heard about Tyler Bennet?"

"Yeah. They killed them? Why?"

"I don't know. But they did. I've encountered some nasty people."

"So what can I do?"

"I don't think I should get you involved. It's not safe."

She rolls her eyes. "Whatever. I'm involved now. Why did you come here? Just tell me that."

"They're shutting down the roads."

"Yeah. The I-10 is backed up. I thought that might be about you."

"I can't get to where I need to go by myself."

"So you need a driver?"

"Basically. But I think..."

She interrupts me. "Let's go."

"Laney...I can't ask you to do this."

"You can't stop me." She's already standing up and shoving things into her purse.

"What if I'm lying?"

"I'll tell them you threatened to kill me. Meet me outside."

"What about your brothers?"

"My aunt is coming over. Worry about her."

Two minutes later she slides into the driver's seat of her van. I'm trying to decide if I should be a passenger or hide in the back.

She tosses me a pair of reading glasses. "I took these off the counter."

I put them on and check my reflection in the visor mirror. "What do you think?"

She takes them off my face and tosses them into the back. "Too intellectual. You look like you might know

how to fly a spaceship, or try to nail UCF coeds by
getting high and talking about social justice."

"Heh, that's half true. I'm just not sure how to get
through the checkpoint."

"I got that covered. If they stop us I'll play some death
metal. In this crappy van, they'll assume we're just white
trash."

"Here's to stereotyping."

"And my angsty teenage years."

[54]
SMALL WORLD

WE WERE WAVED THROUGH A ROADBLOCK on the I-5 and thankfully I never had to endure Laney's full playlist.

On the way, I texted the number Tyler gave me before he was killed and received very specific instructions on getting to Markov's house behind the gate in an already gated community on a remote corner of Walt Disney World property.

We had to go through three private security checkpoints to get here. Markov had pre-arranged everything so all I had to do was introduce myself as Mr. Stone and we were waved through without having to show a driver's license or even let my picture be taken.

Laney twice jokingly suggested we make out so we looked like a couple. At least I think she was kidding. Under different circumstances...

At the last gate at the edge of a driveway, a man dressed more like a valet than an armed guard – although I could spot two weapons on him – steps out of a small stone guardhouse, inspects our van then lets us through.

Another man, college-aged and dressed in a polo, is waiting for us outside the front door.

It's a mansion, but not a massive one. Aside from the extra security features, it's just like the others in the reclusive neighborhood.

"Hello, I'm Brian," says Markov's assistant. "If you can follow me in, I'll let him know you're here."

I hold Laney's car door open for her, but she doesn't need any more help than that.

Brian takes us through the foyer into a spacious living room filled with Disney memorabilia. It has the tasteful look of a gallery, more than a children's playroom.

After getting us two bottled waters, Brian leaves us alone.

"So who is this guy?" asks Laney.

"I guess you could call him a spymaster."

She takes in the decor. "Man, I should think about becoming one."

"I'm surprised you haven't been hired to be a lobbyist for some aerospace company."

"Those blood-sucking corrupt jackals? Cost plus contracting is why we're not on Mars."

I guess I struck some kind of nerve. "I see."

"Besides that, I don't have a college degree."

"You should finish that." I reply, then realize she's heard that a thousand times and has a lot more to deal with in life than I do. I get the sense that her father was never around and her mom has some kind of illness.

"Or find someone else who has a better use for your skills," says a booming voice from the hallway.

We look over and see a short elderly man using two canes to maneuver himself into the room. Dark hair and beard, robustly-built, he reminds me of a dwarf from Lord of the Rings.

Markov notices Laney's crutches resting by the couch. "Ah, another quadruped like myself."

"Four legs good, two legs bad," says Laney.

Markov smiles and takes the chair opposite us. "What an appropriate quote given the circumstances." There's a faint Russian accent, but his enunciation sounds more like an Oxford professor.

I look at Laney, not sure what I missed.

"Animal Farm," she says. "By George Orwell, an outspoken critic of Russian politics."

Markov raises a finger, "Yet an ardent socialist himself, who had difficulty dealing with how the use of force to control one aspect of human behavior would inevitably lead to trying to control other aspects and ultimately lead to totalitarianism."

He waves his observation away. "But we are not here to discuss politics of that nature. We're more concerned with the nuclear weapon a hundred miles over our heads."

"Two-hundred and thirty," corrects Laney.

"Yes. I should be more precise around you. I read some of your blog posts."

"You did?"

"When you were at the front gate."

It would figure that the old spymaster would have his tentacles everywhere.

"So you're like a spy?" asks Laney.

"I'm an old man people sometimes ask questions, then promptly ignore. Usually for the better."

"So you know the situation and what happened to Tyler and his father?" I ask.

"Yes. Tragic. Very tragic."

I take the black square and set it on the table. "Well, I brought this. Can you clear things up now?"

"Mr. Dixon, I left the magic wand that does all that in my other jacket pocket. Things are very complicated."

"Yes. Yes, they are. But right now I've got a target on me and can't take a piss without worrying a Russian kill team or a renegade US agent is going to murder me."

"And yet, you find yourself in the delightful company of an attractive and intelligent young woman. I always thought that was a trope of action movies. I'm beginning to think there's some kind of pheromonal effect at work."

"Chicks love a bad boy," says Laney. She slaps my knee. "You don't get any badder than this one right now."

"Indeed." Markov calls to the other room. "Brian, would you take this device and call our friend in computer forensics at the National Air and Space Intelligence Center?"

Markov's assistant materializes and picks the square up off the table. I feel a strange separation anxiety as he walks out of the room.

"Is that...safe?"

"With Brian? I should hope so. He's actually Lieutenant Brian on loan from the Office of Naval Intelligence. We need to make sure it is what you say it is."

"Why would I lie about that?"

"Good question. But apparently you were in the custody of a renegade DIA agent for several hours. Anything is possible. I'm a cautious man."

"Living in Disney World."

Markov smiles. "They have the best, non-invasive security in the world. And I'm quite fond of the place. When I was a boy I used to watch Disney cartoons in a basement in Leningrad, afraid the KGB would bust in at any moment. When I saw a film reel of Walt Disney's Wonderful World of Color introducing Disneyland, you can imagine the effect it had on a boy living under a frozen tyranny. Ah, I've digressed. Mr. Dixon, I believe you. I just need to make sure the facts agree with my assessment. I've made that mistake too many times."

Brian steps into the archway and nods to Markov. "It checks."

"And there we go," says Markov. "This little square our friends risked their lives to retrieve is what we are afraid it would be. And soon, within days, the crew of the K1 will have another. If they don't improvise before then."

"I heard there's a rocket already on the pad at Baikonur," says Laney. "People thought they were doing a satellite launch in three weeks but the schedule got moved up. Which is weird, because I heard from a friend at Moscow Polytechnic they're still inspecting the telescope mirror for one of their payloads."

Markov grins at her. "It would seem your network is even more extensive than my own. Brian, would you check on that?"

There's a small smile of satisfaction on Laney's face. "A lot of us space geeks like to talk. Russia has their share, China too."

"I bet. When this matter is settled, we should talk about your goals, Ms. Washburn."

I interrupt them, "After you two are done friending each other, can we talk about how we're going to clear my name?"

"Mr. Dixon, in a period of time measured in hours or days, but less than weeks, nobody will care who you are." He points to a small cabana on the other side of the pool. "There's a guest house with cable, high-speed internet and a fully stocked kitchen. You're welcome to stay there until events have come to their conclusion. Meanwhile, the rest of us are trying to solve the larger problem."

"Do the rest of you have targets on their heads?"

"Tyler did. As did Peterson and Bennet. And I don't know if you've checked the news in the last few hours, but the manhunt for you has moved to west Georgia – where a former Navy SEAL who matches your description has been breaking into cabins and going out of his way to be seen by authorities in order to lead the attention away from you."

What is he talking about? "I don't understand..."

"If you're on the run, our nemesis, Zhirov, doesn't know that we have the square and are aware of what he's up to. Likewise, neither does Silverback."

"Silverback?" asks Laney.

"A mole within US intelligence who has a number of people unwittingly working for him," says Markov.

"Yikes."

"Yikes, indeed."

Markov's rebuke stings. Suddenly I feel like a very petty man. "Okay. I get it. What can I do?"

"Right now, I need the two of you to tell me everything I need to know about rockets, space stations and anything else I should know."

"That's a lot," says Laney.

"I'm a quick study. Just start and I'll ask questions as we go along."

[55]
STRATEGY

MARKOV KNOWS way more than he initially let on. As we paint the broad strokes about the current technical state of the space industry he starts drilling down into specifics about craft, equipment and who has what.

While I was able to explain things from a pilot's perspective, Laney has the real information about what is flying over our heads, how long it takes to prep a launch, what kind of shifts crews sleep in, and a myriad of other details that would have put any of my professors or instructors to shame.

Twice she corrected me about engine capacities and the cubic volume of different craft.

"Yeah, but the PPTS has 33 cubic meters of pressurized volume on the older system. The new one gets 37 with the improved scrubbers," she explains to Markov's amusement.

"Um, right. That's true."

"I think they're sending the wrong person into space," he observes.

"We try to keep the real brains away from the things that go 'boom,'" I say, trying to save face.

As we talk, he takes notes, occasionally passing them to Lieutenant Brian who goes into another room to make phone calls.

I'm not sure what Markov is thinking about, but he keeps asking questions about the layout of the K1 and its telemetry system.

"It also has a laser," I point out.

"It does?" says Laney, surprised.

I almost let out an "Ah hah," at having some information she doesn't know.

"They tried to burn a hole in my space capsule. Thankfully, Capricorn had me turn my heat shield towards the station."

"So the Russians have a defensive system onboard the K1 they can use at close range?" He does some calculations on his pad. "I assume the effective range would be 1,500 miles or so due to curvature and assuming no attenuation?"

"Yes," Laney and I say at the same time.

"This presents an interesting challenge. In a conventional situation the solution would be to try to take out the K1 using a high-velocity object and destroy it in orbit. Unfortunately, a near miss would result in them detonating the nuclear weapon.

"The second choice is to bring an explosive device with enough ordnance to destroy the K1, or at least the module holding the weapon. The problem with that is two-fold; getting close enough to do that and the aforementioned near miss scenario. Not to mention the repercussions from the Russians."

"If it's the Russian's problem, why don't we just let them deal with it?" I ask.

"Radin is in even more of a delicate position than we are. While Silverback has our intelligence agencies hamstrung, Zhirov has his ears everywhere – plus, there's not much Radin can do. Zhirov controls access to space. Even the Russian Army space wing's launch centers are controlled by him.

"Oddly enough, the proper course of action is covert intervention by the US. Zhirov's goal is taking power in Russia, not outright confrontation with America. That's why he's been expending every effort he can to capture you. He'll use the nuke, no matter what, but he wants to save it for embarrassing Radin."

"They can't just send some commandos to get him?"

"They would never get close."

"What about appealing to the crew of the K1?"

"The two commanders are Zhirov's chosen men. They control access to the compartment that contains the weapon."

"Wait? Are you saying the other crew aren't in on this?"

He shakes his head. "Not all. In fact...let's just say that you were able to escape with the assistance of someone onboard."

"Wait, what? They were trying to kill me."

"Yes. Or at least the commanders were. But at least one person on the crew was actually working with us. They're the reason we knew the weapon was onboard. When they started getting elevated radiation readings and took it to Roscosmos, the pushback made them suspicious. So they took a geiger counter on a spacewalk next to the bulkhead and confirmed their suspicions.

"This cosmonaut was then in a precarious position. Nuclear weapons in space are specifically banned by treaty. Making any kind of noise about this would have serious, if not fatal, consequences."

"With all your inside information, how come Tyler is dead?"

Markov looks at the floor, avoiding my gaze. "I explained to him the likelihood they were going to have him killed. He naively thought that his status as a senator was somehow going to protect him – at least from physical threats."

"And Silverback still got him. Why is he still active?"

"One, I'm an old man people rarely listen to. Second, Silverback is very likely more than one individual. I suspect that he or she is working in concert with someone who has influence at the highest level."

"But Silverback knows about you. Yet here you are." I'm taking my frustration out on the one living person that has an idea what's going on.

"Are you asking why Silverback hasn't killed me yet? The answer is very simple and Russian. I don't know who Silverback is, but I have my suspicions. I also have dossiers on a number of government officials containing extremely incriminating information. Affairs, bribes, most of it minor, but enough to remove any of them from their position.

"While I have my own security, my real protection comes from the fact that should I die from anything resembling suspicious circumstances, those dossiers would find themselves immediately released and a great number of people would be embarrassed and exposed – Silverback among them. It's a lot like Zhirov's weapon. It's what's keeping his enemies at bay. Fortunately for me, these dossiers are digital and not stored in any one place. Which brings me to what we need to do. While Silverback's reach is extensive, we do have allies, but we have to act very quickly. Ms. Washburn, is there someone to look after your brothers? It would probably be best if you came along with us."

"Me? Uh, yeah. My aunt is visiting for a few days."

"Hold up. Are we going somewhere?"

"I can't tell you that until we're there. But I would appreciate your advice. I'm pulling some favors and putting together a team."

"A team to do what?"

"Our only option; steal the nuclear weapon that's onboard the K1."

SPACE OPS

FOUR HOURS LATER, our helicopter touches down on a tarmac near a hangar at the far end of Cape Canaveral Air Force base. I get chills thinking about the last time I was this close to an airport.

As I help Laney, and Brian assists Markov out of the helicopter, an athletic silver-haired man in a black polo gets out of an SUV and joins us.

"Dr. Markov," he says, shaking the old Russian's hand.

"Admiral Jessup. I believe you are aware of my companions?"

Jessup gives Laney a nod then stares at me for a moment, sizing me up. "So this is our fugitive?"

"We're pretending he's under custody," says Markov. "I'd appreciate it if you didn't run out and collect the reward just yet."

"I'll take it under consideration if he promises not to steal anything." He gives me a very intense look that I can't tell if it is a joke or not. He relents and turns back to Markov, "So this is your team?"

"Indeed. Is this the facility?" Markov nods to the building. "May we go inside?" He quickly ambles towards the door on his canes.

Jessup hesitates. "Well, you need security clearances..."

"And you have the power to grant them, don't you?" Markov faces Laney and me. "Mr. Dixon and Ms. Washburn, tell anyone what you've seen in here and I'll shoot you myself."

I believe him.

Jessup shakes his head, apparently used to Markov getting whatever he wants. He takes out a keycard, unlocks the door and follows us inside.

It doesn't look like a cleaning crew has been here in years. Jessup takes us past an abandoned security desk.

"What's an Admiral doing on an Air Force base?" asks Laney, no longer able to contain her curiosity.

"Besides holding my nose? We rent this space from our pretend pilot friends." He takes us through another door and down a corridor.

"This operation started with an NRO project back in the 1960s. They wanted to build a space station specifically for spying on the Russians. They got as far as a mock-up and a facility a few miles up the road. However, by the time they figured out the logistics of everything, satellite technology and the SR-71 were advanced enough at that point to handle most of what we needed.

"But the idea kind of stuck. The Navy liked the idea of having our own reconnaissance birds and strategic space capabilities. Congress gave us a little budget to play with some ideas. Some clever, others not so much.

"One idea, straight out of the Naval Intelligence handbook, was finding ways to intercept or manipulate satellite surveillance.

"Some of our folks thought up a crazy scheme to put a mirror-tap over Russian spy satellites and control what they saw or even faking images. Another idea was to outright steal one of their birds to get a look at what made it tick.

"Of course the problem was two-fold. The first was having a vehicle that could sneak up on a satellite. The second was having a way to do all the crazy things we wanted. We played with everything, from robotics to little space-suited monkeys. This way..."

The next room is the main section of the hangar. The few working overhead lights illuminate various machines and equipment covered in plastic. There's a small mission control room and sectioned-off zones with rocket engines and workbenches and tools.

"My predecessor eventually convinced a secret congressional committee to give us the budget when he stopped talking about space monkeys and gave them something they could wrap their heads around.

"We called it Space Ops, a squad of Navy SEALS trained for space operations and the gear they'd need to pull it off." He sweeps his arm around the hangar. "A lot of this was built by SpaceX and other outfits in their backrooms. Come over here and I'll show you the main attraction."

We go through a barrier of black rubber slats and enter a chamber with a tall capsule under a tarp.

"Help me out, Dixon," says Jessup as he hands me one end of the tarp. We pull it down, revealing a very close copy of the Unicorn.

"Look familiar?"

"Yeah. I know a guy who would rent one to you for a hell of a lot cheaper than what you probably paid for it."

"But not like this." Jessup walks around the vehicle to a large hatch, twice as big as the one on the Unicorn. It seems too large for a vehicle this size and would unbalance it.

He turns the handle and pulls the massive door open. "The real money is in what's inside..."

Instead of seats and control panels, the capsule looks empty. I try to focus on a sharp cone-shaped shadow and realize I'm actually staring at something.

Jessup uses a pocket flashlight to show the outline of the blacker than black thing. It's two-meters wide and shaped like a rifle bullet. Other than the shape, I can't see any surface features.

"This material absorbs just about everything you can throw at it."

"What good does that do inside the outer capsule?" I ask.

"It doesn't stay there. The DarkStar is its own spacecraft. It launches from the capsule after it achieves orbit. A counter thrust cancels out the ejection. Assuming – big assumption – that everything works right, to any observers on the ground, the launch looks textbook. We have the second stage eject some chaff, making radar surveillance a little hazy, just for good measure."

I stick my head in to get a closer look at the spacecraft. "How does it dock?"

"There's a hatch on the bottom."

"Interesting. Wait, this thing is obviously too small for propulsive landing and if the hatch is on the bottom, where's the heat shield? It's not the light absorbing stuff is it?"

"No. It's inside."

"Inside? How does that work?"

"It's not for the craft. It's an inflatable heat shield for the occupant."

"Hold up...you mean re-entry is a space jump from orbit?"

"Yep."

"Jesus. Your SEALS are even braver than I thought. That's never been done. An inflatable shield has never been human-rated."

"This craft has a whole bunch of firsts associated with it," says Jessup.

"How many times have you sent this model up?"

He shakes his head. "Never."

"Good luck on that."

We turn around at the sound of footsteps. A stocky man with a buzz cut and impossibly straight posture is standing there. He looks like the man Captain America wants to be when he grows up.

Jessup introduces him. "This is Captain Prescott, he's the brave soul that has agreed to ride this thing – assuming we can get it on top of a rocket."

"AFI ten," Laney whispers to me.

Prescott gives my hand a firm shake. "Mr. Dixon. I understand you're going to tell me how to fly this thing?"

"Me?" I turn to Jessup. "I don't know the first thing about it. Where are your technicians and the people who made this?"

"Congress stopped funding four years ago. Right now the entire support crew for Space Ops consists of the people in this hangar and a few volunteers making their way here. The Captain is retired and volunteered for the mission."

I size him up. "Where did you do your astronaut training?"

"Aside from playing Star Wars as a kid? It'll be here with you in the next few hours."

[57]
CRASH COURSE

PRESCOTT IS SMART. Real smart. He's in Bennet and Peterson's league. Possessing all-around intelligence and athleticism, he could have been a physicist or pro quarterback.

As Laney pours through the dusty manuals for the DarkStar, I give Prescott a crash course on space survival, starting with the suit.

The Space Ops suits are based on the iCosmos ones, but are predictably all black and the gloves and hands have built-in electromagnets for adhering to the outside of a space station.

"Modern spacesuits are light years beyond the ones used just a decade ago," I explain to Prescott. "More so than the pressure suits of the last century. Once you step inside, the onboard intelligent assistant will let you know if you're doing something stupid."

"I suspect that will be a constant thing." He grins.

"Yeah, try not to poke a hole in the suit or take your helmet off to get some fresh air. The more important thing is understanding what it means to work in zero-gravity." I hold up the glove. "I'm sure these magnets are a clever idea, but I'm not sure I would trust them my first time out. You don't want to reach for something and find out that you're drifting away from the space station."

I think of the example Bennet gave me. "Once you step outside your craft, you have to imagine that you're a mountain climber – you never take a break unless you're fastened down to something. You're under the constant threat of falling off that mountain. While your suit has some built in jets that can take you back to the station or your craft, that's only if things are actually all working. If you get a power failure or some kind of software glitch, you might find yourself in an even more dire situation. Your first priority is something to hold on to. Your second is air. Everything else is a distant third."

Prescott picks up what I'm telling him fairly quickly, asking a few questions here and there, but never needing me to repeat anything.

Laney and I do our best to explain the controls of the DarkStar as we try to make sense of them ourselves.

While we do this, Jessup and Markov work on their scheme to get this onboard an iCosmos flight without anyone knowing what's up.

Because iCosmos is able to rapidly recycle its rockets and maintains a packed launch manifest, at any given time there's a rocket heading to the pad just a few miles away from us.

The Navy and the Air Force contract launches from them frequently and can do emergency launches, bumping commercial contracts. The key is to get this quickly on top of an Alicorn booster and not have it appear suspicious.

After getting a rudimentary understanding of the DarkStar and the suit, we all step into a dusty conference room to go over the layout of the K1.

Laney fires up the projector and the familiar cross-shape of the station fills the screen giving me a moment of pause.

I put what happened behind me and focus on explaining which module probably contains the nuclear device.

"I'd imagine that under the current situation at least one of the commanders is inside that section at all times. But before you get to them, you have to gain access to the space station." I turn to Markov who has been watching from the corner. "Can we get any help from your friend onboard?"

"Yes. Our insider will let you in through the airlock they use for EVAs. They will use the excuse of checking an air sensor they've rigged to give a malfunction warning. After they've let you inside, you'll wait until they return to the main crew section."

"And should I abandon the DarkStar at this point?" asks Prescott.

"Is there an advantage to doing that?" Markov asks me.

I think it over for a moment. I know he means beyond providing Prescott with a way to return home. I get the chilly realization that the Captain expects this to be a one way trip.

"No. Prescott will need to be tethered to the DarkStar until he gets to the K1. At that point he can use a magnetic clamp to attach his tether to the K1. With sufficient slack it won't affect things, unless they do an orbital position change, which I don't expect. I think the most prudent thing is to not abandon the DarkStar."

I see Laney watching me out of the corner of her eye. She's thinking of all the situations where having another craft so close to the K1 could compromise the whole mission. But I think she also understands that neither of us want to send this man on a suicide mission – well, more of a suicide mission than it already is.

"And once inside, how would you recommend I proceed to the secure module? Should I take off the suit?" asks Prescott.

"Good question. I was able to maneuver through the K1 with mine fairly well, but I'm sure it also cost me several seconds compared to how I would have moved in just my thermal. I guess that depends on whether you want maneuverability or body armor. I had mine on when I escaped the K1. Your goal is different. If it were me, I'd keep it on because some of those cosmonauts are built like gorillas."

I can see Prescott weighing the matter over. "I think I'll go without the suit."

Translation, he's going to stealthily sneak through there and kill anybody who gets in his way. He's thinking offensive. I'm thinking defensive. I get an image of him crawling through the modules with blacked-out face paint and a commando knife in his mouth ready to slice enemy throats.

After going through the technical specifics, Jessup joins us to discuss the tactical details.

"We worked out a variety of different entry techniques," he explains. "One is a knock-out gas. The problem with that is each module has its own air handler and sensors that will shut the hatches if they detect a foreign substance. Sadly, before this project was closed down, we were working on a reactive agent that could spread through an entire facility then change into an anesthetic. As far as weapons go, we have some gloves with stun guns built into the palms that will allow you to keep your hands free."

I want to ask where these tools were when Bennet and Peterson were conducting their clandestine operation, but keep my mouth shut.

"Stun gloves are great," I reply. "But how do we get the commander in the secure module to let Prescott inside? If they've figured out how to hot-wire the bomb, the moment he sees an American face poking his nose into the porthole he's liable to trigger the device."

"We are hoping they have not improvised a trigger yet," says Markov. "But in either event, we need a way to get Captain Prescott into the module."

Prescott steeples his fingers and thinks it over. "What if I kill the other commander and hold his head near the porthole?" asks Prescott.

I'm about to laugh at the morbid joke then realize he's serious. Jessup and Markov take it into consideration while Laney and I exchange quick glances.

These are the stakes. Prescott's solution is ruthless, cold-blooded and exactly the kind of tactic it takes to win.

"May I suggest a simpler way?" asks Laney.

[58]
COUNTDOWN

"WHY DON'T YOU just give the man an injection and knock him out?" says Laney.

"Trust me, I'm not eager to kill anyone," replies Prescott. "But that doesn't always work and getting close enough to someone with a needle is tricky. Even with a combat syringe."

I gloss over the fact that I'm not even sure I know what a "combat syringe" is supposed to be. "Listen, I'm no pacifist and these commanders are fully onboard with the whole nuclear option, so sending them to heaven doesn't really bother me all that much. But there's another consideration here. How exactly would you plan on killing this cosmonaut so you can use him for your puppet show?"

"A knife to the throat. It's kind of our specialty."

"Charming. To my knowledge this has never been done in space before. But I have seen a video of what happened when an astronaut tried to slice open a bag of cranberry sauce for a Thanksgiving dinner. It could have been the outtake of a Quentin Tarantino murder scene. A human heart pumping gallons of blood through a gashed jugular is going to be far worse."

"You have a point," says Prescott.

Yes, and I still have a very vivid image in my head of Peterson leaving a trail of blood through the K1 right before she died before my eyes.

"What about strangulation?" asks murder machine Prescott.

"Yes...if you're not worried about the effect that will have on the commander's face. Bulging eyes and burst veins might be a tip off that something is amiss."

"Mr. Dixon, I hope you understand this is not a game where we get a do-over. The stakes are far too high," says Markov. "If the Captain uses anything other than a non-lethal on the commander and it fails to work, so does the mission."

"I get that. I'm not trying to take the pacifist approach. Hell, I put bullets in three men yesterday because I didn't see any other way out." As I say it, my words make the memory more intense.

"So you understand the need to use whatever means necessary?" asks Markov.

"Yes. I would tell the Captain to try anything that didn't put him at greater risk."

Laney holds up her hand. "Okay, may I suggest an alternative approach?"

"Yes, Ms. Washburn?" asks Markov.

"Well, if the danger is in getting Captain Prescott close enough to the commander to use something to incapacitate him – whether it's lethal or non-lethal – then the solution would seem to be use your spy onboard the K1. Maybe she can?"

"She?" replies Markov.

"You kept avoiding a gender specific pronoun. That usually only happens when you're trying to indicate a female when normally you'd assume a male. Anyway, why not let her do it?"

"Interesting assumption," Markov says, not actually confirming her observation. "The problem is that this person has limits to what they will and won't do. I think this may push them too far if we ask them to help kill their commander."

"And that's why it should be a non-lethal, like a fast-acting paralytic. Could the Captain pass her a syringe that she could then use?"

"Perhaps. Captain, what do you think?" asks Markov.

"Well, I'm a soldier. I'm not really familiar with the whole social engineering solution. But Dixon makes a very compelling and graphic case as to why I shouldn't knife the commander. And strangulation puts me in close quarters with someone who has a lot of combat training. I don't doubt I could take the man out, but it might not be as clean as I like."

I interrupt. "And he has the advantage of having spent months in zero-g. In your case, we're not even sure if the anti-nausea drugs will do their job, let alone how quickly you can adapt. No offense."

"None taken. Dr. Markov, I can certainly pass a syringe to your operative, if you think they'll go for it."

"I believe if they understand this is the least violent of the solutions, they will accept this solution. This still leaves us with the second commander. After you gain entry to that module, you need a way to deal with him."

"You could use your knock-out gas once he opens the door," I suggest. "It's a small enough chamber that the gas will quickly fill it before the air handler has a chance to pump it out."

"That could work," says Prescott. "Here on Earth that's how we'd incapacitate someone in a similar situation. When we practice infiltrating enemy submarines we do that. We also have special rounds that are designed to go through people but not hulls."

"Spaceships and stations are different than submarines," I reply. "Some parts are literally as thin as a Coke can. You're in a balloon waiting to pop."

Prescott makes a note of this in his little journal. "Okay. I'll need a gas mask. Is there a problem if I strap one to my chest inside the space suit? I'm not sure what exposing the filter to extreme cold or vacuum would do."

I get a sinking feeling at the realization of all the different variables going into this. "I think you should be fine with that."

There are so many things that can go wrong. We don't even have a chance to do a dry run. And the man we're sending up to do this has never even been in space before.

Granted, neither had I until a few days ago, but I had the benefit of years of training and weightlessness onboard our vomit comet airplanes. I knew as much as you could know until actually doing it.

I tell myself to relax. Prescott is the best of the best. He's built for this intellectually and physically. His combat experience far exceeds my pilot and astronaut training.

Markov checks his phone. "Hmmm. Unfortunate news. The sensor unit malfunction on the US/iCosmos station that prevented you from docking has spread to another module and they're afraid their water supply may be contaminated with bacteria."

"Oh wow," says Laney. "That's horrible."

"Yes, it is," he replies. "It would seem they asked the Russians for help and they declined – not surprising. Now they're requesting an emergency resupply from iCosmos. Captain Prescott, it looks like we will be sending you into space quite shortly."

"You clever bastard," says Admiral Jessup. "How did you arrange that?"

"Sometimes serendipity must be seduced."

[59]
STATE OF THE ART

THE ALICORN ROCKET used to send the Unicorn spacecraft into orbit consists of two stages: The upper and the lower stage.

The lower stage is the big cylinder on the bottom that uses nine engines to send the upper stage to the edge of the atmosphere, disengaging at about Mach 10 then falling back to Earth where it uses the carefully calculated fuel left onboard to land on a platform at the far end of the iCosmos assembly bay.

The second stage pushes the Unicorn into orbit, reaching 17,500 miles per hour, then heads back down to Earth top first, using a heat shield to slow it down before it does a somersault and lands like the first stage on another pad adjacent to the assembly bay.

There's a third landing pad for the Unicorn to land on, but I have no personal experience because I decided to take a side trip to Rio.

After landing, each component of the rocket is pulled into the iCosmos assembly bay where they're inspected for damage and any parts that need refurbishing are replaced.

The entire rocket, all three sections, are designed to be reused like a passenger jet. This reusability is why iCosmos, SpaceX and Blue Origin have been able to radically change space travel.

It hasn't come easily or cheaply. These companies were the pet projects of some of the richest men in the world who had a grand vision about the future of space.

Several years into this era, the improvements and changes are still happening. The iCosmos assembly building is like one huge machine. Rockets go out one side, come back used through another, and are carried along on tracks as robot arms inspect the surface. AI diagnostic software checks the internal systems and the engines are X-rayed for stress.

Before this period, the most expensive part of a rocket launch was the cost of the rocket itself – even the Space Shuttle. Its side boosters were dumped into the salty ocean making them more costly to reuse than just buying new ones – although you'd never know that from the magic of government contractor accounting. The main tank burned up on reentry and the shuttle itself had to have the engines rebuilt after every launch and the tiles resurfaced. All of this added up to a billion-dollar price tag per launch.

The contractors who worked on the shuttle and its successor, the SLS, really didn't have much interest in solving the problem they were paid handsomely to solve – that was until the upstarts came along and changed the game.

Now the single biggest cost to getting into space is fuel. It takes roughly the same amount of fuel to put the Unicorn and its payload into orbit as it does to send a 727 around the world.

On the bigger rockets they're using to send materials to the US/iCosmos station, the cost per pound is much less.

All of which leads to the current state of affairs where rocket launches are cool, but they're no big deal, to the point that while security is extremely tight around the iCosmos facility – it's still located on an Air Force base – this isn't anything like an Apollo launch of yesteryear.

After thousands of launches, we have a humongous data-set that tells the AI that supervises the launch what's going on at any given time. While there's somebody with their finger over an abort button, it's mostly ceremonial.

In the old days the abort button was just a trigger to make the thing explode. Now there are a dozen different scenarios, from exploding the first two sections after the crew section ejects, to a slightly more graceful abort that splits the sections apart and allows them to all land back on the pad.

While this hasn't made us complacent, everything has become more routine, like commercial air travel. There are ground crews to inspect the engines and fuselage and checks and balances in place to make sure they did their job.

The biggest variable now is the payload. While you can predict what kind of stress an engine will go through and the wear on related systems, if someone stowed a cylinder of acetylene gas in the cargo section and used a valve that wasn't rated for the degree of vibration you'll encounter on take off, your perfectly fine rocket will explode because someone goofed.

Every rocket has a launch supervisor and a payload master. For my mission, the supervisor was Renata. The payload master was an engineer named Greene, who supervised all the things loaded into the Unicorn and made sure the variables wouldn't cause the whole thing to crash.

We've already got an insider with iCosmos who will change the launch profile for the upper stage, making it possible for us to get the DarkStar into a trajectory that will bring it to the K1 without it looking like we're trying to actually aim for the Russian space station.

The most difficult part about getting Prescott into space is going to be on the ground – getting the iCosmos payload master to sign off on the fake-Unicorn capsule.

Markov's trick for that is to get an Air Force payload master to commandeer the launch while not letting it be publicly known that's what's going on.

As Laney and I try to cram everything else we can into Prescott's über-man brain, our Russian strategist is working diligently to make sure that when we load our payload onto the truck and drive it up the road, through the iCosmos security gate and into the assembly building, nobody pops the hatch and spots a Navy SEAL hiding inside our mystery rocket.

The obvious solution would be to ask our CEO, Vin Amin, the man who has the keys, permission to do this, but he's an unpredictable risk. If he says "no" and goes public, we're screwed. If he says "Let me think about," and asks one of his government contacts, we run the risk of Silverback finding out and the K1 going boom.

He's already dealing with the fallout of my shenanigans.

We're in a classic ask for forgiveness later scenario. He'll either love us or hate us. Right now we have to make sure we don't get caught.

[60]
MISSION STATEMENT

WHILE I HELP FILL PRESCOTT'S HEAD, people begin to file into the hangar as Markov and Admiral Jessup call in favors. There are eight Navy and Air Force personnel who have clearly worked together before. It's a testament to the amount of trust they have for the two men that they're ready to jump in and get to work without a lot of questions.

Jessup walks each one by me, says something to the effect, "You've never met this man before," and they give me a nod then go about their business setting up an impromptu tracking station in the control room and making sure the DarkStar and its shell are flightworthy.

The manuals are tossed back and forth between us as we try to make sure all the systems are up and running.

Few of them were the original members of the Space Ops crew and the exact specifications are a complete mystery. For all we know, turning the thing on could cause it to blow up.

Prescott puts on the suit and starts to drill, running through the switches and referring to the manual. I want to point things out to him, but know better. If Bennet taught me anything, it's when to back away and let the student teach himself .

"You want me to give you twenty?" I ask Prescott.

"That'd be great," he replies, running a finger down a line of text.

I look over at Laney as she confers with some techs about the spacesuit radio equipment. She might possibly be the most informed person here.

The authority she's been given is a testament to how dire the situation is and the confidence Markov has in her. I think it's well-placed.

The back door raises to let the carryall truck inside. I use the opportunity to step outside and get a breath of night air.

The Cape has always been a special place for me. The launchpads and buildings are spread out between mangroves and serene bays. It's an odd mixture of nature and technology, the past and future.

To the north, the gleaming complexes for NASA, iCosmos, SpaceX and others are brightly lit. I can spot two BFRs, "Big Fucking Rockets," standing on the launchpad waiting to fly into space. Each one weighs more than a battleship and is half as tall as the Empire State Building.

We live in an incredible age. People like Laney get it, so do some of the general public. But I think they're still in that early phase like the internet in the 1990s.

Yes, they know space is an industry now. Sure, they may know of someone who is peripherally involved. But they don't realize how big things are going to get.

If you look in the right direction you can see the US/iCosmos station as it flies by. Every other week a BFR launches with more hardware for it. When it's finished, the K1, the ISS and all the other space stations before will seem like tiny preludes to the future.

The US/iC will rotate in space, giving it artificial gravity. I think the moment people on Earth realize there are people walking around, behaving very much like life down here, yet in space, they'll begin to understand what it's all about.

The US/iC is just the first of many stations being planned. Smaller ones, bigger than the K1 and the ISS, are already coming online. There's even talk by the Chinese to build something even more massive than the US/iC – an actual city in space.

Then there are the spacecraft being built in orbit – ships for going beyond our orbit, to the Moon and the outer planets.

It's an exciting time to be alive.

"It'd be a shame to lose all this," says Laney as she manages to sneak up behind me on her crutches.

"Yeah, I was just thinking about that. This EMP would be bad."

"Technically it's an NMP, a nuclear magnetic pulse, but yeah." She nods to the people in the hangar. "There's a good team in there. Captain Baylor, she's smart. She'll be handling operations."

"With your advice, I hope." I seriously mean that.

"Oh, yeah. They're too short-staffed to kick me out. Let's just hope we can pull it off."

"You're a real trooper. A couple hours ago you had no idea what you were going to get pulled into."

She lets out a laugh. "Are you kidding? This is the kind of thing every space geek dreams about. Well, that and aliens coming down and asking me to go for a joyride. Heck, it's good to be part of something."

I take a look at the people going over equipment, inspecting the DarkStar and planning Prescott's mission. "Yeah. I'm just glad I don't have to be in hiding anymore. At least not here. Not in front of them."

"It must have been hell," says Laney.

"You have no idea. I'm just glad..."

"You don't have to run anymore?"

"Well, I'm worried what will happen if the crazy Russians set off the nuke. That's for sure. But it's nice to stand still for a moment."

I'm still worried that at any moment we're going to be raided by a bunch of soldiers descending from Black Hawks. At least I won't be alone.

Markov joins us outside. "There they are. The fugitive and his accomplice. Have you told everything we need to tell our Space Commando?"

"I'm letting him go over a few things without me breathing down his neck," I reply.

"And he is ready?"

"He'll have to be. There's only so much you can teach someone in this short amount of time. It took me years to get into space."

"Indeed," says Markov. He turns back around and returns to the hangar.

"I guess I should see if there's anything else I can tell Captain Awesome."

[61]
ASSEMBLY

BEFORE WE LOAD THE DARKSTAR onto the carryall truck, Admiral Jessup takes a stand on the flatbed to address us.

"I'll keep this short. We need to have this craft loaded onto here and taken up the road in twenty minutes. We're all used to working in gray zones. Trust me, this isn't gray. I have the authority to act on clear and present dangers – but Congress and the President have the ability to retroactively take that authority back." Jessup points a finger at me. "This man risked everything to bring us valuable information. He's not an officer, not a soldier. He's a private citizen who acted above the call of duty and because of that, even right now he's still in harm's way."

I get a few nods of approval, but I feel like an imposter.

Jessup continues his non-speech speech. "If this goes wrong, hell if it goes right, they can prosecute me and all of you. Now is the time to find something else to do if you're uncomfortable with that."

Predictably, nobody raises a hand or bows out. He chose these men and women wisely.

I look over and see Prescott flipping through the manuals on the bench. We're about to suit him up and load him inside the craft for the two hour wait to the launchpad.

For a guy about to be shot into space, then fired from a missile, he doesn't seem too worried.

God, I wish I had more time to teach him what I can.

I'm sure Bennet felt that way every time he sent one of us chimps into space. That's why he and Peterson took the responsibility of getting onboard the K1 themselves. Some things you can't leave to others.

"After we load the craft, we'll take a six person team to the assembly bay. They're expecting an emergency payload." Jessup points to a female Air Force officer with short black hair, "Captain Baylor will be in charge from the moment we leave this facility. She's supervised load-ins before and knows the right things to say. We need to keep the iCosmos ground crew, with the exception of the payload master, away from the spacecraft.

"We don't know who has ears in iCosmos, but even the most sincere person could tell someone who has been compromised and the mission will be a bust. And I don't need to paint a picture for you of the consequences of that. A high altitude nuclear magnetic burst would be devastating, no matter where it occurs. Let's just leave it at that."

A Naval lieutenant raises his hand. "Admiral, what happens if they don't want to give us access to the launch vehicle?"

"Are you asking what happens if they figure out what we're up to? We leave. There's no way we can take this thing up without their help. To be honest, if there is a problem, it'll appear clerical. We just say that we got the wrong information and turn back around." He points to Prescott, "The real stakes are for him. He's got to go up in that thing and pull off a miracle."

Prescott nods then goes back to the manual.

While Jessup supervises the loading of the DarkStar, I go over to Prescott to see if there's anything else I can help him with.

"You got this," I tell him.

"Thanks. I appreciate that. The fact that you're still alive is a testament to your training."

"Hah. No. I'm just really good at running away from trouble. You're the poor son of a bitch who has to run into it." I think about what he's about to do. "Don't cut the DarkStar loose and don't think this is a one-way trip. You're a hell of a lot smarter than I am and I made it back."

"Well, let's just see how things go," he replies.

Man, this guy is convinced that he won't make it back. I mean, I get it, that's the whole point of commandos and special forces types. They're the ones you send in who you know are going to act selflessly.

Back in the iCosmos locker room there's a wall of astronauts – the folks who made it into space starting with Yuri Gagarin and all the way through to the last astronauts onboard an iCosmos flight.

I was looking forward to seeing my name up there, but now realize that I have no place in a line-up with Yuri, John Glenn and Armstrong. Sure, Bennet and Peterson belong in that special category, but I was a guy flying something that had become routine.

Although technically, what I do share with Yuri Gagarin is the fact that neither one of us actually landed in our spacecraft. We both ejected before we hit the ground. He was acting bravely because he knew what he was doing. I was just acting out of self-preservation.

"Are you ready, Captain Prescott?" asks Jessup.

"Yes, sir." Prescott sets the manual down and walks over to the spacesuit. "Help me with this, Dixon?"

"Did you pee first?"

"Twice."

Laney is watching us from off to the side, double-checking the manuals and not hiding her anxiety.

Jessup and Markov come over to give Prescott some last minute notes.

I open the back panel of the suit so Prescott can slide inside. He stops and takes something out of his thermal pocket and hands it to me.

"Take my picture for my kid?" he asks.

"Yeah, sure."

Prescott stands in front of the spaceship and gives a thumbs up as I take the shot.

"Could you hold onto my phone until I get back?" he says as he slides his head through the neck section.

"Of course." I put it into my pocket and check the status lights.

I know he's not ready.

He's willing, but he's not ready.

Damnit, David.

"When was the last time you had a cardiogram?" I ask, looking over his chest panel.

"Never."

"Never?" I reply, trying to sound shocked. "But you haven't done any scuba diving in the past year, have you?"

"I was doing training in Coronado three weeks ago."

Markov steps over using his canes. "Is there a problem, Mr. Dixon?"

"Yeah...um...we don't let someone fly without a cardiogram if they've been doing diving at depth within the last six months. There can be serious heart problems."

"I'll be fine," says Prescott. "I'm sure lots of people go up now with tickers less healthy than mine.

"Uh...I mean it won't kill you...but there's a higher chance of blacking out. It's okay for a passenger, but not a pilot."

I catch Laney watching me. She's about to say something, but I glare at her.

"Can we get a doctor in here to do a test?" asks Prescott.

I shake my head. "There isn't time. They have to stress test you on a treadmill."

I don't have to do this...

"This presents a problem, Mr. Dixon," says Markov. "And what do you propose for a solution?"

"Well..."

Say it.

You came up with this whole bullshit story because you can't let this man go through this.

My mouth speaks before my brain can think."I'll have to go."

"Are you sure?" asks Markov.

No. "Yes. I think Prescott could pull it off, but there are too many variables."

"I got this," Prescott says.

I know his pride is at play here. "I know. But the heart thing..." I grab the sides of his helmet and start to unhook it.

Prescott looks at Jessup. "Admiral?"

"I agree with Dixon. We can't take the risk."

Prescott reluctantly nods and lets me help him out of the suit.

As he unstraps the gas mask and other equipment from his chest, Laney walks over and uses a free hand to help hold the suit. She leans in and whispers into my ear, "AFI eleven."

[62]
SECURITY PROTOCOLS

AS I SIT INSIDE the cramped cockpit of the DarkStar, waiting for the carryall to make its way down the road to iCosmos, I contemplate my most recent life choice.

All I had to do was let Captain Awesome get into the spaceship and let him do the thing he was trained for. But no, me and my fat mouth.

Was it the fact that he has a kid? Or is it that I knew all along sending him up when there was a perfectly disposable astronaut standing by who already knew what all the knobs did?

What difference does it make? I couldn't let him take my place.

But the thing that gets me is that I know this was Markov's plan all along. I'd be angry at him for manipulating me if I wasn't so upset at myself for allowing it to get that far.

I should have bravely volunteered to do this thing instead of contemplating hiding out in his cabana until the whole thing blew over or blew up.

Even Laney, recruited less than a day ago, was ready to jump right in. Hell, if she thought we'd have taken her seriously, she would have jumped at the chance to be in this tiny seat with a control panel inches from her nose.

"How we doing?" I ask into my radio.

"We're almost at the iCosmos gate," says Prescott.

He's riding shotgun with Jessup in his SUV ahead of the flatbed.

We're counting on the pseudo-crisis aboard the US/iC to cut through the red tape a little.

While Markov has enough people inside and out to smooth things along, if someone gets a little too nosey and decides to dot more "i's" than we have time for, this whole thing could fall apart.

As the carryall comes to a stop, I imagine the security guards checking their clipboards and radioing into the complex about the rocket that just showed up.

Each second stretches much longer than it feels like it should, but that's just my nerves and the fact that I'm going to be spending the next several hours inside of this tin can waiting to see if I get to die in space or Federal prison.

I don't mind the tight quarters all that much. When I was a kid and had my heart set on being an astronaut I watched *The Right Stuff* and paid careful attention to all the difficult things the astronauts had to do.

The toughest was being stuck inside the space capsule not able to take a pee.

Alan Shepard, the first American in space, had to relieve himself inside his spacesuit because NASA kept pushing back the launch window past the limit of any human's endurance.

Not wanting to embarrass myself or go nuts in the claustrophobic space, I'd test myself by seeing how long I could spend inside a cardboard box.

After a few failed attempts at lasting more than a couple minutes, I found out I could last much longer if I poked air-holes in the box.

I decorated the box with decals and named it "The Centennial Hawk," because I was neither original nor clever.

At first I'd assume a yoga-like pose and watch movies on a laptop I placed inside as my control panel. Then I started going into some deeper meditation – or the nine-year-old's version of it.

While my box was no one's idea of a sensory deprivation tank, I went on some wild daydreams sitting inside there contemplating inner space.

This would help me out later on in life when I worked as a guinea pig and a trainee at iCosmos. I spent a lot of time in the huge water tank going through various simulations, waiting for instructions. Lately it's been zero-g construction for all the space stations being built.

I could sit in the bottom of the tank for hours and hours. Although my first launch was just a few days ago, I've spent months aboard the simulated crew modules and Unicorn prototypes.

All of this leads me to the fact that I'm totally okay here in the DarkStar.

I'm fine.

It's my safe place.

I'm. Not. Worried. At. All.

"David?" says Prescott over the radio.

"Yeah!?"

"You okay?"

"Yeah, fine. I was just dozing off."

"Wow, man. I can't imagine how anyone could sleep during all this."

Me neither. "What's going on?"

"They're letting us through. The payload master is going to meet us in the hangar and sign off on everything."

"Just like that?"

"We emphasized the point that the capsule had to be kept sealed because of the water and the new filtering system."

"Right. Good call."

"That was Ms. Washburn's idea."

"Of course."

The capsule starts to vibrate.

"We're moving."

"I can tell. Other than the payload master, does it look good?"

"We think so. We could have you launched in three hours. They're using the bigger booster, so there's some room for adjustment – which works out well for us."

Trying to intercept a space station is no easy feat. If you're off by seconds, the whole thing is thousands of miles from where you need to be and that takes more fuel.

Fortunately, they're putting me on top of a fatter version of the Alicorn that has more fuel and thrust. It's less efficient, but nobody is worried about that right now.

Prescott keeps me up to date with what's going on outside, while trying not to be obvious about the fact that he's talking to a trojan horse.

Occasionally he calls into his headset as if he's talking to someone back at the Air Force operations center.

I hear the voices of iCosmos load engineers as they inspect the feeds and cables on the outer ship.

The dashboard in front of me shows the Unicorn controls and the different readouts as it talks to the computers outside.

From my side everything seems exactly like a military payload module should look. The sensors we want to give back correct data are doing so, and the ones that we need to lie are performing admirably.

As far as the engineer's portable computers tell them, this is just a dumb cargo ship waiting to be sent into space.

"David," Prescott says in a half-whisper. "We're good. They're going to rotate the ship, connect you to the rocket and then tilt you upright in the next half hour."

"Wonderful."

"We're leaving the assembly building but will check in."

"I'll be right here. Until I won't."

"Roger that." He lowers his voice even more, "And um...thanks, man. I know what you did."

Yeah, but do I?

[63]
GRAND THEFT

T-MINUS FORTY MINUTES

After I run through all the different things I'm going to have to do to get DarkStar to the K1, I shut my eyes and try to find my peaceful place.

This mission is a flowchart. One action follows another. There are variables, but most of them are known. The less I think, the better my chances of survival.

Wait, that's not right. This isn't about my survival. This is about getting the nuclear device off the station. What happens to me isn't important. The only course of action that matters is the one where the people on the ground will be safe.

T-Minus thirty minutes

I watch the little lines of code whiz past on the screen and occasionally catch one of the strings I recognize.

When they sent men to the moon their spaceship had less computational power than the key fob you use to open your car. Imagine going back in time with a smart light bulb and trying to explain all the things that make that work.

Now a rocket is really a bunch of code attached to some slightly extraneous hardware. Those same engineers of yesteryear would have no trouble grasping all the parts of the Unicorn and the Alicorn. The fact that we use 3D printers to make the engines might come as a surprise, but the design wouldn't be as radical as the fact that right now I'm waiting for a neural network as intelligent as a small mammal to decide if we're good to proceed.

T-Minus twenty minutes

Everything looks good. We're in a perfect alignment for an orbital intercept with the US/iCosmos and the K1 when the DarkStar does its little maneuver.

Let's just hope they don't decide to laser me. I'm pretty sure the wavelength absorbing material that covers this thing is the exact opposite of what you want around you when you're the target of a high-energy weapon.

T-Minus fifteen minutes

We're in the final stage. In less than a half hour I'll either be in orbit or a firework.

I close my eyes to relax for a moment but have to open them when something bright starts to flash unexpectedly.

I reach a hand out to touch the panel but jerk it back in surprise when Vin's face appears on the screen.

"What are you doing?" he asks.

I freeze, not sure what is going on.

"I can see you, David. Did you know that I monitor every launch from a window on my screen? Not many people do."

"Uh...hey, Vin." Should I unbuckle and try to get out of the ship before security gets here? Hold on...maybe I can talk him out of that. "How did you know I was here?"

"When I started iCosmos I didn't want to get complacent. I promised myself that for at least the first thousand people in space I'd watch and make sure that they got there safely.

"That's a hell of a lot of pressure, if you think about it. If something bad happens, I have to watch it live. Imagine my surprise when my terminal tells me there's a live feed in a cargo module where there shouldn't be. When I open it up, who do I see? You. Have you seen our stock price lately? The board of directors is talking about replacing me..."

"Vin..."

He shakes his head and cuts me off. "Everything I've worked for, David – everything is on the line because of you."

"I didn't have a choice..."

"Really? What are you doing now?"

I think about Markov's warning about the reach of Silverback. "I'm not at liberty to say."

"I'm not stupid, David. I could tell Peterson and Bennet were up to something." I see his arms move as he types on his keyboard. "I just spent the last several days in what I'd technically call Federal custody after three of my astronauts caused an international incident."

All my screens go dark except for his video. He just shut me down.

"Vin! Don't!"

"I'm asking you again, what are you doing here?"

"You have to trust me."

"Do you know why it took so long for you to get a seat on my ship? It's because I have the most comprehensive psychological profiles you could imagine. I have maps of all my astronaut's brains and can predict how they'll act under different situations. Every time your name came up, I'd run your profile and come back with the same answer; you didn't have the right stuff. Your reflexes, your knowledge, your skills – those were off the charts. But there was something about your character that said this was a man who was out for himself. The only reason you got your slot was because Bennet pushed for it. I told him you didn't have what it takes. Your brain was nothing like his. You weren't a hero. You were a survivor. Survivors make great test pilots, but they're not leaders of men. And now here you are, trying to steal a quarter-billion dollars of hardware from me after causing the worst disaster of my life."

"Vin...things are complicated. I can't tell you my mission."

"That's not what I'm asking. I want to know why you're the one sitting here."

"Me?"

"Yes, you, David Dixon. Why you? What happened to Prescott?Did he back out? Was he ill?"

"Wait? You know about this?"

He gives me a pitiful look. "David, nobody does anything here without me knowing. Markov said he was sending up a specialist."

"Prescott wasn't right for the mission."

"And you are?"

"I don't know. I guess I have to be."

Vin gives me his sage-like smile. "And here we are."

"Capricorn?"

"I deny everything." He winks at me then presses a button on his keyboard.

My control panel lights up again.

"I just gave you a better insertion path to the K1. Four minutes to launch. Anything I can do for you?"

I think he means if I don't make it back. "Tell my parents I love them. Um, give Laney Washburn a chance to fly. Oh, yes, some kids in Rio helped me out. I forget the name of the neighborhood in Rio. Maybe see if you can get them into a school or something?"

"I'll find them."

"Thank you."

"Have a safe trip. When this is all over you should come out to the yacht."

"Only if you promise to lend me the silver Speedos you had on at Burning Man."

[64]
PROJECTILE

THIS LAUNCH IS JUST AS JARRING as the last the one. While rockets are a thing of beauty to see take off from the ground, being inside one is a slightly different experience. You're stuck between two forces that want to crush you and shake your brain loose from your spinal cord.

There's the rocket below you, burning millions of gallons of fuel in what can be best described as a controlled explosion. Above you is the earth's atmosphere. Maybe that doesn't seem like much, but think about when you were a little kid and stuck your hand out the car window and what it felt like when the wind slapped into it. Now imagine the wind is slamming into you at 7,000 miles an hour.

What's totally different than last time is the fact that I'm not in my comfy iCosmos form-fitting couch. The chair inside the DarkStar is a few straps stretched over an aluminum frame. I'm afraid I'm going to bust through it any second like my fat aunt on a cheap lawn chair.

One time in college a few of my buddies took turns riding around inside the trunk of an old Impala. It was a dumb, dumb thing to do.

When it was my turn, Ross, my sophomore year roommate, decided to go off-roading.

That trunk was a veritable Versailles compared to the inside of the DarkStar.

I'd give anything to be back in there right now with Mad Ross at the wheel, spinning out in the dirt lot behind Target.

I watch the readout as the countdown hits Max Q – the point where the rocket reaches the maximum impact against the atmosphere.

It's not exactly smooth sailing from here, but if there's a point where this fake space capsule is going to crush like a tin can and the rocket rip itself apart from stress, I just passed it.

Don't get me wrong, lots of things can still go horribly wrong. But we just passed a critical point. The atmosphere begins to get rapidly thinner around here and the vibration settles down a little.

I still have the gurgling roar of the rocket to remind me that I'm one misplaced decimal away from oblivion.

I get ready for the kick of the second stage booster as it separates from the primary booster.

BOOM and we shoot forward like a champagne cork from a bottle.

Meanwhile, the primary booster begins its descent back to Earth where it will land on the launchpad – making me kinda wish I was riding that down right now.

I'm now entering the 60 mile-zone that people generally agree is space.

Fun fact: the first manmade object in space was a Nazi V2 rocket in 1942. Space historians and people who like to remind you how there would be no private space industry without NASA tend to gloss over how much those goose-stepping assholes contributed to rocket technology.

Now I'm about to pass the 108 mile record they set, which basically means I'm beating Hitler again.

At this altitude, if I could look out a window, I'd see stars. But I can't, because I'm inside a black bullet designed for stealth.

Six more minutes of burn on the second stage and then we have separation. That's when the real excitement begins.

Right now I'm just doing the same launch profile we've done thousands of times before. The never-been-done-before part comes when the second stage detaches and the fake-Unicorn begins its approach to the US/iCosmos.

In order to make things look legit to anyone tracking on long range radar or telescope, at the same time the second stage engine disconnects, the DarkStar is going to launch from it.

I read the manuals and studied the interface, but I still have no damn idea what's going to happen.

What I can tell is that there's a very large cylinder between my legs like the hump of a long horse. This bad boy is filled with LMP-103S – a chemical that reacts with a catalyst and produces about 30% more thrust than the hydrazine we use on the Unicorn spacecraft.

To really appreciate the situation I'm in, you can't think of me as sitting on top of a rocket as I get pushed into space: Instead, imagine a rocket engine itself with all those tubes and metal guts – and I'm strapped inside there. Basically, DarkStar is all engine and no rocket.

That's how Admiral Jessup's engineers figured out how to put one powerful rocket inside of another – they decided to have the astronaut straddle the most dangerous part.

Sure, there's some heat insulation that's supposed to protect my testicles from frying like eggs, but this has never been tested. For all I know, they melted the last three crash test dummies they put here.

The upside is that I'm pretty sure I'm going to black out the moment the rocket fires. The K1 is on the other side of the earth and I have to race like a bat out of hell to get into an elliptical orbit that will not only match its speed, but put me on a parallel path. All without them knowing I'm even sneaking up on them.

To do this, the DarkStar is designed to pick up another two thousand miles an hour of speed beyond the velocity of the Unicorn.

Most of it all at once.

Did I mention that the main rocket engine on the DarkStar is running between my legs?

Not in some cool this-is-my-pseudo-phalus kind of way. No, this is more of a this-monopropellant-thruster-is-about-to-violate-you-like-no-man-should-ever-be-violated kind of way.

"You ready to go?" asks Laney on the comm.

"No. Not really."

"Too bad. Time to man up."

"Baylor here, I'll be doing the countdown in mark..."

Oh, crap. Here we go...

5

4

3

2

[65]
THRUSTER

THE ROCKET KICKS on and I feel a rumble words cannot describe.

"MOTHER OF GOD!"

"You okay, Dixon?" asks Baylor.

"THIS IS INSANE!"

"I think he's enjoying it," says Laney.

"THE POWER! ALL THE POWER!"

I think I need a cigarette. Holy shit. I just got violated by a mothballed Navy secret weapon and I think I kind of liked it.

Hell. I know I did.

Jesus. Christ.

I don't care if the DarkStar doesn't return my texts tomorrow. There will always be this magical moment I can take with me forever.

In pilot circles there's a kind of physical envelope we all strive for. It's that borderline place between going so fast you're about to black out and the sensation that your body is moving impossibly fast and you're sort of at one with the universe.

Ernst Mach, the guy who got to name a whole unit of speed, once theorized that inertia was the property of the gravitational force of all the matter in the universe acting on a body.

Relativity provided a much better explanation, but in that perfect moment of acceleration you feel like the universe is trying to hold you back – and failing.

For several glorious minutes, the DarkStar thrusted me along that edge.

This is why I became a pilot. And to think I was going to let some Navy squid have all the fun. Not on my watch.

"Hey, Dixon," says Captain Baylor over my comm after the burn. "Did you survive?"

"Survived is an understatement. When I get back I'm changing my relationship status for this machine."

"I'm sure you two will make a great couple. The good news is your trajectory looks great. We're using the spread spectrum radio for telemetry since we can't pick you up on radar."

"What's the bad news?"

"What? Oh, there isn't any. I guess I phrased that poorly. Hold on, Markov wants to speak with you."

"Hello, David. How are you doing?"

"Fantastic." I know better than to mention that I spoke to Vin about the launch. Even within our small group of rocket thieves I have to be careful.

"Well, I'm the bearer of bad news. I have confirmation that Zhirov has his commanders working on a improvised trigger for the nuclear device."

"Um, dumb question, where is the rest of the crew on this? Any chance of getting them to mutiny and save us all some trouble?"

"Unfortunately, no. Although they have not been informed of what is actually taking place, they're not likely to be in a position to try to stop this."

I knew it was too much to hope for. Although the crew of Skylab 4 did a kind of mutiny back in 1973 when they thought they were being pushed too far. Ultimately they returned to work; although NASA never let any of the men fly again.

I imagine the fear of crossing Zhirov goes a bit beyond being forced to retire at your current government pay grade.

"You can expect that at least one or both men will be in the secure module when you arrive," says Markov.

"And your insider, they're all set?"

"Essentially."

"Essentially? What does that mean?"

"I still have to do some persuasion."

"Okay." I have no idea how he's talking to the cosmonaut, let alone what carrot he's dangling in front of them. Fast Passes for Space Mountain? Well...Soviet Premier Nikita Khrushchev did have a hissy fit back in 1959 when he was told he couldn't visit Disneyland because of security concerns.

"I'll let you know."

"Please do. I'm less than twenty minutes out from the K1. I'd like to know that when I knock on the door someone will let me in."

"Baylor here. So, uh Dixon, are you comfortable with Laney Washburn giving you the technical details of the K1? I know she's a civvy, but she knows more than anyone here."

"Is this a joke? Hell, yes."

Laney hops on the comm, "You know you're not supposed to knock, right?"

"Yes, Laney. It was a figure of speech."

"Okay. Just checking."

"I think I'll just poke my head into the main viewport and wave to everyone. Maybe moon them."

"Sure." She gets right down to business. "We got some schematics that show the collision radar for the K1. It looks like the DarkStar will be fine if you leave her at the end of the tether. They won't spot that.

"But as far as you're concerned, they'll definitely be able to detect your suit once you exit. However, since the explosive decompression of the airlock, they've been having issues with the sensors, plus there's debris still floating around the station."

Debris... "Um, Laney. Do you know if..."

"Yeah. Baylor says they retrieved her body. Side note, they're still refusing to turn them over to us."

"Seriously?"

"Yeah. Markov says it's blustering by Zhirov to keep everyone distracted."

"What do they want? Oh, never mind." Me.

"Right. So anyway, once the DarkStar is over the K1, it'll orient itself nose down. You'll need to exit through the rear hatch and use your suit thrusters to make it to the station. Once you're within 50 meters you'll be inside their blindspot. From there you'll need to make your way to the spacewalk airlock on the south end of the station. Got it?"

"Roger."

"Here. Type 'CAMAFT.1' into the terminal. I found out they have a pinhole camera array embedded into the DarkStar's skin."

A screen pops up on my console and I see the tiny white speck of the K1 as it grows closer. "Oh, this is helpful."

"We'll be right here if you need anything. We're going to try to keep the chatter to a minimum though, in case they have an antenna listening for stray signals."

"Got it."

A number counts down the meters as the K1 grows closer. The tricky part, which thankfully, the computer is handling, is figuring out how to match velocity and direction with the K1 without using too much fuel and making it obvious that a rocket is approaching.

Most of my acceleration was compensated for by using an elliptical path that put me on a steep climb where the earth's gravity could slow me down – kind of like a curveball.

Through the walls of the DarkStar I can hear the hissing sound of the micro-jets making tiny course adjustments, accounting for the remainder of my speed.

As the K1 grows from a tiny white pinpoint to a massive cross I get a chill down my spine when I think about what happened here just three days ago.

All I wanted to do was get to safety. Now here I am, about to jump right into the stupid middle.

[66]
TOUCH DOWN

THE DARKSTAR MAKES one tiny little course adjustment and I come to a stop, 100 meters directly over the K1. We're still on the dayside, so the K1 is a brilliant gleaming cross in the middle of four iridescent blue squares of solar panels.

On my display panel the K1 sits perfectly in the middle like a cross-hair over the earth. In a few minutes we'll pass over the horizon into the night side and the K1 will be a giant black square against the glittering lights of the cities below.

I check my suit to make sure my life-support is working then call in to my fellow outlaws below.

"What's the word?"

Captain Baylor is on the comm. "So far we haven't detected any unusual radio signals from the K1. It looks like you're a go for EVA."

"Okay...what's the status of Markov's man or woman on the inside? Will anybody be there when I come calling?"

"We're checking on that..."

"Checking? It's kind of important."

"Hold on."

I finish inspecting my suit and get ready for my EVA out the hatch behind me.

"Baylor here. Markov says to proceed. He's sent a message to the operative."

"But there hasn't been a reply..."

"Affirmative. They may not be in a position to do so. We think it's best if you head to the airlock and wait there."

"Sure." I mean, what else am I going to do?

I lower the seat back and attach the EVA strap to a clip on my waist. It's basically a giant fishing reel I'll use to keep me tethered to the DarkStar until I reach the K1, where I'll attach it to a clamp there.

The nice thing about modern space stations is that they've got more handrails than an old folks home. The challenge is going to be getting from here to there.

The thing about zero-gravity is that although it looks like you're Superman flying through the air, he gets to change his mind about what direction he wants to travel mid-flight. I don't.

To train for this, iCosmos has a huge blacked-out warehouse with a very smooth floor and a robot arm that glides around on an air cushion, supporting you. You kick off replicas of the Unicorn and US/iCosmos modules and fly through the air with nothing to stop you except another surface.

You get a deep appreciation for Newton's First Law of Motion very quickly. All you have to do is misjudge where you plan on landing by a few inches and you'll watch your intended destination whiz past at the same velocity you kicked off.

In real space there's no padded wall to run into. You just eventually burn up in the atmosphere and cremate yourself.

While my spacesuit has jets that fire compressed gas, this is very limited. With nobody out here to lifeguard me, it's important I get it right the first time.

I turn the vent valve and the DarkStar releases the air inside the capsule in all six directions at once so it doesn't start shooting around like a balloon.

This was a clever feature I noticed in the manual. On a ship this small, venting just 20 cubic feet of air would send it flying and defeat the whole "stealth" thing.

The front of the ship is pointed down at the K1 and Earth like the pointy tip of an ice cream cone. When I open the hatch at the back, my eyes are greeted by thousands of stars. The sun is directly behind the door and the DarkStar, true to its name, doesn't reflect any light.

I give myself a few seconds to appreciate the view then push myself out of the compartment. Once I move outside the shadow of the DarkStar I'll be visible to the K1's radar, so moving quickly is important.

There's no way I'll be able to completely avoid detection in my suit, but if I'm just a quick blip, I should be okay.

I think.

[67]
STANDBY

I GLIDE OUT OF THE OPENING, then use the edge of the hatch to bring myself into an upside down position. That's another thing, while you can bend around your center of gravity in space, trying to do a somersault is a practical impossibility without anything to act against.

I gently push away from the DarkStar and begin to move out from behind its shadow. When I'm a meter away I activate the jets on my pack and a tiny spurt of air sends me towards the K1.

It doesn't look like I'm moving at first – and that's a good thing. If I was at running speed, like 25 MPH, that means I'd hit the K1 at that velocity – which is the same as falling from a two-story building and landing on your face.

The tip of the upper spire on the K1 gradually grows closer while the tether at my waist spools out a thin line fast enough to keep pace without getting tangled.

My target is the cross-shaped module at the end of the spire. This is the section that juts upwards from the station.

Although I tend to think of the K1 as built like a cross, it's actually more like a little toy jack.

As I get closer I can see inside the top module through a skylight. Thankfully, nobody is looking back at me.

A few meters from impact, I reach my hands out to soften my fall. I spot a railing around the window near me and grasp it.

Boom. We have touchdown. I think I hit soft enough to not make a big noise inside.

"I'm on the K1," I report into my comm.

I take the tether from my belt and clip it to the handrail.

When I look up at the DarkStar my heart does a flip flop when it's not there.

Duh.

Stealth ship.

Even the tether is invisible past a few meters.

I pull myself along the rails to a set of handholds that lead down the upper module and to the side of the airlock.

Okay. If everything else plays out this smoothly, I'll have a nuclear device in my hands in the next few minutes and be ready to take this thing home.

"OPS, any word on the insider?"

"Hello, David. This is Markov," he says in case the accent wasn't a tip-off. "There's been a complication. I'm unable to reach my operative. We suspect the commanders of the K1 may have restricted the other crew."

"Hold up. Are you saying there's nobody here to let me in?"

"That is correct. Until further notice we need you to stand by."

"And if you can't get hold of your operative?"

"We're working on a contingency."

"Um, Markov, I'm not sure if you realize there really aren't any contingencies. I need someone on the inside to open this airlock. It's not like I brought C4 and can blow my way in."

"I understand that. Please stand by..."

I can tell he's just as frustrated as I am. After everything we've gone through to get this far, to come this close and fall short...

I stand by and stand by some more. It's not the worst place to wait for the end of the modern world.

Below me the earth moves into its nightside and I see the sparkling lights of southeast Asia. The entire half of the Pacific Rim is a glittering crescent.

"David. We've intercepted some chatter from Roscosmos. We have confirmation that the commanders have locked down the crew."

I turn my attention back to the present. "Meaning what?"

"My operative cannot get to you and we think that Zhirov may be planning something imminently."

"Are they going to blow the whole station or use some kind of satellite ejector?"

"We don't know. Either way, the most prudent course of action is for you to return to the DarkStar and come back to Earth."

Well, damn.

[68]
POINT OF ENTRY

WELL, THIS SUCKS. I can't seem to catch a break lately.

My body begins to dangle away from the station and I have to remember to pull myself back in, lest someone looking up from their nuclear device sees me chilling out here.

Okay, so Markov says I have to return. He's obviously very certain that his operative is not going to be able to let me inside. Without their help, I'm in a bit of a bind here.

There are only two EVA airlocks on this station. There's the one a meter from my head and the other one on the bottom of the station, adjacent to the airlocks where spaceships dock.

Both of the EVA airlocks require someone on the inside to depressurize them and unlock the hatch.

While they both have an emergency release – in case someone gets trapped outside, there's no way I can use that and not send the whole station into an alert causing all the sections to seal. At best, I would make it into the upper module and not any further before they caught me.

The whole point of an inside man was to let me inside discreetly. Without that element of surprise, there's not much I can do.

Alright, David, is there another way inside?

Think outside of the box.

With some tools I could take apart a window and go inside one of the modules...except the explosive decompression would send the station spinning and let everyone know they have a visitor. So, dumb idea.

Okay, is there a way I could get them to let me in?

Maybe knock on their door and trick them into an EVA?

Okay, no Bugs Bunny techniques. What if I take out their communications antennas? Would the commanders decide to send someone out here?

Put that on the "maybe" list.

What other options are there?

"OPS, what's the condition of the docking module?"

"Have you returned to the DarkStar yet?" asks Baylor.

"Negative. I'm weighing other options."

"What other options? Markov says you should return."

"I understand that. But he's also not an astronaut. I repeat, what is the status of the docking module?"

"From what we understand there are two Russian craft berthed there. The third dock is damaged from the Unicorn incident and the fourth one is empty. But you can't open the hatch without causing the inner module to decompress. It's not intended for hard vacuum."

"I understand that. Hold on."

"Hold on for what?"

"I'm thinking of something."

"David, you should be planning your return. You don't want to be up there when the nuke goes off."

"No shit. I don't want to be anywhere when that goes off."

"Hold on. Markov wants to speak to you."

"David, I appreciate your bravery but it's time to come home."

"Hold up. There might be another option."

"Perhaps. But if you blow their airlock we believe they'll suspect an intruder and move up their plans to use the device. It could be...counterproductive."

"Yeah, I get it. What if I could get in without them knowing?"

"You would be a miracle worker."

"Well, put my helper on the line, I think I have an idea."

"What are you thinking?" asks Laney.

"I once saw a documentary where Stephen Hawking explained that as a boy he found seventeen ways into his house while his sister only knew of twelve."

"I guess boys are biologically programmed to figure out how to sneak through windows," she replies.

"Well, I did it with yours..."

I think I can hear the sound of her blushing.

"Anyway...I got to thinking. I think I know another way to get in."

"You can't open the docking airlocks to vacuum."

"Yes. I know. I also know that I can't blow the EVA airlock either. Noted. May I continue?"

"Sorry. What are you thinking?"

"I think I know another way inside."

"Go on..."

"The Russian spacecraft docked below, is it standard procedure to leave the hatches open or closed to the inside of the K1?"

"Closed, but not locked. If the station decompresses it's easier to get into. If one of the ships gets a leak the air pressure from the station will keep the hatch...HOLY SHIT DAVID! You're smarter than you look!"

I hear her yell to everyone in our command center. "David figured out a way inside the K1! I'm going to put you back with Baylor while I pull up some manuals of the Russian ship. AFI 12 if you pull it off."

"Baylor here. What is this madness that has your groupie all flustered?"

"First, I think I'm her groupie. Second, I have a plan. I don't go through the K1. I go through the side hatch on one of the Russian ships. I think I can do this without sending the K1 into full-alert."

"Hmmm...Yeah, with the other docking ring damaged they probably shut off the emergency alarms on that section. And if you go through the hatch on one of their birds and seal it back up, you can open the inner lock to the K1. Good call. Here's Markov."

"David, how certain are you that this will work?"

"Not at all. But it gets around the concern we had with using the EVA airlocks. The ships are on a separate system. As long as the K1 has hull integrity it won't cause a problem."

"Alright. Proceed with your plan. But if there is any complication, return to the DarkStar immediately."

"You got it."

Great, me and my big mouth. I had a perfectly good opportunity to go home and I just blew it.

[69]
PRESSURE

DISTANCE IS A DIFFERENT concept in space. From here to the docking module it's just a hundred meters, but I can't exactly stroll there or use my suit jets to go whizzing by. I have to do it like my monkey ancestors did it climbing through trees – hand over hand.

There's plenty of railing to pull myself along. The trick is grabbing it. Gloves on a spacesuit aren't like the type for doing the dishes and a spacesuit isn't just a bag to hold air. They're essentially a mini-pressurized spaceship that keeps you from blowing up like a balloon.

The old ones were basically a bladder that squeezed you like an arm pressure cuff – but all over your body. The modern ones are made from skintight material that's essentially a full-body corset. The exception is the hands and the head.

My helmet is a pressurized fish bowl and my gloves are still the old-style bladder that squeezes the hands and has a habit of causing your fingernails to fall off.

This is fine for light work and maneuvering, but for more physically challenging jobs like building the US/iCosmos, spaceworkers use mechanical extensions where their hands sit inside cozy little pockets controlling mechanical fingers. This works well enough, but the long arms make you look like a chimpanzee – which is why we call them "chimp gloves."

I'd kill for a pair right now. Pulling myself along on the rails is fine for a few meters, but I can really feel it in my hands.

I'm tempted to just yank really hard and let myself soar over the module, but there's the very real chance I might sail past the last hand grip and keep going into space.

On the US/iC they have robot lifeguards that will retrieve you if that happens. There's nothing like that on the K1.

I move down the EVA spire and start crawling out along the storage module, hoping there's nobody inside who can hear me.

I could take a shortcut and move through the gap between the solar panels and the station, but I'm terrified of clipping a panel or getting caught as they make their orbital adjustment.

Even up here in free fall, there are tiny bits of atmosphere that drag on the massive surfaces. Every 45 minutes the panels change their pitch slightly as the K1 goes into and comes out of the part of its elliptical orbit that brings it closer to the earth. I'd prefer not to get stuck like a fly on a window wiper blade.

"How you doing, Dave?" Laney asks over the comm.

"Awesome. All that time I spent on the monkey bars at recess is really paying off. If Amy Schweiger could see me now."

"Was she your first crush?"

"No. My first bully. She tried to pull anyone off the bars when they crossed them. Never got me, best she ever managed was pantsing me."

"So you were that clueless about women even back then?"

"I reckon."

"How do your fingers feel?"

"I think the nails are still attached, if that's what you mean."

"I heard some astronauts used to have them removed for long space walks."

"About the most I'll consider doing is shaving my...So, how is Earth?"

"Fine, I guess. Can't wait to get off it. Markov still hasn't heard anything. There's lots of chatter on the Russian side. The US is getting a little antsy."

"What happens when intelligence agencies start intercepting the words 'nuclear' and 'space'?"

"Do you have all your porn backed up to an EMP-proof medium?"

"I think the magazines under my mattress are safe."

"What's a magazine?"

"Hilarious."

I swing over the outer pylon so I'm "under" the station and start pulling myself back towards the center. I spot the two Russian ships berthed on the docking module below me.

I try to take my mind off the fact that I'm 200 miles over the planet. "So, you made any progress on the Russian manuals?"

"Yep. You know Russian, right?"

"Mostly just a working knowledge of what switches do what. But I wouldn't trust myself to take something apart without instructions."

"The Russian Army used to have their equipment designed so an illiterate kid from the middle of the Ukraine could repair them."

"Guess what? A functionally illiterate kid from California is going to have a try at that."

"I've marked down what tools you brought that you'll need to get inside."

"Excellent. Because I am now descending the lower pylon towards the docking module and I can already see Ivanka."

"Ivanka?"

"My sweet, sweet Russian ride. I realize that I've stolen...hold on...I forgot about the ambulance...eight vehicles so far. Nine if you count the rental car I'm probably not going to return. Ivanka will be ten. Although technically I'm not stealing her."

"Just violating her."

"She's asking for it – all shiny and metal like that."

"Well, you're going to need some help so you don't blow it. Literally. There's a safe way to get that hatch open without setting off the charges or causing it to explode from the internal air pressure. And then there's the bad way."

"I vote the safe way. I'm working my way down now."

My handrails have sadly come to an end. In order to work on the hatch I have to position myself in such a way that I don't drift away.

Laney is way ahead of me as she explains where to find the hooks to clip my belt tether. "There are four on the nose section and another above and below the hatch."

"You're a lifesaver."

Zero-g mountain climber-style, I attach myself to one and push myself to the other and stick a finger through the opening and refasten the tether.

"Boom. I'm over the hatch."

"Great. Now stop saying "boom" and look for a small circle with the words 'Vozdushnyy klapan vykhlopnykh.' You read Cyrillic, right?"

"Like a glove."

"You're not inspiring confidence down here."

"Not so much up here either. Found it. Now what?"

"Take your hex tool and insert it into the slot and turn to the right."

"Okay. Ready to proceed."

I give it a twist and my hand gets pushed back from the pressure of the escaping air. If I hadn't been expecting it, I might have let go of the tool, which would have been bad.

"Give it about two minutes, then see if you can feel any air coming out."

I count backwards to zero and check with the palm of my glove. "Nothing."

"Great. Captain Baylor just gave me a thumbs up. Which I think means we didn't set off any alarms. You ready to dismantle the hatch so you can put it back together again?"

"You got it."

I spend the next twenty minutes taking apart the release mechanism so I can open the door from the outside. It'd be a two-minute job on Earth, but I don't have a convenient place to set my tools down or any of the small parts I remove. If I lose something up here, it becomes a satellite.

At last I'm able to unlock the door and swing it open. I then tediously replace all the parts so I can seal it. If I don't do that, I'll depressurize the K1...again.

"Hatch shut. I'm inside."

"Okay. You know how to work the manual airlock from here and equalize pressure?"

"Yes, ma'am. Starting now."

The PFFFFFTTTTT sound of air entering Ivanka is inaudible at first but soon grows louder before equalizing.

"Capsule air pressure equalized with the K1. Ready to equalize suit pressure."

I feel a cold rush of air as my suit fills with the atmosphere of the K1. My nostrils are immediately greeted by the scent of melting plastic.

I think that's normal. But I can't really remember.

"Okay Dark Ops, ready to cross the threshold and commit an act of piracy."

"Proceed, David...carefully."

[70]
INVADER

I RELUCTANTLY slide out of my spacesuit. I have to take it off to get to the gas mask I strapped to my chest and the other tools I didn't want to expose to hard vacuum and freezing cold.

For a brief moment I consider leaving it on for the added safety factor it provides as lightweight armor, but ultimately decide it'll cut down on my mobility. Also, although the backpack has a slim profile, the last time I flew through the K1, I didn't exactly do it gracefully.

I shove the suit into a cargo net on Ivanka's bulkhead then put the tools into my thermal suit pockets. Afraid I'll electrocute myself, I shove the stun glove into a pocket by my ankle.

I take one more moment to adjust the radio over my ear and send a final message back to Earth.

"About to enter the K1. I'll be silent for a while."

"Go ahead and leave your channel open so we can hear you, David," says Baylor. Now that the technical part is over, she's taking point on the commando part of the mission.

Right now there's a room full of people listening in down there, silently passing notes.

I've been there. In stressful situations, like this, you choose one person at a time to help the astronaut through.

This can either be a friendly voice or someone with technical know-how.

Back at iCosmos we have a couple of NASA veterans who'll get on the comm with people during extended spacewalks and tell you stories and jokes to keep you company.

It's incredibly reassuring to listen to someone who made it to space in a different era talk you through a complicated situation.

Right now I think I'd like Prescott to tell me some Navy SEAL tales that don't involve throat slitting or mission failure. Instead, I have to settle for radio silence and the constant hiss of the K1.

A space station is filled with hundreds of noises. The best description I've encountered is that it's like living inside an old motel air conditioner.

Besides the hissing sounds of the air vents, there's the variety of hums and knocking sounds coming from everywhere. Because a space station is free-floating, vibrations really don't have anywhere to go.

One of the virtual reality simulations we do is called "Knock Knock." The point of it is to see how quickly you can find a mysterious rattle inside the space station. More than a game, this could come in handy if someone's scientific spinny-thingy is going to vibrate loose an entire module.

I push Ivanka's hatch all the way open and slide into the docking module. Directly in front of me there's bright yellow tape across the hatch where the Unicorn was docked. I guess they don't want to take the chance that someone will try to use the damaged docking collar.

The hatch to the upper pylon is closed. I put my ear to the metal and listen to the hum of the station. Reasonably confident there's not a troop of Russian space marines on

the other side, I spin the wheel and open the entran
the next section.

Last time I was here, I was in a bit of a rush. Now I'n
taking my sweet time. Nuke or no nuke, I don't want to
run into the commanders or anyone else unprepared.

I reach the end of the lower pylon and stop myself
before gliding into the junction that leads to the four
different modules and the upper spire.

Everything is quiet. The emergency lights aren't
flashing like last time, so there's that. But I don't hear
people talking.

The secure section is at the end of the module to my
left. At least one of the commanders must be inside there
with the nuke.

The main crew section is directly ahead of me. This is
where the kitchen and the sleeping quarters are located.
Behind me are the laboratories. The other side is the
storage section.

Which way?

If I want to get into the secure section I'll need one of
the commanders to use as a puppet. I take the stun glove
out, slide it over my left hand, then shove the combat
syringe into that sleeve so I can get to it quickly.

Okay, all I need to do now is to just slip past all the
other crew and paralyze a Russian combat-veteran.

Perfect.

Maybe it would have been a better idea if Prescott was
here instead.

[71]
REC ROOM

I FLIP A MENTAL COIN and pull myself down the module leading to the secure section. If I encounter a commander I need to get him alone, and not in the middle of a bunch of cosmonauts who might not be too happy to see my smiling face again.

The section is a long tunnel of connected modules extending over a hundred feet. The part with the bomb is supposed to be close to the very end. From the look of things, half that section is closed off.

I glide along the passageway, keeping an eye on the small cubby holes lining the sides that occasionally lead to add-on modules. I don't want to get brained by someone hiding in the shadows with a monkey wrench.

I come to a stop a few feet below the window on the access hatch for the secure module. Using the handle as a support, I slowly raise my head up to play peekaboo through the window.

I'm sure there's some stealthy SEAL way to do this using a mirror or spit and bubblegum. I just steal a quick look then duck back down like a two-year-old playing hide and seek.

The next section appears empty. The hatch at the far end is shut, so that means at least one of the commanders is probably behind there.

Ever so gently, I give the wheel on the hatch a twist to
see if I can get it to open....except it doesn't budge. I try
the other way and still have no luck.

Just to be doubly certain, I read the Russian
instructions on the hatch to make sure I'm doing it right.

Yep. This sucker is locked from the inside.

So that's going to complicate my whole Weekend at
Bernie's routine with the lifeless body of a commander if
I get the chance to make him lifeless – there's nobody in
this section to put on a show for. They're secured by two
sealed doors.

Wonderful.

I push back towards the junction and try to think of
another option.

I could try taking the door apart. I just have to make
sure that I do it quietly. I'll also need more substantial
tools than the one I used to penetrate Ivanka.

Surely, somewhere on this station I can find them. But
before I go on a scavenger hunt I need to get my captive.
It'd be awkward digging through a tool chest only to have
one of them find me first.

At the intersection I veer left and push myself into the
crew module. There's a hatch slightly ajar at the far end.

I pass canvas pouches lining the walls holding
belongings. There are workstations with laptops and
loops on the hull to slide your feet into so you don't drift
away.

Past this area, there's a kitchen section across from a
small table where the crew can take communal meals as
their condiments float in front of them.

Interspersed among the space hardware and quick fixes
of patch cords and handwritten signs telling you what not
to touch, there are photos and cartoons stuck to the walls
like you'd find in any other workplace.

200 miles up, in the most inhospitable environment you can imagine, people are still people. I notice a number of XKCD comics, popular among the smartest of nerds, with little yellow Post-It notes attached saying things like, "Sergey, this is a Star Trek reference," or "Sergey, -sudo is a command that gives you ultimate control over a computer."

Poor Sergey, it's not enough he doesn't get nerd humor, he has to be reminded of it by his co-workers.

I pass the closet that holds the toilet. For a decade the Russians were beating us in the arms race for the best way to use the john in space. The one on the ISS used to break down occasionally, forcing astronauts to use "Apollo bags" – which was an invention that never really caught on like Tang or Velcro. Although none of those were actually invented by NASA. They probably consider heat shielding a much better invention to lay claim to than doing number two in a plastic bag that seals with a pre-attached sticky strip.

There's a very dark period of my astronaut guinea pig experience I prefer not to think about that involved sitting in a chair that could rotate in any direction up or down and having bodily functions as technicians watched.

I repress that memory as I float through the last hatch and enter a section of small closets holding sleeping bags. Each little cubicle has photos and decorations belonging to individual astronauts.

Early concepts for living on space stations involved communal sleeping bunks that astronauts could use in shifts. While this is fine for a 19-year-old sailor on a submarine, it's not a viable solution for professionals used to having their own homes. Even a tiny section to call your own and retreat to is better than nothing.

I'm a little worried that I haven't seen any astronauts; not even someone catching a nap.

I reach the end of the module, do a flip and make my way back towards the junction.

The section directly ahead is the labs. To my right is the storage section. I decide to head towards there.

There's a sealed door midway down the module. The crew might be hanging out on the other side, doing who knows what.

There's no window, so I put my ear to the hatch and listen.

The only sound is the hundreds of vibrations and hums of the station.

I float back and take a look at the wheel to the hatch and realize there's a crowbar wedged into the spokes, preventing it from being opened from the other side.

Well, that's kind of weird.

I quietly slide it free and stow it in a fabric pouch so it doesn't drift into my skull later on.

I turn the wheel as slowly as possible. When it makes a "click" I push it open and peer inside.

The next section is dark except for the blinking of dozens of tiny lights.

I pull myself a little further inside and suddenly feel an arm go around my neck and squeeze tightly until the little blinking lights fade.

[72]
CAPTIVE AUDIENCE

I'M PRETTY SURE I'm not dead. For one, I'm still thinking, which is a good sign. For another, although I can't see, I'm pretty sure that the afterlife isn't just the sound of a bunch of Russians arguing.

They're going too fast for me to pick up. All I can gather is they've been trapped in here until I opened the door.

From what else I can surmise, I'm not exactly being heralded as their rescuer – my hands and feet are bound.

I'm not sure how many times someone has been tied up like this in space, but I can tell you that not only is it uncomfortable, I keep banging into the wall.

"Prostite! Prostite!" I say in Russian, begging their pardon.

Someone whips off the hood. A man with a head shaped like an orange points a finger at me and shouts in Russian, "It's him!"

There are four others in the module. I recognize the red-haired woman, Sonin, from the first time I was up here. There's another woman, a little older with blond hair and two men. Neither of them was the one that stared me down in the Unicorn.

"Why are you here?" asks Sonin.

"Why have you tied me up?"

"You ask questions not," growls the round-headed man.

"Let me guess, you're Sergey."

"See! He is spotter!"

"That's spy, Sergey," says Sonin. "Why are you here?"

Sergey isn't having any of this. "We must tell Commander Yablokov!"

"Yablokov is the one that locked us in here," says the blond. "Let's see what the American has to say."

"I say you let me go and we talk about this like civilized people."

The other man watches me quietly from the sideline. I can see he's holding something behind his back.

I nod towards him. "And tell this guy to lay off whatever he's got planned?"

They ignore my plea to be set free.

"Okay... So we're just going to hang out here while your commanders start World War III? Fine. I can chill."

"What do you mean?" asks the blond woman.

"Hi, I'm David Dixon." I manage to tumble around and bring my open hand towards her.

"You are not amusing. Last time you were here we lost a crew member."

"Well, if he was helping your commanders with what's in the secure section, then it wasn't much of a loss. Two good people died up here because of what you assholes are hiding."

Sergey turns red, raises a fist and kicks off towards me.

Sonin pushes him out of the way. "Nyet!" She turns to me with an equally angry expression. "Explain everything now!"

"Fine. You just want the broad strokes? Your boss back in Roscosmos, Zhirov, had his pals smuggle a nuclear weapon up here so he can use it to threaten President Radin in a coup attempt. Right now your commanders are squirreled away in the secure module trying to figure out how to make it go 'boom' without the trigger chip my friends stole."

"This is lie," says Sergey.

"Then why did I find you locked inside here?"

The blond is the first to speak up. I get the sense she's the nominal leader of the group. "Commanders Yablokov and Domnin said that one of us is a spy selling state secrets to the Americans. They secured us inside here while they are searching the station for evidence."

"Right. That makes sense. Except for the fact that I've been in every section of this station except the secure section – which I assume only they have access to – and didn't run into your crack team of detectives scouring for clues. So either this was just a ploy so Yablokov and Domnin could enjoy some man-on-man quiet time away from your prying eyes, or they're lying to you."

"This bomb, what would it look like?" asks the man floating in the corner.

"They described it as a suitcase nuke, which I guess means roughly suitcase-sized."

"And what is the yield?"

"Nobody told me. But enough to cause an EMP that would wipe out the power grids and telecommunication systems, plus fry most anything that has a circuit board."

"This is a lie," insists Sergey.

"Life is full of disappointments, pal."

"And why are you here?" asks the woman.

"I'm the fucking cavalry. I volunteered to come up here on a one-man mission to try to steal the nuke before your boss back on Earth pulled the trigger."

"Your plan doesn't seem to be working very well," says Sonin.

"That's all a matter of perspective. A few minutes ago I didn't think I was going to have any help. Now I have all of you." I try to give them a smile that's far more cocky than I feel. "So who wants to let me out?"

Sergey blurts something that sounds a lot like, "Let's beat him until either blood or the truth spurts from his cracked skull."

"Sergey, watch him," says the blond as she pulls the others into a floating huddle.

My bodyguard brings his round face in front of mine, waiting for me to do something.

"So...you read any good XKCD cartoons lately?"

I watch something flicker in his eyes. For a brief moment I think he's about to hit me. Instead he growls, "They are not funny. You are not funny."

"Maybe not intentionally."

The conversation comes to an end and the others drift towards me.

"Sergey, cut him loose," says the woman, then adds, "If he does anything suspicious hit him."

"He already looks suspicious to me," Sergey replies as he unties my hands.

I rub my wrists and fake a smile. "I'll work on that. So can we try this again? I'm David Dixon." I hold out a hand.

He stares at it for a moment then reluctantly shakes it. "I still believe nothing."

"Well, let me tell you everything I know and then you can decide."

[73]
BAD INTENTIONS

I GIVE THEM ALL THE DETAILS I CAN, while watching their reactions. I know one of them is Markov's insider, probably Sonin or the other woman, Vera, but I keep my mouth shut. I never went to spy school, but I imagine that rule number one is probably don't tell anyone that you're a spy – and rule number two is to never call out another fellow spy.

From their questions, I can tell they already knew something very shady was up. The commanders cut them off from talking to Roscosmos and rushed them into this section on short notice.

"Alright, hypothetically, let us say that we believe you. What is your plan? And how did you get here, by the way?" asks Vera.

"That's top secret." I don't actually know if it is, but better to keep my invisible spaceship a secret for as long as I can. There's the distinct possibility that one of these people could be an insider for Zhirov.

"I got in through one of your spacecraft berthed below." I almost said "Ivanka." That would have been interesting. "As far as my plan, um, well I was going to try to subdue one of the commanders and get him to let me into the secure module where I was going to use a sleeping gas to knock out the other."

"This plan is a stupid plan," says Sergey.

"Well, yeah, pal. You're right. I didn't have a whole lot of time to come up with a better one. Maybe the politburo here can think of something better."

The other man, who had been fairly quiet until now, Yves, speaks up in precise English. "How do you believe the commanders are going to detonate this bomb?"

"Um, with a detonator?"

He gives me a slightly condescending smile, which I'm sure I deserve, "Yes. But how will they deliver the bomb?"

"Deliver it? We're at the perfect altitude. I was thinking they were just going to press the button when their boss downstairs tells them to."

For some reason this assumption starts another debate that I can barely follow as they argue in Russian.

Sonin explains the discussion to me, "We believe that Yablokov is capable of this, but not Domnin. He is very..."

"Politically motivated," interjects Sergey.

"Well, this is interesting. All along we were working on the assumption the plan was for them to act as suicide bombers."

Sergey shakes his head. "Nobody loves Zhirov that much. Yablokov might do it for the...kink? Is that the word?"

"Close enough." I think he either means thrill or sense of duty, which could be the same thing. "So if you don't think their plan A is to blow the whole station, then what are they up to?"

"Could they eject it from the EVA airlock?" asks Sonin.

Yves shakes his head. "No. That would only put the payload in a slightly degraded orbit from us. If they detonate the bomb while we're in the same hemisphere, we could still be affected."

"Perhaps they plan to load it into one of our spacecraft?" says Vera.

"But there are only five seats in the other," points out Sergey. "That would leave us short one for reentry."

"Sergey, I don't think your commanders are planning for you to make the trip back to Earth. In fact, I'm kind of surprised they left you alive so far."

His face can't hide his reaction. "Commander Yablokov would not kill his own crew."

"Commander Yablokov would put a bullet in your head in a heartbeat," says Yves. "Domnin would do the same if he was promised a promotion. They're military men first and foremost. They came over to Roscosmos from the Army Air Force with Zhirov."

"Then why are we alive?" asks Sonin.

"Because Zhirov hasn't asked them to pull the trigger. This is still some kind of bargaining chip?" Yves asks me.

"Yes. I don't even think Radin knows what they have here yet."

"What?" blurts Sergey. "We must radio down and tell them!"

He starts for the door but Sonin and Vera grab him by the pant legs.

"Slow down there," I say. "The moment you send any kind of transmission down to Earth with the words 'bomb' and 'Zhirov' in them, one of his lackeys is likely to tell your commanders and the jig will be up."

"Is it settled then that they're going to use a spacecraft?" asks Vera.

Yves scratches his chin as he floats in mid-air thinking this over. "The prudent thing would be to abandon the station and take both of the spacecraft back down to Earth."

"But that still leaves the commanders with the bomb. Domnin may be the political animal you say he is, but if he's cornered, he might not hesitate to blow the thing out of spite. There's also the chance that Yablokov might not give him a choice. And there's the possibility that they have some other way of getting the bomb where they want to. We'd look pretty silly skedaddling out of here if that was never what they wanted."

Yves snaps his fingers. "Of course. They're not going to use the spacecraft. They'll use the EVO."

"EVO?" I reply.

"Extra Vehicular Orbiter. It's basically a small satellite launcher as big as a trash can. You eject it from the airlock. When it gets a few hundred meters its thrusters fire. After it reaches the right orbit a mechanical pusher releases the payload. Domnin said ours had malfunctioned, but I believe he was lying."

"How fast does it go?"

"Maybe two or three thousand miles an hour after a full burn."

I think it over for a moment. "That would give us five hours before it's far enough away from the station that they can set off the bomb. Regardless of which direction they send it, we'll run right past its orbit five hours after that. So when they launch it, they launch it. There's no going back."

"We have to stop them from getting to the airlock," says Sonin.

"Not so fast. We don't know if they have a dead-man's trigger on that thing. We could yell 'surprise' and the whole station goes boom."

"So what is your suggestion?" asks Vera.

I think it over then shake my head. "It's not a very good one..."

[74]
STING OPERATION

CAPTAIN BAYLOR CALLS INTO MY EAR. "David, are you okay?"

I completely forgot I still had the microphone and earbud in place and think I'm having a psychotic breakdown.

"I'm all good," I reply. My Russian hosts look at me like I'm even more insane than they already believe me to be. "My friends back on Earth. Give me a second. Hey, Baylor. So I met some new friends. Yablokov and Domnin gave them a forced time out and locked them into a storage section."

"Have you been able to capture one of the other commanders?"

"Well, no. It seems they decided to barricade themselves behind two doors in the secure module. There's no way to get to them without a plasma torch and catching their attention."

"That's...unfortunate. Unless you can think of something soon, I suggest that you and your friends make it to the nearest vehicle and hightail it back to Earth before the nuke goes off. We just got intel that Radin placed Zhirov's puppet candidate under arrest for unspecified reasons."

"Wait, what?"

Markov takes the comm. "Hello, David. It would seem that Radin has decided to play his hand on a three-dimensional chessboard."

"Does he know that Zhirov has a nuke?"

"He hasn't taken any direct action to suggest that he does. Arresting Milov is a typical Russian maneuver. We should have seen it coming."

"What does this mean for us?"

"Not good. By going at Zhirov indirectly, Radin is chipping away any advantage to using the nuclear weapon as a bargaining chip. This likely means that Zhirov will have his men detonate it sooner rather than later. Which could be any moment."

"There's a cheery thought. The crew here seems to think that at least one of the commanders, Domnin, wants to get out of this alive and Yablokov wouldn't mind either."

"And how would they do this?"

"The most likely scenario is they use a small rocket called an EVO to send the nuke away from the station and detonate it when it's on the other side of the Earth."

"Could you use this rocket to get it to a higher orbit where the nuclear device wouldn't be a threat?"

"Not likely. Right now we're trying to guess if they made a dead-man trigger or not. If they didn't, then all we have to do is wait for them to pop out of the secure module and bum rush them and take the nuke."

"And if they did?"

"Well, that would be the dumbest of dumb ideas in the history of dumb ideas."

"And what is your plan for that situation?"

"Um, something?" I look at the Russians who have been patiently listening to one side of the conversation. "My boss says Radin just arrested Milov. He thinks

Zhirov is going to go nuclear very shortly and make it look like it was Radin's fault and stage a coup."

"Yebena mat'!" says Sergey.

"No kidding. So we need a plan real fast. If they don't have a trigger, we ambush them. If they do...um we think of that when we get to it. Any suggestions?"

"We need to know if they have a trigger they can set off right away," says Yves.

"Yes. I thought I just said that?"

He shakes his head. "That means we need a way to know. Right now they should still be in the secure module. One of us can go to the command section and watch the monitors. There's a camera aimed at both hatches." He scratches his chin. "This trigger. Would it be taped to their hand?"

"Probably. That's what I'd do...if I was suicidal and homicidal."

"Okay. We need someone to go to the command center and watch. The rest of us should wait here. If they don't have a trigger we can make it to them before they finish opening the inner airlock."

"Sounds great."

"I want to kill these men," says Sergey.

Man, he sure flipped the bit fast. "I know where you can find a crowbar to do that."

"And what if they do have a deadman's trigger?" asks Vera.

"We hide," says Sergey.

"Basically." I think it over for a moment. "Yablokov would be the one with the trigger, right? He probably thinks Domnin won't push it if things go south. They still have to get to the EVO, right? Where are they stowed?"

"There are two directly above us," says Yves.

I passed right by them without noticing. "The airlock faces the other side, right? I doubt Yablokov is going to do an EVA alone with the bomb. They'll probably both go up there."

"Perhaps, but what good would that do if Yablokov has the bomb and the trigger?" asks Sonin.

"Um...yeah. How are the EVOs programmed?"

"They're not," says Yves. "They're controlled from the command center. Each one has a frequency."

"That's it...Those two have to go outside to load it. Then they have to come back inside here to send it on its merry way. We do a little switcharoo while they're coming back into the airlock."

"A switcha-?" asks Vera.

"One of us is already outside. We unload the EVO without them knowing. When they send it away we dismantle the bomb."

"Outside? In space?" asks Vera.

"I was thinking inside here... Oh, right. Yablokov still has his trigger. Dumb idea."

"What if we take it into one of the spacecraft?" asks Sergey. "The one you snuck aboard? There, perhaps we could dismantle?"

I think it over for a moment. I'm a little surprised that he was the one to figure that out. "Yeah, that could work. There are a lot of 'ifs' in there. Let's just hope they don't have a deadman trigger."

[75]
HIDE AND SEEK

"I'VE GOT BAD NEWS," says Sonin as she sticks her head through the open hatch, carefully keeping her voice low. "The helmets. They're gone. All of them."

We'd sent her out on a reconnaissance mission to the upper airlock section, since she was the smallest and most agile. Two minutes later she returned with the dire news.

"What do you mean, 'gone'?" asks Sergey.

"Gone as in they probably locked them up in the secure section to keep you guys put," I reply.

Smart move. And bad for David. This means that there's only one astronaut working for the forces of light with a complete spacesuit. This one. Unless one of the Russians knows how to breathe vacuum, this operation just fell squarely back on my shoulders again.

"Okay. We need an alternate plan," says Vera, casting a look at Yves.

Suddenly Sergey perks an ear up like a mastiff listening to the sound of a can opener. "I think the secure section inner door just opened."

I don't stop to question how he could tell over the cacophony of Darth Vader sounds that fill the station. As a pilot I know to trust the instincts of someone who is familiar with their hardware.

There's no time to think. I have to react.

"Stay here!" I say in a harsh whisper then kick myself towards the open hatch.

I grab Sonin by the shoulder and pull her through then slam the door on her crew behind us.

"What are you doing?" she says, casting a nervous glance towards the other end of the station where the secure section is located.

I ignore her for a moment, grab the crowbar and wedge it back into the wheel that keeps the door shut, locking her comrades back inside.

I pat her on the back, and make a downward gesture towards the intersection.

A quick thinker, she gets it and pulls herself along by the straps then takes a dive down the docking spire. With my nose inches behind her feet, I follow her as she descends into the module.

CLANK!!! The outer door opens above us.

We're still only halfway down the module. If Yablokov and Domnin catch us playing hide and seek, this game is going to be over real quick.

Sonin yanks on a cargo net and sails faster towards the bottom. As soon as she reaches the lower junction she does a somersault like a cat, lands on her feet then presses up against the recess under the wall.

There's some muffled Russian talking above me, growing louder. I reach the junction, but not as gracefully as the space princess.

I try to find something to push from, but she saves me the trouble by scissoring her legs around me and pulling me under the overhang.

I grab a handle by a hatch leading to one of the two remaining vehicles and try to make my body go as flat as possible.

Sonin puts a finger to her lips – I guess I was being too noisy – then points to a reflection on the window at the bottom of the junction that overlooks Earth.

It's night below us, so the window acts like a mirror, showing the top of the main junction as a white disk.

One shape flies by towards the storage section. Another appears to go up towards the command section just below the upper airlock.

Sonin looks at me wide-eyed and nods. She instantly gets why I put the crowbar back in place.

If the commanders found that missing, they wouldn't just know that their captives were free to roam the station; they'd also know that somebody else had let them out.

In the category of things that would cause Yablokov to pull the trigger and make things go "boom"; an unknown person onboard the K1 is probably pretty high up.

We wait a tense minute as the commander checks the storage section. Finally, his shadow crosses back over the white disc of reflected light and he pulls himself up into the command section.

I whisper to Sonin, "We have to get into separate spacecraft."

"What?" she mouths.

I point towards Ivanka. "My spacesuit is in there. I have to do an EVA. You need to hide in the other one."

She nods her head in agreement. Out of nowhere there's a loud banging sound like a pipe hitting a radiator, over and over.

I give her a confused look.

"My crew is creating a distraction," Sonin whispers. "So we can get inside the spacecraft."

Got it. Back in the storage section they must have figured out our only course of action.

I give a nervous glance upwards, afraid Sergey or whoever's ape-like banging is about to bring Domnin and Yablokov running.

Sonin shakes her head. "We did that the first hour they locked us in there. They don't care. Ready?"

We go to opposite ends of the docking section and check our hatches.

Sonin gives me a thumbs up. We both pull the handles open at the same time then carefully close them, doing our best not to make too much noise.

I spin the wheel until the air-seal is secured.

And here I am, back inside Ivanka.

I work my way into my spacesuit as I bounce around the cabin, trying to avoid smacking my head on the bulkhead and failing.

Helmet finally on, suit lights all good, I vent the air from Ivanka and pray the commanders think it's just one of the many many sounds coming from the station.

After the ship has reached a vacuum, I open the side hatch I'd dismantled just a little while ago and drift outside.

Using the handrails outside the docking junction, I work my way over to Sonin's ship. She's got her face pressed up against the window.

If I was hoping for some kind of silent words of wisdom, I'm out of luck. She looks just as confused and scared as I feel.

[76]
STALKER

I WORK MY WAY up the docking spire towards the underside of the module where the EVOs are stored. From my perspective, through a gap between the panels and the station, I can see the tubes where they're launched.

As hiding places go, it's not exactly the best. Technically speaking, with Asia below me, I'm actually trying to hide in plain sight of about 4 billion people. Let's just hope none of them look up.

Laney's voice shocks the hell out of me. "How's it going?"

"Quiet, I'm trying to hide."

"You're in space. There's no sound."

"Then why am I hearing you?"

There's a long silence. I guess they decided to stop transmitting.

"Okay, I'm here. Put Laney on."

"Now you want to listen to me?"

"Obviously. What happened to Baylor?"

"She's right next to me. I'm moral support and technical. She's operations."

"Wow, you guys have an org chart and everything. When is the company picnic?"

"We don't know when yet, but my money is on Guantanamo for the location."

"Great. I love Cuban food."

"Noted. So we haven't noticed any large explosions in space and the end of Western civilization, yet. So that's good."

"We've come closer than I care to think a couple times. The commanders hid the crew helmets."

"We heard. Then things went silent."

I forgot about the open channel. "Right. A cosmonaut named Sonin is in the other craft. I used Ivanka as an airlock. Now I'm hiding here waiting for the commanders to shove the nuke into the EVO unit."

"Then you're going to do the switch. Right?"

"Something like that."

"You know they probably have a camera aimed at the EVO launchers."

"Yeah. I guess that would make sense."

"That means you need to move your ass quickly as you can to retrieve the bomb because if they see you on the monitor..."

"Boom goes David."

"Boom goes my satellite television."

"Got it. It'll take them a few minutes to cycle through the airlock. And they might not even have a dead-man switch."

"Or they might. Want to take that chance?"

"No, ma'am."

There's a flicker of light on my face shield. At first I think one of my instrument lights is acting up. Then I realize on the stealth suit none of them are all that bright. In fact, I think you can only see them from my point of view.

"Something wrong?" asks Laney.

"There's a flickering of light hitting my helmet."

"Where did you leave Sonin?"

"Right!" I look down and see her spaceship. The light is coming from her porthole.

At first I think she's making some kind of Morse code signal, then I realize it's just frantic flickering as she tries to warn me about something. I wave a hand at her and the light stops.

I point upwards towards the EVA airlock. She flicks the light on and off.

"Is it aliens?" asks Laney.

"I wish." I see a glint of light from overhead. "Hold up. I think they're on the move."

I slide my helmet's black visor into place. According to the manual, it's supposed to reduce the amount of light reflected from the suit to almost nothing. It does a fairly good job without rendering me blind.

Since we're on the night side over Earth, I risk poking my head over the edge to get a better view of what's going on above me.

One of the commanders is working his way around the rails. There's a tether fastened to his belt leading ten meters back to the waist of another astronaut holding a large hardshell case. Copious amounts of red duct tape are stuck to his free hand – which I assume is the dead-man switch.

It's practical, but rather absurd. Yablokov, the one I assume is holding the bomb, looks like a balloon tied to Domnin as he makes his way to the EVO.

Rather than have both men with only one hand free, they decided to have Domnin pull Yablokov over to the EVO.

The fact that they have a dead-man switch out here tells me how paranoid they are about having someone try to stop them – even 200 miles up.

I keep a watch on them, but remain motionless. While I might blend in as a shadow, quick movement on my part might get me noticed.

It takes them several minutes, but they finally reach the EVO tubes. Domnin pulls in his fellow commander and they both use their waist tethers to clip to a rail next to the launchers.

I duck under the module above me when they're looking the other way.

After securing themselves, they open the release doors to the EVO and place the case inside. Domnin makes some adjustments to the EVO then shuts the panel.

I watch as they return to the airlock and count off the seconds it'll take for them to enter and shut the door.

Once I'm sure they're inside, I slide out from my hiding position and move as quickly as I can, hand over hand, to the EVO tube.

In my head I count off the seconds as they go through the airlock cycle and pumps fill the chamber.

Satisfied they're not coming right back out, I pull open the release on the top of the EVO, take the suitcase, then shut the door.

Moving back down to my hiding spot is difficult with just one free hand. I'm too afraid to let go of the suitcase and don't dare let it dangle from a tether where it could serve as an atomic anchor ready to bash into the K1 or me.

Finally, back under the shade of the module, I call down to earth. "So...um...I think I have a nuclear weapon. Um, now what?"

[77]
SUPER POWER

EARTH IS A GIANT HALF BLUE, half black marble below me and I've got a nuclear weapon in a suitcase...

Holy crap – I have nuclear weapon. I mean, it's scary and all, but wow. I'm like a one-man nuclear power.

If I ever had any plans of super-villainy, now is the time to pursue them.

And...I got nothing.

I'm interrupted by the slightly more sober responsible people back on Earth. "David, this is Baylor. We're getting someone on the line to help with this."

"Uh, great. Why didn't we think about that before?"

"We did. We're not all just sitting around down here waiting for you."

"Is this the man with the nuclear device?" asks a male voice.

"Yes?" I say hesitantly. "Who is this?"

"I'm Major Lewis with Army Ordnance Disposal. Is the device in a container?"

"Yes. It's a large plastic box."

"Okay. I need you to set it down on the floor and check the sides for wires."

"Um, Major, there's no floor here."

"The ground, whatever. We just need to make sure that it's not rigged with some kind of anti-tampering trigger."

Did they just call the guy in the middle of the night without telling him what was up?

"I'm in space. So we'll have to make do. I'm betting they didn't put a booby-trap on the case."

"We need to be sure before we open it."

I don't think he understands the kind of time constraint we're working under. I undo the latch and feel my scrotum shrink to nothing.

"Nope. No hidden triggers."

"What? How do you know?"

"Because I just opened it." I stop squinting and stare inside the case at the round device with a cord running to a smaller black box.

"You shouldn't have done that."

"Right. Next time I'll remember."

"Okay, Dan, I need you to describe to me what's inside the case."

I don't bother correcting him about my name. After I explain what I see, he asks me to check a serial number and confirm some details.

"Alright, Dan. You're looking at an NK3 nuclear package that would normally be the payload of an air to ground missile. It sounds like they've modeled the detonation system on an old Soviet mobile delivery system. The small box – that's the detonation trigger. It can either activate a timer or go off immediately."

"Got it. So now what?"

"See that yellow cable that runs from the box to the cylinder?"

"Affirmative."

"I need you to pull that from the cylinder connector. Let me know when you've done that."

I reach a nervous hand to the cable, afraid I'll screw up and grab the wrong one.

Slowly, as if the fate of the whole world, not just half, depended on it, I unplug the first cable. Beads of sweat drift off my face and splatter on the inside of my helmet.

"Done. Okay, now what?"

"Did you detach the cable?"

"Yes." My fingers are starting to shake. "What's next?"

"There is no next. You disarmed the device."

"Just like that? Huh, I was expecting more..."

"Yes. This isn't some Hollywood movie, Dan."

"David. My name is David."

"Okay. Anyway, this hardware was meant for Russian military to operate. With the exception of the potential booby-trap on the case, they don't really expect any other party to actually get this close to their bomb."

"Oh. I guess that makes sense."

A green light flashes on the smaller box. "Hey, there's a light that just turned on."

"Does it say 'Zaryad' or 'Taymer'?"

"Zaryad. That's Russian for "charge", right?"

"Well, fuck," he replies, sending my testicles deep into my chest.

That's one word you don't want to hear coming out of the mouth of the nuclear weapons expert who's supposed to talk you through the most critical bomb defusal ever.

"What's wrong?"

"That means they just tried to blow up the device," he replies.

WTF? I stare down at the cylinder that was just seconds ago plugged into the receiver.

"This could have been ugly."

"No shit. Good thing I didn't wait to see if the thing was booby-trapped."

"Yes, but normally that's advisable," Lewis says defensively.

"David, this is Baylor. Did you just say that they tried to blow up the bomb?"

"Yeah. Crazy. Huh? Did things just go south down there?"

"This is Markov. We haven't had any changes in developments. Precisely where are you over right now?"

"The Indian Ocean."

"Interesting. I do not think that was a strategic target."

"No?"

"No. I think the commanders set off the device because they know that you have retrieved it from the EVO."

Shit. They probably spotted me in my hiding spot from one of the cameras around the station...

"Baylor here. David, ditch the receiver and get out of there as quickly as you can!"

I grab the detonator box and fling it in one direction and the cable in another. They sail off into space and vanish. "I just got rid of the bomb parts."

"Great. But don't throw away the bomb. They might be able to retrieve that. And if they don't, the casing could burn up in the atmosphere and poison millions."

Wonderful. I hold the handle tightly. "The thought never crossed my mind." Um, sort of. "When you say get out of here?"

"Get back to the DarkStar. Now that Yablokov and Domnin know you have the device they'll be coming for you."

Damn it. I kind of thought once I had the bomb it would be game over.

Guess again, Dan.

I grab a tether from my belt, lay it across the open case then shut it over the strap so I can sling it around me like a backpack.

With both hands free, I quickly pull myself up the docking column and past the junction module.

Although the Russian escape craft are directly below me, something tells me that Yablokov and Domnin have already cut off that escape route. I just hope Sonin and the others are okay.

I make it over the junction and start sliding up the spire to where the DarkStar is tethered.

I never heard the gunshot.

In fact I don't even know what just happened until there's a loud popping sound on my suit, a sharp pain in my side and I lose my grip.

I'm knocked off the spire and air hisses out of my suit making me spin around like an out of control balloon.

"FUCK!" I scream as I fly away from the station and feel everything get cold.

Darkness starts to creep in over the corner of my vision as I lose oxygen.

[78]
DEATH SPIRAL

SANJAY IS ABOUT TEN METERS ahead of me in the wreck of the alien spaceship. His bubbles hit the ceiling and roll backwards like a level trying to seek the higher ground.

Somewhere behind me Bennet is taking the rear, letting the two of us be the first to explore the crashed Xixanox alien battle cruiser.

That is, the first non-actors and crew to explore the set.

Built in an unfinished nuclear reactor cooling tank in North Carolina, for the last three months it'd been home to a massive movie production shooting underwater scenes on one of the largest sets ever built.

"Don't let your man get too far ahead of you," Bennet says on the underwater radio.

Sanjay is like a kid, eager to explore this new terrain.

Vin heard about the set and had us drive up from the Cape to see if we might be able to use it for space training.

While it sounded cool to me, Bennet thought it was a waste of time. The Xixanox cruiser looked nothing like anything we could expect to encounter on the US/iCosmos station or anywhere else; unless steampunk aliens influenced by H.R. Giger invaded.

Still, it was fun to explore something that didn't look like it was built on the Boeing factory floor.

It was easy to pretend we really were on some alien ship about to make contact – and probably not in a happy way.

When Sanjay reached for the handle I sensed it was a bad idea. This part of the set seemed more flimsy than the rest and was already deteriorating. Pieces of Styrofoam bobbed on the ceiling and curlicues of paint that never dried formed in the corner.

I tried to stop him but was too late. As he pulled on the door, the whole wall collapsed and Sanjay was quickly covered in a cloud of debris.

"Shit! Sanjay is down!" I kicked forward to help free him when another wall collapsed on me.

A metal truss pinned me to the floor, knocking the air out of my lungs. I could spot Sanjay's terrified face just a few inches from my own. His air hose had been severed and was flapping around like an angry serpent.

"Hold..." My words were choked off by a spray of water as a crack in my mask let in water.

I took a deep breath and shut my mouth.

Sanjay reached a hand towards me. I snatched his wrist and pulled him out from under the truss using all my strength.

I was still stuck but managed to get to my knees, lifting the wall on my back.

I tugged Sanjay by the belt and pushed him past my body, shoving him out of the collapse.

His fin kicked my mask, almost knocking it loose as he swam back down the corridor, leaving me alone.

I tried to inch my way free, but the weight of the wall was too much. I felt my thighs ready to give.

The weight was too much and I fell to the floor of the pool. Water trickled into my mask and everything went blurry.

Fuck, I thought, this is how I die. Underwater in a pretend spaceship.

As I resigned myself to my fate, a powerful hand grabbed me by my ankle and yanked me away.

It was Bennet to the rescue.

The entire rear section of the set collapsed and a cloud of dust rolled past us.

Not waiting to see what else was going to go wrong, he pulled on my shoulder and pushed me towards the way we came.

He followed me all the way to the edge of the concrete pool and waited until I rolled onto dry ground before getting out himself.

Sanjay was already out of the tank, helmet off, hands on knees, coughing out water.

I ripped off my mask and took my first breath in what seemed like forever.

I laid on my side, the air tank still stuck to my back, catching my breath.

Bennet climbed out and leaned over me. "What the hell, Dixon?"

"COUGH...set collapsed."

"No kidding." He reached down and picked up my fractured mask. "What about this?"

"Must have been rebar or something."

I was too confused to understand what he was angry about. "I had to help Sanjay."

Bennet shoved the cracked mask in my face like I was a dog that pissed all over the rug. "What about this?"

I shook my head, not getting it.

Disgusted, he yanked the other mouthpiece from my chest and waves it in front of my nose. "What is this?"

"Back up," I said between exhausted breaths.

"Why didn't you use it?"

"No time." I made my way into a seated position and pointed to Sanjay. "What about him?"

"He's dead," said Bennet.

"What?" Sanjay blurted.

"You left this idiot down there."

"I had a torn hose!" Sanjay protested, understanding that Bennet was talking more than metaphorically.

While this wasn't an official astronaut training test, it was clearly enough of a trial by fire for Bennet to see what we're made of.

Bennet shrugged him off and turned his attention back to me. "How did you fuck up, yoga boy?"

"I saved Sanjay."

"I would have made it," said Sanjay.

"Go back to fantasyland," growled Bennet. "Dixon. Tell me how you fucked up?"

"I needed to secure my own air supply first."

"Why?"

"Because I'm under extra stress and increased exertion. Not doing so could kill us both."

"If this had been a..." Bennet glanced over at the underwater set and rolled his eyes. "A goddamn whatever, you'd be dead because you panicked."

"I didn't panic."

"Oh, you didn't? You acted perfectly calmly and rationally?"

"No..."

"You goddamn panicked." He shoved a finger right between my eyes. "You acted, but you didn't think. The impulse was right but the instincts were all wrong."

"I'm sorry..."

"Get this gear loaded up in the truck. I'm going to go call our boss and tell him this was a stupid idea."

When Sanjay and I finished loading the equipment, Bennet was standing in the middle of the parking lot with a cigar in his mouth staring up at the night sky.

I left Sanjay to sulk by the truck as I walked over to Bennet.

The only light was the stars and the orange glow of his Arturo Fuente, a rare indulgence. I stood there in silence, letting him have his moment of peace.

"Do you want to die up there?" Bennet asked.

"You mean like of old age from a heart attack as I have zero-g sex with a couple of space hookers?"

This got me a blast of blue smoke in the face. "Let me rephrase the question. Do you ever want a chance to go up there?"

"Yes. Hell, yes. Without a doubt."

"Then next time you do what you're trained. Not what your little impulses tell you. What were you trained to do?"

"Secure my own air supply any way I can."

"Then what?"

"Lend assistance."

"Then what?"

"Get to safety."

"What happens when you skip step one?"

"I jeopardize the mission?"

"People die, David. People die."

[79]
REACTION

THROUGH THE DARKNESS, underneath my gasping breath, somewhere beyond my panic – my body reacts. I don't think. I don't analyze. I let instincts take over – not the ones I was born with, but the hard-earned ones from spending countless hours at the bottom of a practice pool, floating in mid-air in the Vomit Comet with a blacked-out helmet or dropping from an airplane with my eyes closed and no sense of up or down.

This is what Bennet tried to drill into us. It's not enough to be clever in a tight spot. Survival depends on not having to think.

Right hand goes to the pouch on my thigh and grabs the plastic stick. Left hand probes my side, searching for the spray of air...there it is.

Put my rubbery fingertip on the leak.

Push the yellow gooey plastic stick into the hole.

Keeping pushing.

This is just like fixing a tire. Except I think the puncture went through the passenger.

One step at a time.

Let the stick do its job.

The hissing is starting to slow. That's good or the air is completely gone.

Wait a beat...take a breath.

Yep, there's air in here.

I'm still spinning.

Spread my arms wide and slow down.

Something white is flying towards me fast.

Deep breath.

Alright. I'm spinning less. There's the white thing again.

It's an cosmonaut in an EVA pack going full speed.

Is this a rescue?

No.

This is an attack.

That's probably Domnin heading straight at me while Yablokov is somewhere with a gun. Not Bennet's gun, but some specially modified thing with a wide trigger for an astronaut glove.

Damn it. They shot me.

Stay cool, David.

Turn your body so the suitcase is facing towards them. Use it as a shield.

Jesus Christ. I'm using a nuclear bomb to block gunfire.

"OPS, this is David. I've been hit. I have the hole in the suit sealed. I have a hostile inbound. Question; what happens if a bullet hits the nuke?"

Lewis takes the comm. "The slapper detonators won't do anything. Hexanitrostilbene is very stable. But if you get a leak in the plutonium casing that could cause a contamination issue...but you're in a space suit. However, if the bullet hits the plutonium and goes through you...well...you'll be dead too soon to care."

"Right. I'm going to assume these assholes would rather not put a hole in the bomb, so I'm using it as a shield."

I spin until my suit jet stabilizes my rotation so I'm facing away from the K1.

BAM!!! Something – probably Domnin – just slammed into my back.

He's trying to pull the case away from me.

The strap is slipping over my head as he lifts it free.

Hold up...let him.

I go limp and allow Domnin to get the case off my shoulder. As he slides it along my arm, I grab the strap with my right hand and give it a yank.

Although this doesn't free it from his grasp, it sends me flying backwards behind him where I hit his EVA pack.

I slip my left arm under his left shoulder, grappling him from the back.

Alright, I don't think he saw this move coming – neither did I.

Now what? In any moment Yablokov is going to start shooting, regardless if his boy is in the way.

The world starts to spin as Domnin activates the thruster on his pack.

Flames lick my visor and I quickly let go as his side rocket nearly burns a hole in my suit.

Damnit! Dumb move on my part. He almost melted through. Good thing this stealth suit is heat resistant.

He's already flying back to the K1 with the nuke.

My suit rockets have only a small amount of burn left. Better make it a good one.

I light them up and chase after him.

From my left thigh pouch I pull out the black blade used to cut through straps and anything else that gets in the way. It's my only weapon.

BAM! I hit the back of his EVA pack.

I quickly grab the handle on the top with my right hand and use it like a pommel horse to swing over him.

With the knife blade in my left fist, as soon as I see his visor, I slam it into the plastic as hard as I can.

The tip goes in about an inch, just over his eye.

Domnin goes through a range of emotion from terror to elation as he realizes the blade stopped short of touching him and the self-healing polymer in his helmet has sealed around the puncture.

Enjoy the moment, pal. I know how these helmets are made.

I give the knife a twist and the slit ruptures, cracking the glass. His entire face shield explodes.

The blood vessels on his skin rupture and blood pours out his nose and eyes. The poor son of a bitch made the fatal mistake of trying to hold his breath in a vacuum.

CRACK! I feel the vibration of something – probably a bullet – as it hits the top of Domnin's EVA pack.

I push myself backwards so his body and the jetpack are between me and the K1 – which is growing closer real fast.

We're heading towards the base of the main tower, below the upper EVA airlock where Yablokov has found a position to take shots at me.

We're moving a hell of a lot faster than I'd like. There's no time to try to commandeer Domnin's rocket pack. I can only get ready to use him as a human air bag.

BAM!!! We slam into the module. It feels like I just fell off a house and landed on the sidewalk.

BANG!!! The nuke just bounced off the outer wall and ricocheted into my shoulder.

Shit...we're all bouncing backwards.

Damn you, Newton.

Think fast. We're about to be in wide-open space with Yablokov free to take shots all day long with his damn space rifle.

[80]
LAST STAND

CRACK!!! A bullet grazes the top of my helmet and my head jerks backwards. It's so goddamn loud I'm positive it split my skull. Nope. Still here.

Thank god these things are designed to deflect micrometeorites.

I pull myself into a ball behind Domnin so I'm a smaller target. The nuke is drifting to the side, still in his grasp.

Maybe I should reach for it?

THWACK! THWACK! His body jerks back and forth like a puppet being yanked around.

Blood streams out of his chest and shoulder.

Christ. Yablokov is trying to hit me by shooting straight through his friend!

"David, what's your status?" asks Baylor.

"Fucked? I'm floating around out here and Yablokov is shooting at me. Fortunately I have Domnin's dead body and his EVA pack to use as a shield."

"Did you say you're using him as a shield?"

"Yes. But Yablokov is still taking shots."

"David, that's not good."

"No shit."

"I mean you'd be better off using the nuke to block the gunfire."

"Well, it's out of reach." I glance at Domnin's death grip on the strap. "Um, my reach."

"What I mean, is that those EVA suits use a monopropellant that could be set off by a bullet-strike."

"Oh. So I should just turn myself in? Great idea."

"No. Sorry. Just be aware of that."

"Yeah. Got it. Thanks."

Okay, the crazy Russian is shooting at you and it turns out the nuclear device is a better shield. Maybe if I reach over and grab Domnin's arm I can get it to swing the pack back at me...

The moment I grab his triceps a bullet hole emerges a centimeter away from my fingertips.

I pull my arm back in and try to ball up as small as I can again. The EVA hits me in the visor as bullets strike the corpse over and over. How much ammo did they bring up here?

The K1 is getting smaller, but that doesn't mean much. If Yablokov has a good scope, he can shoot at me for miles. There's no air resistance and the actual gravitational effect on the trajectory is insignificant.

Making matters worse; he's got the sun behind him, making it hard for me to spot him.

I notice there's a bulge in Domnin's thigh pocket. It's a gun. Stainless steel, and specially designed with a wide trigger and some kind of funky recoil suppression, you'd almost think it was a tool. I guess it is, but for putting holes in people.

Alright, David, go for it.

I reach a hand down, trying to keep it concealed behind his body as long as I can and snatch the grip.

THWACK! A bullet goes through his thigh and grazes my knuckle. A trail of blood shoots out like a geyser then freezes into small drops.

Okay. We have a gun, but Yablokov has a space rifle. This isn't quite fair.

You know what? Don't give him time to think about it either. I snake an arm around, grab the controller for the rocket pack and push the forward button.

Flames erupt right next to my helmet and the EVA suit hurtles towards the K1.

The nuke drifts backwards and I grab the handle with my left hand, not letting it drift away.

I straighten my body out as much as I can so I have a tiny profile.

THWACK! THWACK! THWACK!

I feel the vibrations as Yablokov unloads into Domnin as we fly towards him.

I can't even imagine what the corpse looks like now. The droplets of blood are like tiny red comets flying away from him.

The K1 begins to dominate my field of view and I spot Yablokov floating over the top of the EVA spire in his own pack. He's got a long silver rifle in his hands.

I raise my gun and fire at him. It's a wild shot, but he sees the explosion of gas from the cylinder and knows he's now a target.

He presses a button and his rockets send him downwards, behind the top of the spire.

I've got a few seconds before he takes up another position.

Move fast, David. Any moment now and he's going to come creeping around the side of the station from a remote position and start shooting at me.

But which way?

Out of the corner of my eye I spot a shadow moving across the solar panels to my left. That slick bastard. He went way the hell out from me to do that.

I yank the nuke off the strap and clip it to my remaining tether. I then turn Domnin's body towards the direction his pal is heading and push the forward thruster.

Flames lick around me as the rocket pack shoots forward and upwards towards the trajectory of the shadow.

Using a rail, I pull myself around the spire, to the opposite side of Yablokov, cutting off his sneak attack.

As I reach the other end, Domnin's dead body is floating right towards the other commander.

Confused, and thinking with his gun and not his brain, Yablokov momentarily starts firing rounds into the already ripped apart cosmonaut.

Yablokov decides he'd rather take the shot at me than Domnin and brings his rifle to bear on me.

I only have a second to get my shot.

[81]
ADRIFT

I BRACE MY GUN against the side of the spire and take careful aim. Not at Yablokov, but the canister at the back of the EVA pack with all the warning stickers on it.

Sparks fly an inch from my head as Yablokov fires a round straight past Domnin and almost into my head.

The two are about to collide.

I squeeze my trigger.

BANG!

BANG!

BANG!

I hear every shot because the only place for the vibration to go is into me.

It's the last one that sets off the explosion I can see, but not hear.

Domnin's EVA pack rips apart in an orange ball of flames that swallows Yablokov.

Parts of Domnin and his suit fly off in a dozen directions.

Yablokov spins wildly out of control, but somehow manages to stabilize himself. His jets fire and he rotates towards me.

As the flames die down I can see that his helmet is cracked and his face charred.

I can't tell if the burnt thing looking back at me is alive or dead. All I know is that it's filled with fury.

His thrusters blaze and send his carcass directly at me.

I unload the rest of the magazine into his chest. A pointless effort. He's already dead.

I try to jump out of the way, but the edge of his EVA hits me hard in the shoulder.

Tendrils of blood and fuel flow from him and his pack as his furious trajectory sends him into a solar panel.

Blue and black glass panels break apart and shatter into thousands of pieces.

I feel the station shake and try to cover my face plate from the debris. Tiny shards rain against my suit.

There's another impact and I look below as the burning corpse smashes into Ivanka.

The impact is followed by an explosion and the entire docking section lights up in an orange ball when his exploding EVA pack sets off the fuel on the other craft.

BOOM!!! The sound makes its way through the station and into my suit through touch.

I feel the station rattle and lurch as the explosion tears the lower section away.

My grip is knocked free and I go flying – choosing to hold onto the nuke instead of trying to make a futile grasp at the rail that's now too far away.

As I drift helplessly away from the K1, the wreckage of the docking section floats off like a severed limb in the ocean current.

"OPS...holy shit. Can you reach the K1?"

"Patching through," says Baylor.

Tense seconds go by as the K1 grows smaller and smaller.

I try my suit jets, but they're all spent.

"David?" asks Sonin, sounding far away.

"Thank god! Are you okay?"

"The hatches are sealed up. What about you?"

"I got the nuke. We should be able to find it from my suit transponder."

"Wait, why don't you bring it back to the K1?" asks Baylor.

Sonin swears in Russian. "We don't have any EVA suits. We don't even have any working spacesuits. By the time a resupply makes it here..."

"I'll be out of oxygen," I reply.

The K1 is already a small dot. It's like a little jewel. A deadly one, like any interesting gem, but beautiful no less.

I hear Laney protest in the background, "Let me talk to him! David?"

"What's up, Glitter Menace?"

"What about your reserve rockets?"

"Used them to tackle Domnin."

"Okay...maybe we can improvise something? What about the EVO's?"

"They have to be initiated from outside the station."

"Damn it. What about...there's got to be something!"

"Kiddo, all that matters is the mission. I've got the nuke. The bad guys are dead. We'll be able to retrieve this thing before I become a shooting star and all will be right with the world."

"No, it won't. Don't give up." I can hear her sobbing on the other end of the comm.

"I'm not. I'm just accepting the idea that there are no more alternatives. Make sure that Vin finds those kids in Rio that helped me. If that happens, I'll die a happy man."

The earth is so big and beautiful right now. I'm on the day side and night is approaching – It's such a wonderful metaphor for what's happening.

Bennet, Peterson, Tyler, they all died for an important reason I get now. I know why they did it.

I can hear the static of the open channel, but neither Laney nor I know what to say.

"David," says Markov. "You've done an admirable thing."

"Thanks. Look after Washburn for me."

OPS goes quiet as they try to figure out what you tell a guy about to die.

Finally, I speak, trying to put a brave face on everything. "Hey, Laney, it's so beautiful up here. I can't wait for you to see it one day."

[82]
FALLBACK

I LOOK AT THE LIGHTS down in the night side and imagine each one is a living person. Maybe they are.

"David..." cries Laney, tired of the silence, "if only the DarkStar hadn't been destroyed."

"Yeah...is it?"

"You said all the ships were destroyed in the explosion?"

"I meant the Russian ones."

"Wait...Hold on...checking telemetry. Yeah, it's still there."

"Well, that's a relief. Too bad it's about a kilometer away now."

"I can control it remotely."

"Wait? What?"

"Yeah, dumb ass. If you tethered it, I'll use the control rockets to burn through the line. Hold on. We're logging in now. Got it."

"Shit? Are you saying I'm not going to die?"

"Not from lack of oxygen. But you'll still have to do the high altitude reentry on the inflatable heat shield. Nobody has ever tried that before."

To hell with the martyr bullshit. I want to live. Or at least die trying to.

"I think I can deal with those odds."

So this will be interesting...

David Dixon will return...

THANK YOU!

Thank you for reading this! If you enjoyed it, I hope you'll consider writing a blurb on Amazon, Goodreads or your favorite book site. Publishing is still driven by word of mouth and every single voice helps – especially yours!

Don't be afraid to say hello on Twitter. There's a 99% chance I'll answer back (and yes, it's really me replying!)

If you'd like to know more about my upcoming books and other projects, please stop by my website at **AndrewMayne.com** and sign up for my newsletter. I've been known to send advance copies and other cool stuff to people who sign up!

You can follow me online at:
Twitter.com/AndrewMayne
Facebook.com/AndrewMayne

I also have lots of videos about writing and other topics at:
YouTube.com/AndrewMayne

I do a weekly podcast on creativity that can be found at:
WeirdThings.com.

Please check my "Also by" section for all my other titles!

Best,

Andrew Mayne
@AndrewMayne

About the Author

Andrew Mayne, star of A&E's Don't Trust Andrew Mayne, is a magician and novelist ranked the fifth best-selling independent author of the year by Amazon UK. He started his first world tour as an illusionist when he was a teenager and went on to work behind the scenes for Penn & Teller, David Blaine and David Copperfield. He's also the host of the WeirdThings.com podcast.

Also by Andrew Mayne

ANGEL KILLER
NAME OF THE DEVIL
PUBLIC ENEMY ZERO
KNIGHT SCHOOL
THE MONSTER IN THE MIST
THE MARTIAN EMPEROR
THE GRENDEL'S SHADOW
GAME KNIGHT
HOW TO WRITE A NOVELLA IN 24 HOURS

23658779R00212

Printed in Great Britain
by Amazon